Sense, Sensibility, & the Mediterranean Sea

KC McCormick Çiftçi

To anyone who learned that thoughts are worth more than feelings and is unlearning that now.

One

No matter how Eliza felt about sticky Michigan summers, there was something special about being home again. Even if it wasn't really home anymore. She curled her legs up onto the seat of the porch swing, reaching for her lemonade. It was so hot that her ice cubes had barely stood a chance, transmuted into wetness on the outside of her glass rather than coldness inside it.

"Whoo," she exhaled, fanning herself. "So hot!"

Eliza's mom Susan quirked an eyebrow in her direction from the yard, where she was pulling weeds...in the middle of the day...when it was ninety degrees with a humidity rating Eliza couldn't even bring herself to look at with both of her eyes open.

"You live in Turkey, dear," said Susan. "And you think *this* is hot?" She shook her head at her daughter. "What's going to happen to you when your plane lands in Antalya?"

"I'll manage somehow." Eliza smiled, eyes dropping to her lap where her phone was sitting. Because as much as she might not be that excited about the peak summer heat, she was definitely excited to be seeing Deniz again.

She picked up her phone, scrolling through their recent text messages. It was getting late in Turkey, but if she had learned anything about what her boyfriend was like when he was back in his parents' village, he was a night owl. Not like her, adjusting to her parents' schedule: in bed by ten and up at six for coffee. No, Deniz was frequently texting her when it was evening in Michigan, making it the wee hours of the night in Turkey. She didn't remember him being like that in Antalya, but nobody could be too much of a night owl with stacks of papers to grade and early morning classes to teach.

A message was waiting for her from Deniz; she must have missed it in the very rare moment that she wasn't glued to her phone.

Can I pick you up at the airport?

Eliza smiled to herself, her fingers already flying with her response. ...no. Thanks, though.

Three dots popped up, suggesting Deniz was working on his response, but nothing came through. She decided to put the poor guy out of his misery, sending another message to follow the previous one.

Just kidding. Of course you can pick me up. Did you really think I'd rather take the tram? Dude, I'm going to be barely coherent by the time I come to the end of my 18-hour journey. Public transportation would be unwise if I don't want to wake up at the last stop of the tramline.

Deniz's response came quickly. Wow, that was a joke, huh? It was a pretty weak one, if I do say so.

"Yeah, right," she scoffed. I'm rolling my eyes at you so hard right now. You can say whatever you want, but I know you believed me, at least for a second.

Maybe. I thought I had overstepped on your American independence. Or on your friendship with Crystal, since I'm pretty sure she's going to be eager to see you, too.

Leave it to Deniz to be concerned about Eliza getting quality time with Crystal, her oldest friend and current roommate. And while it was true that Eliza had missed Crystal all summer (she had stayed in their apartment in Antalya while Eliza had returned to Michigan), it wasn't quite the same as missing Deniz, her crush turned nemesis turned friend turned boyfriend.

So she told Deniz just that. Crystal can deal with it. She might miss me now, but she's about to see so much of me she's going to be sick of me. Actually, maybe I should be worried about the same thing happening with you...

His response was immediate. Not possible. I've missed you too much this summer. Be warned: I might not let you out of my sight again for a very long time.

The man normally had a way with words, but something about that didn't sound quite right. Um. Was that supposed to sound creepy or...?

Definitely not. You have to remember that they didn't teach us "English for flirting and seduction" in my university courses.

Eliza laughed out loud, imagining a college-aged Deniz taking diligent notes on his lined paper about proper flirting technique. Good to know. So you're telling me there's a hole in the curriculum? Maybe I should suggest a seminar to Dr. Yılmaz. I'd be happy to teach it.

She knew the laughing emojis Deniz was sending her now were sincere, and she could almost picture him throwing his head back and laughing from deep in his belly. That was one of her favorite surprises when the two of them had begun dating, seeing the unbuttoned version of him. The side of him that laughed with abandon, that relished a good meal, that expressed his normally closely kept emotions openly. She had had no idea just how passionate and free Deniz Aydem could be (apart from kissing her for the first time right in the middle of Kaleiçi), and the time they had spent together had been full of happy surprises.

What are you up to today, anyway? she wrote. I miss you.

The rapid fire responses she had been getting died out instantly, almost enough to make Eliza wonder if she had said something wrong.

She was still scowling at her phone when her mom stepped up onto the porch. "If I didn't know you were texting that boyfriend of yours, I would think there was something wrong with you," Susan teased. "Giggling away up here like a schoolgirl."

Eliza stilled the porch swing so that her mom could take a seat next to her before the two of them began rocking again, setting a new, gentle pace.

"How is Deniz, anyway?" Susan asked.

"He's good." She smiled at her mom, wishing she could introduce this woman she admired so much to her new boyfriend. Alec, Eliza's ex-boyfriend, had been bad news, and Eliza knew Susan had worried about her the entire time they were together. Even if her mom was a bit wary of Deniz, Eliza knew she had nothing to be concerned about. He was a good guy, and Susan would come to see that for herself. Just as soon as he was back some place where he had better phone coverage. Video chatting had been an impossibility the entire time he'd been in his parents' village, but she was grateful they could at least text each other.

"What's keeping him busy these days? Do you know yet when he'll head back to Antalya?" Susan's interest was genuine, even if she didn't mask the concern she was feeling.

"Well, you know he's in the village, right?" Off her mom's nod, Eliza continued. "His sister is there now, too, so he's been keeping busy spending time with her."

"I see. He's close with his sister, then?"

Eliza nodded. "Really close. She's younger than him, and I know he feels like he needs to look out for her. And also push her. Support her to their parents."

A wrinkle of worry appeared on Susan's face. "What do you mean? Why does he need to do that?"

"It's nothing sinister, Mom. Just...you know. Parents worry about their children. Especially the baby of the family. Or so I hear." She leaned into her mom's side, elbowing her ever so slightly. "You didn't worry about me at all when I moved to Turkey?"

"That's different," said Susan. "You were moving to a new country, just about as far away from me as you could get. There would have to be something wrong with me *not* to worry about you doing that."

"I don't know. It might not be so different. Deniz mentioned something yesterday about Cansu—that's his sister—wanting to move to London for a bit. Some kind of work exchange program for her there." She planted her eyes on her mom's face, eyebrows wiggling with mischief. "So ask me again why her parents might worry about her."

Susan sighed. "You got me there. Parents...we're all the same, I guess. No matter the country, the language, or even the age of our kids, if they go away from home, we're going to worry about them. Or maybe even try to talk them out of going in the first place."

Eliza nodded. "Yeah, it seems pretty universal, doesn't it? And at least when you were sending me off to Turkey, you knew Crystal would be there with me eventually. For Cansu, this is a new and unknown adventure, something really exciting. But I'm sure for her parents it's scary to think about. Far away from them. Not someplace they can get quickly or easily if she needs them. A language they don't speak."

"That's right." Susan was quiet, thoughtful. "That worried me, too. I mean, I don't know a word of Turkish, so if something had happened to you, what would I do? It's the same for them. At least Deniz speaks English. And Cansu does too, right?"

"She does. I haven't met her yet, you know, but I talked to her on the phone a few times. Her English is really good, and I'm sure she'd have a great time in London. Or I should say, she *will* have a great time in London. Because if I know Deniz, he's going to be the one to convince both her and their parents that she needs to take this opportunity."

"That's wonderful that she has such a supportive big brother," said Susan. "And that he has her."

"It is. Like me and Crystal, in a lot of ways. I mean, I know they're *actually* siblings, but—"

Susan was shaking her head. "There's no reason a close friend can't take the place of a brother or a sister. No reason at all." Eliza's mom was one of three children, close to both her brother and her sister. As an only child herself, Eliza had always appreciated both her mom's relationships with her siblings and her encouragement of Eliza forming close friendships of her own.

Talking about Crystal reminded Eliza just how much she missed her friend. Even though they'd been video chatting regularly, it still wasn't the same as ordering takeout together or sipping a beer on the beach. She was happy things were going so well for Crystal at her new job that she'd stayed in Antalya this summer, but it still felt wrong that the two of them were apart. That Crystal was missing out on everything that made Michigan summers great...and that Eliza was missing out on everything that Crystal was experiencing there.

Changing the subject, Eliza smiled at her mom. "So, when are you going to come visit me? And don't give me some answer just to appease me. I'm holding you to it this year!"

Susan smiled. "I couldn't do that to you, Eliza." She paused, surveying her garden, her pride and joy. "You know the thought of flying—especially all the way to

Turkey—just about gives me hives. But I want to be there. To see where you live. And, of course, to meet Deniz. We'll make it happen just as soon as we can."

Eliza clapped her hands with glee. "You're going to love it, Mom. And I'll give you all my best advice for making that long flight bearable."

"What about Deniz's family? Do you think I could meet them, too?"

Eliza shrugged. "Apart from talking with his sister on the phone, I haven't met anyone. Honestly? I don't know..."

As exciting as it was to imagine her mom visiting, walking the streets of Antalya together, there was a new, unexpected thought niggling at her stomach. Her mom meeting Deniz...would that be too much too soon? Deniz hadn't exactly offered to introduce Eliza to *his* parents, after all. Maybe things weren't that serious between them. Or maybe his parents didn't approve. Either they knew he had an American girlfriend and they weren't happy about it...or they didn't even know she existed. And either way, that wasn't good.

Susan patted Eliza on the shoulder. "You look serious all of a sudden, kiddo. I didn't mean to freak you out with all the parent talk. It's going to be months before I come there anyway, so let's just table that topic for another day."

Eliza forced a smile, knowing full well that Susan Britt could see right through her, but still appreciating her mom's willingness to play along. "Of course. It's going to be such a blast!"

Two

"How long does it take to reply to a freaking text message?" Eliza grumbled to herself the next morning. Upon waking, she had fumbled around on her nightstand for her phone and was dismayed to see that Deniz was still AWOL. It wasn't like him not to say goodnight or to check in.

Maybe his phone is out of credit. Or he doesn't have coverage. Or, I don't know, a cow ate it. That could happen, right? And it would take ages for it to come out on the other side, what with all those extra stomachs...

Eliza groaned as she flung herself out of bed and gracelessly into the day. Some people might begin their mornings with meditation or mindfulness, but she, apparently, began hers with cow digestive systems and boyfriend-related frustrations.

She couldn't help but worry that maybe something had happened to Deniz. Barring any cattle-related phone confiscation, there was a genuine possibility that something was wrong. He wouldn't not text her just for the sake of not texting her...would he?

Before she could second guess the merits of double texting without having received a response, she fired off a message to Deniz. **Are you okay? Haven't heard from you, so...just wondering, I guess.** She hit send before she could give in to the urge to reread her message ten times and ensure it didn't come across as too desperate. Too needy. She just...wanted to know what was going on with Deniz, that was all. To make sure everything was okay.

When a response didn't come immediately, she flung her phone onto her unmade bed and huffed out of the room in search of coffee and a distraction.

In the kitchen she found Susan—alone, Eliza's dad having already left for work hours ago—sitting at the kitchen table with her own mug and a newspaper, no doubt open to the crossword puzzle. Susan's glasses were perched at the end of her nose and the coffee next to her had grown cold, lost as she was in working through the mysteries and challenges her puzzle had presented her.

Susan looked up at the sound of Eliza's shuffling feet. "Good morning, honey!" A smile spread across her face as she greeted her daughter. Ready to leap to her feet, she asked, "Can I make you a cup of coffee?"

Eliza shook her head as she gestured to her mom to sit back down. "Thank you, but I've got it under control. Believe it or not, I actually manage to caffeinate myself all on my own just about every day of the year!"

Susan wiggled her eyebrows. "Except when you sleep through your alarm and Crystal has to make it for you?" she teased.

A groan snuck out before Eliza could stop herself. "I never should have told you about that morning if I wanted to keep any credibility whatsoever in this family." She shook her head. "It was *one* time!"

Susan pursed her lips. "Sure, *that* was one time. But don't forget, dear daughter of mine, that I was there throughout your entire childhood, so I have a pretty good idea just how many stories like that you have up your sleeve." She started counting on her fingers. "There was the night you were *so sure* there would be a snow day the next morning that you turned your alarm off. And that time you were anxious about a presentation at school and pretended you were asleep no matter how many times I called you, shook your shoulder, flipped your lights on and off." Susan smiled. "I had to admire your commitment that time. Not that it worked."

Eliza shuddered. "And the presentation was a disaster." She was at the sink now, filling the kettle to boil water. "If I remember correctly, that was the turning point for me. The end of all that childish foolishness."

Susan's forehead wrinkled with a frown. "What childish foolishness?"

"Being scared of something I couldn't control, I guess." She placed the pour-over dripper on top of her favorite mug, inserting a filter and measuring out her ground coffee while she waited for the water to boil.

Susan had been quiet, watching her daughter and waiting for her next words. When Eliza looked up, she gave her an encouraging nod. "Care to elaborate?"

Eliza sighed. "I guess I mean being controlled by my emotions, to be honest. I'm sure it won't surprise you to hear that I was a bit anxious as a kid, but somewhere along the line I made a conscious decision to change that. To be the one in control, rather than being subject to the whims of my feelings."

"Am I a terrible mother if I didn't realize that was happening?" Susan's concern was deepening with every sentence her daughter spoke.

"Of course not." Eliza shook her head. "*I* didn't even know that's what I was doing. Trust me, if it had been a conscious decision, we probably would have talked about it at some point. It's not like I could ever keep a secret from you."

"Then where did this realization come from?"

Eliza shrugged. "Honestly, I'm not sure. It seems like the kind of thing I would have uncovered in therapy, but I haven't been recently. It's not exactly the sort of challenge I'd want to take on in a language I barely speak."

"You couldn't find a therapist who speaks English?"

"Okay, you got me there. It's not like I've actually looked for one. It's just convenient to have the excuse of the language barrier." Eliza took the dripper off her cup, stirring in cream and a spoonful of sugar while she thought about her next words. "I guess some of this self awareness has just come from reading. Either reading non-fiction and applying that to myself, or, more often than not, reading fiction. Getting inside a character's head and realizing, 'Oh shit, this dysfunction of theirs is actually something I can relate to. And apparently it's something I can overcome rather than just live with for the rest of my life.'"

Susan was nodding. "That makes sense, and I can relate. I can't even tell you how much I've gained from all the miles I've walked in fictional characters' shoes. If I had to be addicted to something, I'm certainly glad it's books."

"Same here. Reading them and definitely buying them. Speaking of which, I'm planning to head to the bookstore today to fill up every empty square inch of my suitcase. Do you want to come with?"

Susan pulled a face. "Do you even have to ask? I'll drive."

It wasn't until Eliza and Susan had made it to the bookstore that Eliza heard from Deniz.

Sorry about that. Things have been crazy here. How are you? That was all his message said.

Eliza's eyes nearly goggled out of her head as she read the message. "Really?" she said out loud. "I mean, really? What the heck happened to you, dude? Where did you disappear to?"

Susan was the one to respond, naturally. "What's going on?"

Eliza held out her phone for her mom to read the message. "He disappeared, and he's not exactly being forthcoming with what happened."

Susan quirked an eyebrow in her direction. "And...what? Do you think he was doing something shady? Or do you think he was just genuinely busy?"

"I...I mean, I don't think he was cheating on me or anything. I just don't like that I didn't know where he was."

"Hmm." Susan was quiet, thoughtful. "It seems like, for as much as you've been priding yourself on being in control of your emotions—"

"I know," Eliza interrupted. "I know, trust me. I'm not exactly doing a great job being the chill girlfriend I pride myself on being, cool as a cucumber."

Susan shook her head. "I didn't bring it up for a 'gotcha' moment or anything like that. I think it's good, actually. Relationships sometimes bring up old things that we haven't healed fully, giving us a chance to work through them again."

Eliza groaned. "That's great, Mom. It sounds super fun, you know? Like, why don't they advertise that on the dating apps? 'We'll help you find the love of your life *and* unearth a bunch of old shit from your childhood, too.'"

"It's not that bad, Eliza. And you're not special in this. It happens to all of us, or at least to all of us who let ourselves be vulnerable in a relationship. I learned plenty about myself over the years with your dad, and I'm sure I'm a stronger, more self-aware person now than I was when we met."

Eliza nodded. "There's just one slight difference between me and Deniz and you and Dad. You two have been married for what? Thirty years? And Deniz and I have barely even started dating."

Susan held up her hand. "I'm not going to argue the finer points with you, Eliza. I'll state my piece one more time, that being, of course, that exploring the emotions that come up when you don't hear from your boyfriend is a perfectly reasonable use of your time. Shoving them down won't make them go away, and there's nothing to be embarrassed about by talking about them."

Eliza made herself smile despite the stress ball that was lodged in her stomach now. "That's more than one piece, but I'll take them all into consideration."

Brightening with a genuine smile, Susan put her arm through the crook of Eliza's elbow and pulled her toward the store. "Wonderful. Now let's have some fun."

When they returned home a couple of hours later, Eliza and Susan were both weighed down with books. The bookstore they had visited was an old favorite from Eliza's childhood, shelves stocked both with new releases and with a wide variety of secondhand and rare books. Eliza had picked up the new Kate Austen novel that had come out while she was in Turkey, along with a bag stuffed to the gills with historical romances. The shop had a promotion going where that bag could be filled to the brim and still only cost ten dollars, so Eliza had seen no reason to hold herself back.

True, fitting them all in her suitcase was going to prove a challenge that even her Tetris skills couldn't master—unless Tetris skills somehow translated into making things weigh less, too.

Susan's shopping bag was full of books on health and spirituality, inclined as she was to seek out new ways to expand her consciousness in both of those realms. And while Eliza was neither the most spiritual nor the most interested in alternative health, she always respected someone seeking to better themselves in whatever form it took.

While they regrouped from all the energy spent perusing bookshelves, sorting through covers, and scanning the blurbs on the back, they sat on the couch in the living room, sipping the iced coffees they had brought home with them.

"That was just what I needed," said Eliza. "And always the best way to spend a morning."

"Agreed," said Susan. "Though now I'm feeling spent. I think a little cat nap before we do anything else is just what I need."

Eliza smiled at her mom and nodded, retreating to her own room so that Susan could stretch out on the couch in peace. Eliza could use this time to look at her suitcase, look at her shopping bags full of books, and cry internally about the impossibility of reconciling the two.

After her door was closed but before she could begin her packing-induced emotional outburst, her phone started to vibrate in her purse. Pulling it out, she saw Deniz was calling her—and a video call, no less.

She swiped her hair behind her ear before answering, trying to ignore her racing heart. Was something wrong? How did he even have the bandwidth to call her right now?

"Deniz?" She answered the phone, waiting for his face to come into view. When it did—and she saw the familiar background of his apartment in Antalya—she felt the tension in her belly come unknotted. It all made a little more sense now, both why he was online and why he had been unavailable for the past day.

"Eliza!" His grin was huge and genuine, filling up the phone screen. "I miss you."

"I miss you, too." She surprised herself with how much she meant those words—and with how uncomfortable that vulnerability made her feel. Still, she couldn't *not* say them back to him. They were the truth, after all.

"How are you doing? What are you up to?"

She moved the camera to show him the bags from the bookstore. "Oh, you know...just making irresponsible financial decisions. I mean, I didn't spend too much on the books, but if I have to pay the airline for a second suitcase, then this will definitely turn out to have been a foolish move."

Deniz was smiling and shaking his head. "It's never irresponsible when we're talking about books. I'm sure it's cheaper to bring them yourself than it is to have them shipped here, so...great job then. Maybe I can read some of them, too." His face darkened for just a flash, so quickly Eliza almost missed it. "I was a little concerned that you were mad at me," he admitted. "You didn't text me back, so..."

Eliza's stomach dropped. Was she going to have to admit her complicated feelings from earlier this morning already? She had hoped that conversation could wait until she was back in Turkey, talking to him face to face. It was easier to be vulnerable with the reassurance of time together, anchoring hands on arms, all those good things. Saying it over the phone and then hanging up, well, that could be the perfect set-up for both of them to overthink things, to play the others' words over and over in their heads until they had thoroughly taken them personally.

"Eliza?" Deniz's question interrupted her thoughts. "It's okay, really, if you were mad at me." He sighed. "I know I disappeared on you for a while there, and I am sorry if that made you worry or feel like I'd abandoned you."

A small, warm feeling peeked through Eliza's anxiety. How was it possible for him to be this tuned in to how his actions made her feel from that far away?

Deniz continued. "I don't know if it was your intention, but I definitely got concerned myself in these last few hours. I was hoping you were okay, and also hoping that you weren't frustrated with me and giving me the silent treatment. Now that I know you're okay—it looks from here like you still have all of your parts—I'm wondering if the other thing is what's happening."

Eliza sighed. *Here goes nothing.* "I...maybe? I was definitely worried. So when I heard from you and it seemed like nothing strange had happened, I did feel a bit...miffed? Is that a good word for it?...that I hadn't heard a peep. Like it was that easy for me to be out of sight, out of mind."

Shaking his head, Deniz answered her concerns. "I can promise you that you were never far from my mind, Eliza. No, I wished I could have texted you many times, but...I just couldn't." He looked like he was holding something back, debating whether to share it with her. Finally, he gestured to his surroundings. "As you may have noticed, I'm back in my apartment."

"I *did* actually notice that." She smiled. "So is that what kept you so busy for the past 24 hours?"

"That's a big part of it. Of course, I had to say goodbye to everyone in the village, too. Visit my relatives, kiss my grandparents' hands, figure out how to carry all the cheese and eggs and tomatoes they all wanted to send back with me on the bus." He smiled then, remembering something that Eliza wished she could picture right along with him. "I did manage to convince my grandmother that I absolutely cannot keep a chicken on my balcony. She didn't accept that store-bought eggs could be a decent replacement for fresh ones, but I reminded her we have a weekly bazaar here, too."

Eliza could picture Deniz's relatives...vaguely, at least. He had shown her photos at his apartment once when she'd asked about his family back in the village. "That sounds absolutely delightful," she said. "I would love to go there with you sometime." She'd never been to Isparta, the province Deniz was from, and she was curious about village life, too.

But at her words, a shadow passed over Deniz's face. His smile, so sincere moments before when he was remembering his grandmother's words with fondness, no longer reached his eyes. "That sounds nice," he said. "I might not be going back for a while, though."

"Oh, of course. I didn't mean anytime soon." Eliza tried to camouflage her disappointment with a chipper tone. "Actually, I think I'm just missing good village cooking. Let's go to Çakırlar for breakfast when I'm back."

Deniz brightened. "Ahh, now you've said the magic words. In just one sentence, you invited me to my favorite meal *and* reminded me that my girlfriend is—finally—going to be back by my side."

Smiling back at him, Eliza couldn't shake the feeling that something was amiss. That either something had happened between Deniz and the rest of his family that made him want to keep his distance...or that, for some reason, he wanted to keep her away from them. Time would tell which it was, but regardless, Eliza's anxiety had settled in for the long haul.

Three

Over the course of the next few days, Eliza let her concerns about Deniz's family fade into the background. When he regaled her with heartwarming stories of village life, she didn't make any comments about wanting to visit. If he wanted her to be there in the future, he would invite her. But after having suggested it herself and having the idea shot down, she wouldn't be making a vulnerable declaration like that again.

One day, Deniz video called her from Konyaaltı beach, and Eliza had to stop herself from changing her flight right then and there. Between the beautiful turquoise water, the sound of the waves, and the breeze rippling Deniz's dark hair, she felt homesick...homesick for Antalya, the city she'd lived in not even for a year.

She wouldn't say it to Susan, but she couldn't wait to be back there. It was the quintessential struggle of someone wishing to be in two places at the same time—Eliza still wanted to enjoy every moment she had with her family, to take advantage of every perk her family home in

Michigan offered...but she also wanted to be on that beach with Deniz. To stay up until all hours talking with Crystal about anything and everything. To wake up on a Sunday morning and spend long, leisurely hours eating a massive spread of village breakfast items in Çakırlar. Maybe even to get back to work, especially since she had a new job waiting for her.

"Are you trying to make me jealous?" she asked Deniz, who wore a smug grin as he turned, panning the camera to give her the full view of what she was missing.

"Who, me? Never. I'm just trying to remind you of what's waiting for you here, in case you feel tempted to stay away longer."

"I already know what I'm missing." She raised her eyebrows, focusing her gaze on him rather than on the surrounding scenery.

Deniz grinned. "That's the right answer, of course." He moved the camera closer to his face. "You can get a nice beach in a lot of places, but there's only one Deniz Aydem."

"You're ridiculous." Eliza laughed. "I'm pretty sure I'm supposed to be the one saying that, not you saying it about yourself."

He shrugged. "What can I say? I love myself." His expression deepened then, sincerity showing through his playfulness. "I really miss you, Eliza." He gestured around himself. "That's pretty much why I'm here, you know. Just trying to keep myself distracted so I'm not moping around missing you constantly."

Eliza's heart bloomed at his words, but she didn't let that show on her face. "I miss you, too." Reflecting on what he'd said, a thought occurred to her. "And while it's sweet that you're missing me so much, I don't *actually* get any joy from you being lonely and miserable while I'm gone. Why don't you and Crystal meet up? You can commiserate with each other about how sad and empty the world is without me in it."

Deniz nodded. "That's not a bad idea. I think Barış and Jack are around, too…maybe we could all meet up for drinks or something." He paused a beat before shooting Eliza a mischievous grin. "Did that make you jealous? Are you going to come back early now that all your friends are hanging out without you?"

Eliza gave him the stink eye. "No way. I know you're all just going to be talking about how much you miss me, anyway." She paused for a second before continuing. "No, that's not entirely true. I'll definitely be jealous, and there is a teeny tiny part of my brain that regrets suggesting it. Like if all of you hang out without me, you might realize that I'm *not* actually the glue that holds our whole friend group together."

Shaking his head, Deniz barely let her finish before he began addressing her concerns. "We don't actually need you around because you're the glue. We need you here because you're the best company, possibly the worst dancer, and by far the cutest one of us all."

"Hey!" Eliza feigned insult. "If *I'm* the worst dancer, then what are you? How could you possibly bestow that dishonor on me?"

"There there, my dear darling girlfriend. Please recall that I said '*possibly* the worst dancer.' It's not decided yet, you know. And if you're wondering who else is in the running for that distinction...it's me. I'll admit it."

"That's more like it." Eliza grinned as memories from the first time she had seen Deniz dance came flooding into her mind unbidden. "I will never forget that night in Kaş as long as I live. Forcing you to stay out on the dance floor to give Jack and Barış some alone time. I mean...actually...I don't know if I can say I'll 'never forget it' since there are probably details I already didn't remember the very next day."

"Hmm." Deniz raised an eyebrow. "I seem to remember Crystal telling you over and over in great detail how many times you dragged me out onto the dance floor. How you wouldn't leave me alone all night." A devastating smile started at one corner of his mouth, spreading across his face. "That was the night I first suspected you might have feelings for me, too. They were just buried under layers of contempt and inhibition."

"Nothing a little *rakı* couldn't see right through, huh?"

Deniz nodded. "Indeed. It gave me hope, you know. Having fun with you that night. It made me think we could actually be friends."

"Ha! And how wrong you were? Is that what you were going to say?" Even as the words were coming out, Eliza wondered why she couldn't just have a sweet, honest moment with her boyfriend. Why did she have to deflect every damn vulnerable feeling that came her way?

But Deniz was undeterred. "You know I wasn't. Well, I suppose I *was* wrong in a way. Or I just set my sights too low. Being friends with you would have been enough to sustain me through all the cold winter nights in my uninsulated apartment. But being your boyfriend? That's like being in a toasty cabin with the wood stove burning at full blaze."

"That is...the sweetest? Strangest? metaphor I have ever heard. Thank you? I think..."

Deniz glanced at something Eliza couldn't see off camera. "Oh, we...I mean, I should go. Hurry home soon, okay?"

She nodded. "I will. Call Crystal. I'll talk to you soon."

They blew each other kisses before ending the call, and once Eliza was alone again in her room, she felt something. Or rather, an absence of something. Even from thousands of miles away and limited to a virtual presence, Deniz had warmed the now-empty space. Eliza couldn't believe she'd ever thought him cold and indifferent.

His presence had become a source of comfort. By his side had become a place she felt she fit...and it was still so early in their relationship. She couldn't help but wonder how things would develop between them once she was back in Turkey.

The flutter of excitement that stirred in her belly at that thought was uncomfortable. Eliza's previous relationship, the one that had ended before she got the job offer in Antalya, had nearly put her off relationships as a whole. Alec had been possessive and controlling, and there had been times during the years they were together that Eliza had lost sight of who she was as an individual. It had been a process to recover from that relationship, and it still made Eliza want to pump the brakes now, even with someone as good as Deniz Aydem.

"I've got to dial it down," she said out loud to herself. "Definitely no more talking about meeting the family...what the hell was I thinking? But also, I can't get obsessive about him. He can have...hmm...one night per week. Or maybe two. And I'll promise to have a friend date with Crystal every week, too. And no inviting the boyfriend to tag along on friend date night, either!"

Thinking about Crystal reminded Eliza of her oldest, most constant friend. Her roommate in Antalya, her sister in everything, and the one person who knew her better than anyone else. Possibly even better than her mom. And it shouldn't have surprised her that thinking about Crystal made Eliza realize just how much she missed her.

Can we have a video chat? She texted Crystal. I miss you so much I'm barely functioning.

The three dots signaling that Crystal was typing her response appeared. Duh! And I miss you too. Can we chat tomorrow? Lots going on tonight and I want to give you my undivided attention.

Eliza supposed it was better to spread out her conversations with uplifting people, to share the wealth across two different days rather than injecting herself with a dose of both Deniz *and* Crystal on the same day and then being deprived for the rest of her vacation. I guess I can wait until then, she wrote, letting herself pout to match the emoji she deposited at the end of the message.

Of course you damn well can. If you need something to do between now and then, please feel free to go buy me all the spices and sauces I can't get here. I'm sure Mama Kim would hook you up with *gochujang* and fish sauce if you asked nicely.

Chuckling to herself, Eliza sent back a thumbs up emoji. Red pepper paste would definitely go far in their kitchen exploits, but she wasn't sure she wanted to gamble on bringing a bottle of fish sauce back. As tasty as it was, if that bottle broke on her books, the cleanup would be a nightmare. She'd find some other way to make it up to Crystal.

The rest of Eliza's day had been just the right amount of uneventful. She had settled into such a comfortable routine with her mom and her dad, Dave, that it was almost like their evening routine was a dance they had choreographed in advance. Or in some ways, it might be like Eliza had regressed back to her high school days, the last time she had lived at home with her parents, but she tried to avoid thinking of it that way.

Whatever the explanation, the three of them prepared their plates and settled into their spots on the couches to watch the next episode of *Baker Street*, one of Eliza's favorite detective shows, which she'd been rewatching from the beginning with her parents.

Two and a half episodes later, she switched off the television, gently shaking both of her parents' shoulders as she collected their ice cream bowls and carried them to the kitchen. She had dozed off herself, and when she had woken up a few minutes ago, the Sherlock Holmes retelling was still playing out on the screen, even though its full audience was unconscious.

"I'm going to bed," she told her parents once she'd loaded the last dishes into the dishwasher. "If you two night owls want to keep watching, you go right ahead. But I'm too tired."

"Good night, honey," said Dave, stifling a yawn. Susan just smiled and waved.

Eliza drifted off to sleep so effortlessly that the next morning she didn't even remember pulling her hair into a loose bun on the top of her head. But sure enough, it was still there in the morning, so she must have done at least some fraction of her usual bedtime routine.

She knew she shouldn't—had heard every argument against it that there was, in fact—but she reached for her phone the next morning as she was rubbing the sleep from her eyes. Everyone who knew anything about mental health and productivity harped on about starting your day on your own terms, not immediately checking your phone's notifications or social media newsfeed.

But what if I missed something? Eliza thought to herself. When she was in Turkey, she checked her phone in the morning to make sure that no one back in Michigan had texted her something urgent. After all, what if there was an emergency? What if someone was sick or injured? How was she supposed to know that if not for her phone?

She applied that same logic now. Deniz and Crystal didn't really have a way of getting in contact with her that didn't come through her phone. So if there was something she needed to be informed about, this was the way it was going to happen.

Now, of course, it rarely, if ever, happened that a "quick check of her notifications" was actually quick. It *usually* resulted in Eliza scrolling through her social media feeds and junk emails until the second alarm she had set the night before reminded her that it was time to get up and start her day.

Today was different, though. A message from Crystal, sent hours before Eliza had woken up, was waiting.

Literally can't wait to talk to you today. So much to tell you. Are you awake yet?

Eliza chuckled to herself. "You'd think after knowing me for this long, she'd know better than to ask me that at five o'clock in the morning when I'm on vacation."

She texted Crystal back. **Just woke up...at what should be considered a reasonable hour for someone who doesn't have to go to work today. Are you free now? I can make some coffee and then call you.**

Her phone started ringing with an incoming call from Crystal. Eliza groaned, looking at her reflection in the phone as she tried to rub the pillow marks from her cheek and smooth down her hair.

When it was clear her efforts were in vain, she answered the call. It wasn't as if Crystal had never seen her in this state of barely awake and completely uncaffeinated existence.

"Are you kidding right now?" she asked her roommate's grinning face. "You couldn't even wait for me to boil some water?"

Crystal dismissed her with a wave of her hand. "Like you can't make coffee while you listen to me. No, I couldn't wait any longer!"

"You couldn't wait for what? To see my beautiful face or to spill all the hot goss? I assume that's what's got you grinning like that." Eliza swung her legs out of the bed and shuffled toward the kitchen.

"It's not so much about the gossip being good as it is that I just needed to see you, you know?" Crystal's expression was one of eager openness as she worked to get all the words out that she no doubt wanted to share with Eliza. While Eliza was the introverted half of their relationship, Crystal was the perpetual life of the party, the one they all gathered around to listen to hold court. And that was what she was doing now, even if only for her audience of one.

"I know," Eliza answered. "I've missed you, too. Now talk my ear off. Tell me what's up."

"Well. So much, oh gosh. Where to even start?" Crystal paused for a second before deciding her plan of attack and waving her imaginary rejected topics aside with a brush of her hand. "Well, I can tell you all the other unimportant stuff another time. Or when you're back. But. I saw Deniz yesterday!"

"You did?" When Crystal nodded, Eliza continued. "Did he call you? I told him to get in touch with you, but I didn't expect him to do it that quickly."

Crystal was already shaking her head. "No, he didn't call. Honestly, I'd be surprised if he did. I don't know that Deniz and I are, like, friends without you in the equation." She considered that for a beat. "Maybe we should try hanging out sometime? It seems like I should be friends with him, you know? Especially if the two of you are serious and are going to keep doing this dating thing...seems like I should be his girl on the inside. The one he goes to for advice on what to get you for your birthday or what kind of ring you might want for a proposal."

"Crystal!" While listening to Crystal's monologue, Eliza had made it to the kitchen, where her morning coffee preparation was now well underway. She would have her mug prepared and caffeine flowing through her system in mere moments...but it still wasn't soon enough for the turn Crystal's words had taken. "No one is talking—or even *thinking*—about getting engaged anytime soon. What the hell?"

Crystal just shrugged and kept talking. "Maybe not, but it doesn't hurt to be prepared for anything. Good to know that you're so opposed to marriage, though. I wonder if Deniz knows that. Do you want me to tell him when I see him? We're meeting up with Jack and Barış tonight for drinks."

Eliza fixed her friend with the closest she could come to a death glare. Luckily, the fact that she was still in her pre-caffeinated state worked to her advantage, amplifying the effects of the gaze.

Crystal dropped the joke, concern crossing her face. "What's going on, Eliza? Sorry for poking too much fun...you know I never know when to let a good joke lie."

"It's not just that." Eliza shook her head. "I don't know. Maybe it's just too early in the day to be talking about things like my future with Deniz. I made a comment to him the other day about visiting his village sometime, and it got really weird. You just...you made me think about that again, I guess. And with that thinking comes wondering what's going to happen between us and if he and I even have the same ideas of what we want out of this relationship. Or where we want it to go in the future."

"I get it." Crystal's demeanor had sobered to an almost unrecognizable version of herself, the one Eliza usually only saw in professional settings. It warmed her heart to be reminded of how seriously her dear friend took her feelings. "I'm sorry again." Crystal paused, as if weighing whether to say her next words. "And I think I get it. I mean...I think I get why you're concerned." She seemed flustered as the words tumbled out. "Like...it's justified. You're not making this up, and you have every right to wonder what the hell is going on with you and Deniz."

Four

"I'm sorry, what?" Eliza was incredulous, her hands pausing in midair as her mug-choosing and coffee-pouring motions came to a halt. "Did you seriously just tell me my anxious fears were justified with that look on your face? Friend, this is like something from Helping Your Anxious Friends 101! If you're going to say something about the thing that's triggering their anxiety, maybe focus your efforts on diffusing rather than on escalating."

Crystal looked apologetic, Eliza would give her that at least. "Uh, yeah. Sorry about that. Still, isn't it better that I told you this before you had caffeine pumping through your veins and making it even worse?"

"Sure," Eliza ground out through her teeth. "Why not? Now spill." She sat down at the kitchen table, all attention focused on the phone in her hand.

"Okay, so..." Crystal paused only briefly before Eliza's insistent glare spurred her to keep speaking. "Deniz was out at Castle Bar last night. That's where I saw him."

"Okay..."

"He wasn't alone. There was this young woman there with him, and immediately I got worried that he was cheating on you. You know? Like...how dare he? And at one of your favorite places to go together, too!"

Eliza had to pick her jaw up off the floor. "What? Crystal. What's happening right now? Is Deniz cheating on me? Or are you a terrible storyteller and this is just the interesting introduction to some sort of plot twist?"

"Oh my God, no!" Crystal's eyes widened in horror. "I'm the worst. No. No no no. There's definitely a plot twist. I was just trying to tell it to you like it happened to me, but now I'm seeing how—for good reason—that came across wrong. Definitely not my intention at all. I should have rehearsed this story before I started telling it to you."

"I appreciate your remorse. Now, can you please tell me the damn story?" Eliza's words came out through gritted teeth.

"Okay, so, after I finished my beer, I went over to talk to them. I had been glaring at this girl the whole time, which I feel kind of bad about now. But I was really glaring at the back of Deniz's head. Apparently, he didn't feel that, though, because he sure didn't turn around. Anyway, I went over there, and I was all, 'Deniz, what a delightful surprise to see you here. Who's your friend?' You know, like, really playing up the whole 'caught you, asshole!' angle of it all."

"I'm sure he was impressed by your performance." Eliza said, willing Crystal to keep the important details of the story flowing.

"Oh, definitely. But then he just smiled at me and stood up to give me a hug. And then he was like, 'Crystal, this is my sister, Cansu. Cansu, this is Eliza's friend Crystal,' and I just shook her hand and chatted with them and felt like a jerk the entire time."

But Eliza wasn't listening to Crystal's dissection of her own feelings. She was hung up on the last thing her friend had said. "Cansu is there? Why didn't he tell me?" She remembered talking to Deniz at the beach, his glances off-screen and his slip-up of saying "we" instead of "I." Had Cansu been there then? Had she heard everything Eliza had said to her brother?

Crystal was nodding. "She came back from the village with him. That's what they said. She's spending some time at the beach before she makes her big move to London. I guess their parents weren't too happy with either of them, and so she came to Antalya with Deniz to sort of get a break from some drama back home."

"This is so weird. I don't get why he didn't tell me she was there. Why he didn't have her say hi when we were video chatting. It doesn't make sense."

Crystal grimaced. "That's the thing, though. It might *actually* make some sense. When Deniz went to the restroom, Cansu started talking to me. She said it's not just about her going to London, the drama with their parents. I guess some things they were saying, like, 'What if you fall in love with an English guy?' felt like they applied to Deniz, too. They don't know about you, so they weren't talking about you specifically. But Cansu said her brother was still...concerned, I guess. They've been talking about it a lot. She doesn't really know how to help him or even what to say, so I guess that's why she was talking to me. Poor kid. How's she supposed to play relationship therapist to her brother when she's barely been in a relationship herself?"

"Yeah, well. I'll feel sorry for her later. After I stop feeling concerned for myself that I'm hearing all of this from *you* who heard it from *her*...rather than me hearing it from my boyfriend. You get it, right Crystal? Please tell me I'm not overreacting...this is bizarre, right? He should have talked to me. I shouldn't be getting relationship updates secondhand...or rather, thirdhand, if that's a thing."

"Oh, thirdhand is a thing. You know, tracing information back to its source is, like, a really satisfying mini mystery to solve sometimes. Like between seasons of *Baker Street* when you're craving some good detective work. Or at least, I assume it would be. I like to play a game with myself sometimes when a seemingly random idea pops into my head. And the game goes, 'where did that idea come from?' Because they're never totally random, you know? It always comes from somewhere, something I read or scanned past on the internet—"

"That does sound like fun, Crys." Eliza was making no attempts to hide her gritted teeth and uneasy demeanor. "You'll tell me about it another time, okay? I need to go now...think about this. I'm not going to be good company for you right now, anyway."

For the first time since the call had begun, Crystal looked concerned. "You're okay, right? Did I do the right thing telling you this? I know you're going to be back here soon, but I just didn't want to wait and spring it on you as soon as you arrived."

"No, I'm glad you told me. And I'm sure there's a reason Deniz is being like this." Eliza shook her head. "I'm not going to confront him about it, and you don't need to either. He'll tell me when he tells me. *If* he tells me about the family stuff, I mean."

"Are you really going to be able to play it cool? Come on, won't he assume that you and I talked about this? Eliza, why don't you just talk to him openly? Isn't that what's so cool about your relationship with him in the first place?"

Eliza shrugged. "He doesn't know how much I know. I doubt Cansu shared her exact words with him, and honestly, the information you and he exchanged is hardly the stuff of a great scandal. No, it's the whole, 'My family might not approve of my girlfriend' angle that's really interesting to me. But if I know my boyfriend, he thinks he's got that all buttoned up. That no one knows how he's feeling and no one can read any stress coming off of him." She smiled. "I guess he underestimated his little sister, though. I wish I could be there to hang out with her, even if being in the same room with Deniz right now might make me want to shake him and demand that he tell me things."

Crystal cocked an eyebrow. "Uhh...so, you're frustrated with him for not telling you things openly...and you're also refusing to speak honestly with him until he does it first? Okay then..."

Eliza just rolled her eyes. "Don't mock. I have a system that works for me. Now, if you'll excuse me, I've got some nasty and unwelcome emotions to deal with and put back where they belong."

"Whatever you say. I'll see you in a few days, though, right?"

"Are you asking me if I'm still coming back to my home, my job, and my life? Friend, just because I'm having a little drama with my boyfriend doesn't mean I'm going to move back in with my parents forever."

"Just checking!"

Eliza scoffed and shook her head at her friend, both of them blowing each other kisses as they ended the call.

Now it was time for Eliza to get to work. That conversation and its revelations about Deniz's family's feelings about Eliza had stirred up many unwanted emotions. Coffee was no longer a necessity due to the sheer volume of stress-induced energy running through her body. It was awfully early for her cortisol levels to be this high, but that didn't mean she couldn't manage an anxious thought when it came her way.

Eliza retreated to her bedroom, closing the door behind her. Tempting as it was to vent to her mom about what she had just learned, it wouldn't change anything. There was no way that either of them would get more information about the situation by talking it to death, and yet the emotions of feeling outraged and offended were addictive. No, Eliza had been down that path before, and if she wanted to, she could choose it again. Vent to anyone who would listen, and when one person got tired of listening, find another one and start over again from the beginning.

She decided to try something different, remembering all of Crystal's readily shared wisdom about various stress management techniques. Wasn't deep breathing supposed to be a helpful thing?

Eliza took a deep breath in, feeling her chest rising, then let it out again quickly, repeating that a few times until she was convinced it had done nothing. Not a bit of good. *Was there supposed to be some kind of trick to this?* she wondered to herself, as she continued to pant and feel stressed, pant and feel stressed.

Finally, convinced breathing was a sham, she flopped onto her bed and pulled out her phone. When all else failed, nothing beat doom scrolling social media to take her mind off of what was bothering her. If she was going to feel crappy about Deniz, why not feel crappy about everything else at the same time?

True to her word to Crystal, a few short days later, Eliza was at Detroit Metropolitan Airport, waiting for her first in a series of flights back to Antalya. The fact that there wasn't a direct flight from her first home to her second home was, at the moment, the bane of her existence. But the journey would be a welcome respite between the emotions of saying goodbye to her parents and the potential drama that was waiting for her in Turkey.

It was never easy to hug her parents goodbye at the airport. As much as Susan and Dave Britt were supportive of Eliza, as much as they wanted her to live her dreams, and as much as she wanted to live said dreams...there was still a force between them that rebelled against the separation. A force that wished that everyone could live their dreams and fulfill their purposes and be the happiest versions of themselves...preferably from a distance of five miles, rather than five thousand. That force was just another name for love, and Eliza was grateful at every tearful airport departure that her parents weren't the kind to guilt her or beg her to stay. She knew some of her peers didn't have it that easy, and some of them had it even worse, with families who didn't seem to care about their decisions at all.

Eliza loved her parents, though, and they loved her, too. Now that she had dried the tears that had snuck out of her eyes, she was ready for the adventure that awaited her. Her return to Turkey, which was no longer the unknown...and her return to being a full-time girlfriend and navigating all the complicated dynamics that came along with that, which was pretty much uncharted territory for her.

She fired off nearly identical text messages to Crystal and Deniz to let them both know that she was on her way, then popped on her headphones and started listening to an audiobook. If she was going to be zoning out in a series of airports for the next twenty hours, at least she had something to keep her mind occupied while she did so.

Crystal's response came first. Awesome! Can't wait to see you. Where are you stopping between here and there? I want to stalk your flights.

Eliza groaned inwardly at the reminder that her flight was anything but direct, then responded. Boston first, then Istanbul, then Antalya. So, I'll be there...tomorrow?

Can't be soon enough for me! I'm counting down the minutes. Safe travels!

After thanking Crystal and reassuring her she would, in fact, keep her best friend updated about any flight delays, Eliza let herself get lost in the story she was listening to again. While it felt uncomfortable not to have something to do with her hands or her eyes, audiobooks solved the pesky motion sickness that made most weekend trips within Antalya Province unbearable.

Eliza thought back to the first weekend away, the trip to Kaş with their whole friend group. Deniz had been there, too. That was the night they'd first had fun together, the night Eliza had blamed on too much alcohol for far longer than she should have. If she hadn't been so stubborn about it, she might have been able to admit her true feelings for Deniz sooner. But it wasn't as if he'd exactly been forthcoming about his feelings, either. Or about his true non-asshole nature. For the first several months they'd known each other, Eliza had gotten the distinct impression that Deniz prided himself on being mysterious and misunderstood.

Of course, once she'd seen through the act thanks to a series of good deeds and vulnerable confessions, everything had changed.

Or at least she thought it had. She looked down at the phone in her hand again, checking that there was still no response from Deniz to her last message. The two of them hadn't chatted face to face again since their previous conversation at the beach...or since Crystal's bomb dropping about Deniz's family drama. Eliza didn't know if the lack of communication between them was more about her being busy with her parents and friends, her avoiding facing the truth that Crystal had hinted at, or if the lack of communication was coming from Deniz.

Why should I take all the blame for the two of us not talking? It's not like he's been calling me and I've been ignoring it. The thoughts were intrusive, but they weren't entirely unwelcome. If Eliza had to feel a repetitive emotion, something like rage was always more welcome than something that made her feel weak. No, things might be weird or strained between them when she saw Deniz again, but that was better than duking this out on a video call.

In an impulsive and possibly passive aggressive move, Eliza sent off one more text message to Deniz before switching off her phone. Let me know if you're still planning on picking me up at the airport, okay? It's cool if you aren't, but I'd just like to know.

Five

It wasn't until Istanbul that Eliza let herself take her phone off airplane mode. Everything had been on time up until that point, so she hadn't needed to send any updates to Crystal. But her stubbornness and the justified frustration that was keeping her lit from within like a never-ending flame wasn't ready to see whatever sweet response was waiting from Deniz. No, if he had written to say, Of course I'll be there! I'm waiting already! I've got coffee and your favorite flowers and a bag full of books, it would be very hard to stay mad at him. And staying mad at him just might be the thing that was keeping Eliza's mind off how tired she was, how interminable this travel day had been, and just how uncomfortable her legs were already.

She wanted nothing more than to stretch out on her own bed, but as there was still one more flight between her and said bed, she settled for walking laps around the terminal. She had two hours to kill in Istanbul, and she knew beyond any doubt that she had already sat enough for at least the whole next week. Eliza was prone to restlessness, not just the restlessness of spirit that came from being a Sagittarius, but the restlessness of legs that came from having Restless Leg Syndrome. Something she had no doubt inherited from Susan, but which was the only trait of her mother's that she would have gladly given back.

It had taken her phone a few moments to realize it was back in Turkey and send her the standard, Welcome to Turkey! Here are all the details about how your phone works here and blah blah blah text message.

Along with it had come a message from Deniz. No way, I'll definitely be there! If I'm a tiny bit late, don't go anywhere. I promise I'm on my way.

Eliza frowned at her phone like it had grown a second head. Or a *first* head considering that it was a phone. How do you already know you're going to be late? I'm not landing for, like...3 hours? Are you walking to the airport?

Just something I've got to do before I come there. I promise I'm not walking there and I won't make you walk home either!

A sigh escaped from Eliza's lips. "I'm already exhausted from all this travel, and it's only going to get worse in the next three hours. What kind of stunt is this guy pulling?"

Before she could overthink it too much, she fired off a text asking him (more or less) just that. Okay...fair warning, though. I'm definitely going to be very tired by the time I arrive. Can't promise to wait too long, so...you know...

It was vague, but she was fairly confident the message communicated her impending frustration with the situation. She had neither the energy to explain herself more clearly nor the desire to navigate the finer point of airport pickup relationship dynamics via text message. This was a conversation they could have in person...in a few days, perhaps.

I'll be there, Eliza. If you have to wait more than five minutes, your meal is free. Isn't that the sort of promise American restaurants like to make?

Despite herself, she smiled. She'd prefer a clear estimate of when to expect him at the airport, but she still could appreciate the joke. Eliza was also willing to admit (or at least consider) that her exhaustion and the emotion of leaving her homeland behind (again) had made her a little extra sensitive.

The travel gods must have been smiling on Eliza, because her flight from Istanbul to Antalya had departed on time and even arrived early. In fact, she had departed the plane and even collected her suitcases by the time her flight was scheduled to land.

But maybe being early wasn't the best thing when her boyfriend was planning to be a few minutes late. If her flight had been twenty minutes late rather than early, maybe he would already be here, waiting.

Because the truth was, as she scanned the faces outside the domestic arrivals exit, he wasn't here yet. Eliza had hoped he would be, had excitedly anticipated his smiling face being one of the first ones she'd seen upon exiting the airport...and yet, in a sea of friendly hotel chauffeurs and taxi drivers looking for a fare, there was not one familiar smile to be seen.

Eliza forced a smile that she didn't feel, wheeling her suitcases off to the side to make way for the travelers exiting behind her. She scrolled through the messages on her phone, firing off a few updates to people who'd been waiting for them.

Susan had likely been waiting for this text since Eliza had hugged her goodbye the day before. Her mom was inclined to refresh the flight tracker app on her phone every five minutes when her only child was in the air. Now that Eliza was on the ground again, her day could begin. Or else she could finally catch the sleep she had missed the night before due to said flight tracking.

Crystal, of course, responded immediately, considering that she was both in the same time zone and awaiting having her roommate back in her apartment. Can't even wait to see you!

To Eliza's happy surprise, Deniz's response was immediate, too. I'm 2 minutes away. Stay right where you are!

That brought a smile to her face. The promise of only two more minutes, upright and weighed down by her heavy backpack, was encouraging to the utmost. Standing there with all her bags for an indefinite amount of time had felt like torture, but two minutes? 120 seconds? That was nothing.

Before Eliza had even counted to 100 (because of course counting the seconds away had seemed like a great way to pass the time), she spotted Deniz's head making his way through the crowd. If she had thought she felt relieved knowing he'd be there soon, it was nothing compared to how she felt *actually* seeing him there.

It seemed unfair that Deniz was looking better than ever while Eliza was feeling like a swamp thing after twenty hours of travel, but damn if it wasn't the truth. Either he had spent the summer out in the sun lifting heavy things or else she'd just missed him so much that she'd forgotten quite how striking a figure he cut.

Eliza's feet were moving towards Deniz, faster with each step, and they had matching grins on their faces. The distance closed between them, and then she was abandoning her suitcases and flinging her arms around him. Deniz took Eliza in his arms, picking her up and spinning her around. He was talking, but his face was pressed so close to Eliza's ear (and her ears still felt unbalanced from all the ascents and descents and pressure changes) that she only caught a few words. "...you...missed...happy..." was pretty much all she could understand.

Finally, Deniz set her down, stepping back without letting go—his arms were still around her upper back. "Hi," he said, smiling into her eyes. "God, I've missed you so much. I can't believe I'm really seeing you." He pulled her back in for another hug. "Holding you. Kissing you."

Eliza tried to stop him before he went in for the kiss, overwhelmed by all the preparations she needed to do in order to feel ready for her close-up. She definitely needed to brush her teeth. Probably needed some lip balm. And it wouldn't hurt to wash her face, brush her hair, and put on a little makeup.

Apparently, however, Deniz didn't mind. His hands slid up to her cheeks as he pulled her in for a kiss, and a groan escaped his throat as their lips met. Whatever weirdness Eliza had been feeling, spurred by the summer spent apart and the lack of communication in the last days, it was all forgotten in that moment. *This* was what she had been needing. *This* could ground her in seconds, could center her back in the security of a comforting, loving relationship in a flash, doing the work of hours and hours of long-distance conversation.

"Hi," she said when they pulled apart. "I really missed you."

Deniz was shaking his head. "Not as much as me. I can hardly believe you're here now, because it feels like you've been gone *forever.*"

Quirking an eyebrow, Eliza responded. "Was it really that bad without me?"

"Whatever you're thinking, it was worse. I think I barely survived."

"You'll have to tell me all about that."

"I will, but maybe not tonight." Deniz was turning them, leading Eliza by the hand while he wheeled her suitcase in his other hand. "The end of a long travel day is no time to start dissecting family drama."

Eliza nodded. "Probably not." Before she could evaluate whether it was the right question to ask, her tiredness and resultant lack of filter forced her next words past her lips. "Was that what kept you tonight, or...?"

"Ah." Deniz's lips formed a line. "Part of it, yes. I was taking my sister to the bus terminal." He checked his watch. "Her bus is leaving in ten minutes."

Hearing him confirm what Crystal had told her but he hadn't mentioned was a relief; Eliza nearly smiled at the reassurance that her boyfriend wasn't hiding something from her, but bit it back. Instead, she said, "Oh, I didn't know Cansu was here visiting. I'm sorry I missed her."

Deniz's smile was genuine now. "She was sorry to miss you, too, but she'll be back." A new expression crossed his face Was he...embarrassed? "Actually, this time she specifically wanted to leave before you got here to give us some time alone. I told her it was unnecessary, but she insisted."

Eliza's eyebrows traveled up her forehead against her wishes. "I...uh. Wow. Okay. That seems...more direct than I would have expected."

Deniz's cheeks flushed to a deep maroon. "Oh no, I don't mean that. She wasn't hinting at...that. She just knew you would be tired and didn't want you to feel like you had to be social or anything. My sister and I, we don't talk about things like that."

"Oh...okay then. That's good to know. Obviously, Crystal is the closest thing I have to a sister, and she and I *do* definitely tease each other about these things."

He nodded. "Why am I not at all surprised to hear that?" They had continued walking, and by now they were almost to Deniz's car. Eliza could see its lights blinking in the near distance as Deniz clicked the button on his key fob.

"Oh, right!" Eliza blurted the words. "There was something else you said that needed a response from me. It almost slipped my mind in the shock of imagining you and your sister teasing each other about your love lives."

Deniz cleared his throat. "Yes? What was that?"

"Well...you said you assured Cansu that it wasn't necessary for her to leave us alone tonight." She cocked an eyebrow in his direction. "Are you willing to stand by those words now? Did you really mean that you wouldn't appreciate a little alone time with your girlfriend, who you haven't seen all summer?"

The blush that had faded from Deniz's cheeks was back with a vengeance. "Eliza," he scolded, "don't you know I was just being polite?"

She quirked an eyebrow back at him. "Oh yeah?"

"Well, obviously." He was cute when he was flustered. She'd never seen him quite like this before. "I couldn't exactly tell her she needed to go. I mean, that's not really how we do things, you know? Especially when she needed to get away, needed to stay with me. I didn't want to kick her out. So I said the polite things, insisted she should stay." He smiled then. "You should be glad it was Cansu staying with me. If it had been another member of my family, they probably wouldn't have picked up on the need to give a new couple some privacy."

"It would be nice to meet some of your family, though. I wouldn't have minded." Had she said that out loud? Were they going to get into this family thing now, before they'd even loaded her bags in the trunk? "I mean..." Eliza fumbled, trying to change the subject that she had so carelessly broached. "No, you're right. Tonight isn't the time to meet anyone. Another time, perhaps. I'm glad your sister is so tuned in."

"Me, too." They had arrived at his car now, and he pulled her in for another embrace after depositing her bags at the back of the vehicle. "That's just one of the things I'm grateful for in this moment."

"Oh?"

He nodded. "I'm mostly grateful for your safe arrival and because I have you here in my arms, all to myself." He paused, a thought flashing across his face. "I *do* have you to myself, right? I mean...do I get to keep you tonight? Or did Crystal give you a curfew?"

Eliza frowned. "You know, I didn't even think. I think I was so tired and jet lagged, I just assumed I would go home and sleep in my own bed tonight. I even told Crystal I'd see her later."

"Ah, sure. Okay, then." Deniz's mouth was smiling in the corners, but Eliza could see disappointment in his eyes. He was rallying like a champ, though. "I can take you home now, then. Or would you like to eat something first?"

"You didn't let me finish." She smiled as she wrapped her arms around his waist. "I *thought* I would want to sleep in my own bed tonight, but now that I'm here with you, the thought of sleeping alone is unbearable." She frowned then as a thought occurred to her. "Of course, I should warn you that even though I am *very* happy to see you, it doesn't change the fact that I'm exhausted and jet lagged and not going to be much for conversation or...well...anything else tonight. So if you want to drop me at my apartment, I'll understand."

Deniz dropped a kiss on her forehead. "I'll take you home. I know there's nothing better than sleeping in your own bed, and you've never slept over at my place before.

I'm sure it would be good to be home and to see Crystal, too."

"Oh, right. Okay, then." Now it was Eliza's turn to force a smile. Was she going to have to kiss Deniz goodbye again so soon after kissing him hello?

"Um, but..." Deniz was blushing again. Eliza raised her eyebrow again, prompting him to continue. "Would it be alright if I stayed over at your place, too? I promise no funny business expectations. I'd just like to be near you."

"That is possibly the cutest thing you've ever said to me. Did you know that?" While Eliza and Deniz had been a couple for several months, they had been apart for most of that time. They had spent just about a week in Antalya after their initial, "I like you," and "I like you, too," confessions, but there hadn't been time for overnight visits yet. Neither of them wanted to rush things, especially not when Eliza had been about to leave for the entire summer.

But things were different now, weren't they? Eliza was back, which meant they were in the same city...indefinitely. And that meant everything could change. The ways they had been holding back, avoiding rushing things or jumping too far into their relationship too quickly...well, now they would have to reevaluate that. They weren't a long-distance couple anymore, and that meant the nature of their relationship had shifted.

While all those thoughts had been swirling through Eliza's travel-addled mind, she had neglected to answer Deniz's question beyond telling him he was cute. But he had been watching her face intently, no doubt wondering what was going on inside her mind, while she had pondered all the ways in which they were about to take their relationship to the next level.

He nudged her into speaking with just one word. "Eliza?"

"Right." She shook her head to clear her thoughts. "Of course! I don't want to be away from you, either. You should stay." Now it was her turn to feel embarrassed. "I just...this is a new thing for us. The overnight visit, I mean. And I'm thinking about what that's going to be like. I mean, I am definitely too tired to think about...*things*. But that doesn't mean I won't be thinking about them, if that makes sense. And I am wondering if the two of us are just going to lie side by side, staring up at the ceiling and feeling awkward. And if that means that this is a bad idea. Or that I need to drink a cup of coffee or twelve and rally so that our first sleepover can be a *proper* first sleepover and—"

"Eliza." Deniz repeated her name, this time interrupting her with a gentle smile and a reassuring hand on her shoulder. "I am telling you right now that whatever *things* you are thinking about, whatever expectations you have of what is *supposed* to happen during a first sleepover..." He shook his head, smiling at her. "They are all off the table tonight. What I mean to say—and I think I should spell this out in clear language so that you don't read into it—is that, no matter what you say and no matter what you do, I will *not* have sex with you. Not in any definition of the word. So you can put that thought aside and stop torturing yourself with it."

"You won't? No matter what I say and do? That...uh...should I be offended?"

He laughed then. "I'm not saying I'm not interested, Eliza. I'm just telling you I'm not an animal. I can recognize the dangerous combination of extreme exhaustion and extreme overthinking, and I knew that if I didn't spell this out for you in a crystal clear way, you would torture yourself over it until you were literally too tired and too wired to sleep." He shrugged. "This way, I hope you can relax. And sleep. And all that other stuff can figure itself out...*soon*."

"Soon, but not tonight, soon?"

"Exactly."

He kissed her again then, his lips on hers and his hands in her hair conveying the exact depth of the promise of his words. Tonight might be about one jet-lagged woman sleeping like she was dead, but the next time they saw each other overnight, something very different from potential snoring and drooling was in store for them.

Six

While Deniz's presence may have reawakened Eliza, her pulse tripping over itself at his nearness and the promise of more time together, the drive from the airport to her familiar apartment in Konyaaltı had lulled her back into complete exhaustion. The sights out the window of Deniz's car were welcoming and familiar, and in a complete 180-degree turn from her first arrival in Antalya—when she couldn't get enough of the palm trees, the unfamiliar words written on buildings, the *newness* of it all—now she felt at home again, as comforted by the sight of the Mediterranean Sea as she had been by the billboards on I-94 when she arrived in Detroit.

Eliza's eyes had slipped closed despite her earnest efforts to stay awake, to chat with Deniz while he drove. At some point, though, he had gone silent, turning up the music playing on his radio, and Eliza had—probably as he had intended—rested her eyes for just a moment.

But that moment had stretched, and when she opened them again, Deniz was parallel parking his car on the street in front of the building where she shared an apartment with Crystal.

She wiped a hand over her face, thankfully feeling just the sheen of sweat and oil she had spent the last twenty hours collecting and no drool from her adventures in car sleeping. "Sorry," she said, smiling at Deniz. "I guess I fell asleep. Not great company for a drive across town."

"Well, one of us had a long journey today. And actually, it *wasn't* me, driving across Antalya." He winked at her. "I can forgive you for drifting off in the passenger seat. If you'd been driving, that would be a different story."

"For sure." A laugh huffed out between Eliza's lips. "I promise never to drive a car or operate any heavy machinery when I'm this tired."

"On behalf of all the other drivers on the road, I thank you." Deniz opened his door, stretching one long leg out onto the street. "Now, shall we get your things upstairs and get you tucked into bed?"

Eliza followed his lead, exiting the car and meeting him back at the trunk. "Yes, please," she yawned. "I mean, if Crystal will let that happen."

At that moment, the sound of a throat clearing came from the balcony above them. "Excuse me?" a voice called down, indignant. "What did you say about Crystal?"

Looking up to the third floor, Eliza's face split into a grin. There, her torso hanging over the railing of the balcony, was her oldest and dearest friend, Crystal Kim. Crystal wore a grin that matched Eliza's own and was waving her right hand animatedly, bouncing up and down.

"Crys!" Eliza called up to her friend. "Is that really you? God, I've missed you!"

Crystal turned around once, giving a 360 degree view to Eliza down below. "It's really me! Not a holograph." She smiled at Deniz then, greeting him with a nod. "Are you two going to get up here now, or do I need to come down there and carry you?"

Eliza grinned as Deniz closed the trunk of the car. "Coming right up!"

But as they made their way to the apartment door, Crystal fled from the balcony, darting back into the apartment.

They met her on the stairs, out of breath as she jogged down to meet them. "Let me help," she said, taking one suitcase from Deniz. Smiling over her shoulder at Eliza, she panted as she lugged the suitcase up, step by step. "Bet you wish we had an elevator here now, huh?"

Eliza shrugged. "Well, from the looks of it—" she glanced pointedly down at her empty hands, only a backpack on her person "—I'm not exactly the one struggling here. I can take that suitcase from you though, if it's too heavy."

Crystal was already shaking her head. "As if! I'm neither too weak to carry this suitcase nor willing to watch you exert any more effort than you already are. You've done enough!" She wiggled her eyebrows then, a sure sign a cheesy joke was coming. "Your arms must be exhausted from flapping yourself all the way over here!"

Eliza groaned. "See, it's shit like that, those terrible dad jokes of yours, that makes me wonder why I even came back. I'm not even in the apartment yet and I'm already in physical pain from your sense of humor."

"Sorry, not sorry," Crystal chirped. "And don't even tease me like that. I know how much you love me. I know you couldn't function without me." She turned her gaze to Deniz, who was silently carrying Eliza's other suitcase beside her. "Deniz! You're awfully quiet over there."

"Just giving the two of you some time to tease each other or have a love fest or whatever it is you two like to do together. Don't mind me, just silently observing back here."

As they made their way up the last flight of stairs, Eliza couldn't help but grin. It felt like she was home, not that different from how it had felt to walk up the steps to her parents' porch a couple of months before. What an odd sensation it was to feel so at home in two places that couldn't be further or more different from each other.

She smiled at Deniz and Crystal in turn, while waiting for Crystal to open the apartment door. Of course, even more than having buildings or apartments feel like home, she was grateful to have people who felt like home in her life. Overcome with the sensation, she leaped forward and nearly tackled Crystal with a hug.

"Ouch!" Crystal fell into the doorframe as the door opened, making Eliza lose her balance, too. "What the heck?"

"Just missed you," said Eliza, her words muffled along with her face in the back of Crystal's shirt.

"Yeah, I missed you, too, but still. Get off me!"

The two friends tumbled into the apartment with Deniz close behind them, bringing in the suitcase that had been abandoned in Crystal's effort to get away from Eliza. When the door was closed, Crystal granted her best friend the hug she had been looking for, both of them laughing and talking over each other about how good it was to be back together again.

Deniz had opted to give the two friends a moment alone, wheeling Eliza's suitcases into her room before rejoining them in the living room, where Eliza was sipping a glass of water, Crystal sitting practically on her lap.

"Are you hungry?" He asked the question to both women, holding up his phone. "I could order something..."

Crystal gestured to Eliza. "I leave it up to you, friend. If you're too tired and just want to crash, I *guess* I'll understand and not be horribly offended. But if you want to sit and eat and chat and tell me everything that happened back home and dig presents for me out of your suitcase, well...I won't say no to that, either." She batted her eyelashes at Eliza, eliciting a laugh.

"Can we split the difference? I'm exhausted," Eliza admitted, "but I'm pretty sure if I go to sleep now I'm going to wake up at three in the morning absolutely famished." She looked at Deniz and Crystal. "What should we get? *Adana kebab*? Pizza? Some kind of *durum*?"

Deniz was scrolling through his phone, checking out their options. "Looks like the quickest option, assuming that's a priority—" He looked to Eliza for her nod, confirming his assumption, then closed his phone. "The quickest option is going to be me running downstairs and picking up *durum* for all of us a couple of blocks away. Delivery will take longer and probably be cold."

"Do you mind?" Eliza was shaking her head. "No, you don't have to do that. It's okay, really. We can wait. You should stay."

But Deniz was already moving towards the door. "What do you want—chicken? Meat? Drinks?"

"Chicken, please! *Ayran* for me!" crowed Crystal.

"I'll take the same," said Eliza, shooting Deniz an apologetic look. "I wish you would stay, though."

He just winked at her. "I'll be back before you know it. So if you're going to talk about me while I'm gone, you'd better make it quick."

And just like that, he was gone.

"So." Crystal moved away from Eliza to better see her face. "What's going on here? Is Deniz staying over tonight? Did you talk about his sister? Are you two going to...you know...?" She wiggled her eyebrows with her final words.

Eliza shook her head. "He *is* staying, but don't bother listening at the door for sexy sounds, you perv. We already decided that isn't happening tonight."

Crystal's jaw was on the floor. "You what? Why would you—? How does one even have that conversation? Was it like, 'Hello, my dear, I've missed you so much all summer long, now please keep your hands to yourself and keep, ahem, *it* in your pants. Thank you very much for your attention to this matter.'?" Crystal's impression had included an affected upperclass (possibly British, though it bared little resemblance to an actual British accent) voice, with facial mannerisms to match.

Eliza laughed. "Believe it or not, that is inaccurate. But without sounding like characters in a period drama, grown-ups do actually have mature conversations about things like sexual expectations."

"Boring! Glad I'm not a grown up, then." Crystal rolled her eyes. "What about the other stuff? Did you talk about Cansu?"

With a slight nod, Eliza continued. "Just a bit. He was taking her to the bus station tonight before he came to the airport to get me. We haven't gotten into everything yet. I mean, I've only just arrived, and I could barely keep my eyes open in the car. We'll talk about it soon, I'm sure."

But Crystal didn't look convinced. "I hope you do. He shouldn't be keeping anything from you, not if he cares about you like he says he does."

"While I agree that people in relationships shouldn't keep important things from each other, I'm willing to give him the benefit of the doubt, Crystal. To hear where he was coming from rather than assuming the worst."

Crystal shrugged. "Well, you're a better woman than me, then. If the guy I'm dating kept a secret—I don't even care what kind of secret it was—from me, I'd give him maybe half a minute to explain himself before I'd just straight up end things. If you care about me, you'd better make it damn clear."

"Are...um..." Eliza fumbled over her words, struggling to form a sentence. "Am I supposed to skip the part of your response where you mentioned 'the guy I'm dating'? Was that a hypothetical guy?" Off Crystal's sheepish look, Eliza felt her voice rising in both pitch and volume. "Crystal! Are you seeing someone?" She shook her head. "You're one to talk about keeping secrets, friend. Spill!"

"I...will." Crystal wasn't quite meeting Eliza's eyes. "I don't know why I didn't tell you about him, but he's great. Really! We've been seeing each other for about two months now."

"Crystal! Are you telling me that almost the entire time I was gone, you were *dating* someone? That seems like the kind of thing you would tell your best friend."

"It...definitely does. I can't explain it, Eliza. It's not that I'm not excited about him. I swear, that's not it. I guess I was just waiting for you to come back, so I could introduce the two of you. You're going to love him, Eliza. He's...I don't even know how to sum him up. He's just the best. So smart, so funny, so...well, hot."

Despite herself, a laugh barked out of Eliza. "Well, I'm glad about that, at least." She picked up her phone to check the time. "We probably don't have long until Deniz is back, so I'll let you off the hook. You can tell me all about—and possibly introduce me to—Mystery Man tomorrow. But for now, just know that I'm sternly lowering my eyebrows at you, shaming you for not telling me about him sooner. And I'm also happy for you, but that seems less important right now."

Crystal hung her head. "You're right. I'll make it up to you...tomorrow. Let's talk about you, though. Is everything okay? Really? All good on the Deniz front?"

"I can't tell you anything I don't know, Crys. I've barely been back long enough to figure it out." Eliza felt a lazy smile spread across her face. "All I can tell you is that it was just the best thing ever to see him there at the airport. I don't know what it is, exactly, but there's something about that man...it's like coming home and also going on an adventure at the same time. It feels like a dream that I get to be the one holding his hand, doing life with him. I just hope I don't wake up anytime soon."

"That's beautiful, Eliza." Crystal was grinning. "No, I'm serious! I've never seen you like this before. Certainly not with Alec." She pulled a face at her own mention of Eliza's ex. "And you deserve to be happy. You know that, right? Stop waiting for 'the other shoe to fall' or whatever it is that keeps you up nights wondering when this is all going to fall apart. Deniz is a great guy. And he cares about you a lot. And the two of you are happy together. It's good, you know? Just...just let it be good."

"I'm trying to do that," Eliza admitted, "and I'm trying not to get myself so lost in this relationship that I risk breaking my own heart before it's even really begun."

Crystal was quiet for a moment. "Deep," she finally said. "Possibly *too* deep, considering the level of jet lag we're working with. Don't overthink it just yet. Have fun. At least for tonight. At least for the rest of the summer."

Eliza nodded. "Yeah...I mean, easier said than done, but yeah. I'm trying."

Crystal reached over to squeeze Eliza's hand, but before she could say something—something encouraging, Eliza hoped—there was a knock on the door, alerting them that Deniz had returned. The two friends jumped up, Eliza flying to the door at the same time Crystal made her way to the kitchen, rummaging around for plates, utensils, salt and pepper.

"Hi!" Eliza flung the door open with a grin that only deepened as her eyes landed on Deniz on the other side. Was it just because it was still her first day back in Antalya, or was *every* time she saw him after a short parting going to come with a massive helping of joy and a large side dish of butterflies? Still, she knew those things usually faded away, so she should enjoy her butterflies while she had them.

As Deniz came inside, slipping his shoes off on the way, Eliza wrapped her arms around his waist, burrowing her face into his chest and taking a deep inhale. Yes, his smell was at least as comforting and intoxicating as she had re-membered. Possibly more so—she *had* been gone for over a month, after all. Things could change in that amount of time, even things like hormones and pheromones...she assumed. She'd have to look that up later to satisfy her in-ner curiosity, but for now she'd settle for one more lungful before stepping back to help Deniz with the bags in his hands.

After the three of them had eaten, Crystal insisted Eliza head to bed. "I'll clean up here," she said, gesturing to the surrounding kitchen. "Seriously. Do you not think I can handle it?" Eliza's face must have conveyed that she knew Crystal's housekeeping skills a little too well to believe that statement, and Crystal scoffed back at her. "It's not that I don't know how to wash a plate, Eliza. I just typically choose not to." She shrugged. "Anyway, it's none of your concern. Your only job right now is to get in that room, put on your pajamas, snuggle up next to that man over there"—she gestured towards Deniz and his steadily grow-ing pinker cheeks—"and get some freaking sleep."

"But I'm not tired," Eliza said, even as a yawn threatened to sneak past her lips. "I mean, I definitely *was* tired, but I'm feeling so much better now. So much more energized after seeing the two of you..." Was that it? Was she just feeling wired and excited, or was she avoiding the aforementioned snuggling up next to Deniz? And if she was avoiding it, then why the hell was she doing that? It was no secret to her heart, mind, or body that she was attracted to Deniz Aydem. That she enjoyed being around him. That he made her smile and laugh and feel flushed with excitement.

Deniz was the first to move. "Come on, Eliza," he said, taking her hand and tugging her towards her room. "You technically *can* fight the jet lag, but what's the point? Let's get you to bed."

Feeling her eyes widening despite herself, Eliza nodded to Crystal. "Good night then, I guess. See you in the morning!"

"Have a good night!" Crystal's response came with a wink and a wiggle of her eyebrows, and it made Eliza want to revoke her best friend status.

Deniz closed the door behind them as they entered Eliza's bedroom, his momentum screeching to a halt once they were alone in the small room. The only furniture it contained was Eliza's queen-sized bed and a wardrobe full of clothing, so apart from the edge of her bed, there wasn't anywhere for him to sit. He did just that perching awkwardly at the foot of the bed and looking around. "Did you want me to leave you alone for a minute to change?" Deniz asked, his eyes not quite meeting hers.

Eliza shook her head. "It's okay." She flipped one of her suitcases onto its side, digging through to find some clean shorts and a t-shirt to sleep in, as well as her toothbrush. "I'll change in the bathroom after I brush my teeth." Noticing for the first time that Deniz was empty-handed, she asked the question that crossed her mind out loud. "Did you need anything, or...?"

"I didn't bring a change of clothes or a toiletry kit with me, if that's what you mean." Deniz was smiling now. "It would have felt presumptuous and overly optimistic, I think, showing up at the airport with a suitcase of my own."

Eliza laughed. "Oh, you need a whole suitcase? And I thought *I* was the high maintenance one in this relationship." She felt lighter already, laughing once again with Deniz rather than feeling overwhelmed by tension and expectation. "Do you want me to check with Crystal? Maybe her new boyfriend—I know, don't look at me like that, she didn't mention him to me, either—left something here that would fit you."

Deniz grimaced. "No, thanks. I'll stick with my t-shirt and boxers, if that's alright with you, rather than putting on another man's clothes."

"Yeah, that's what I figured." Eliza shrugged then. "I had to ask, and I figured it was better than offering you these." She held up the pair of small plaid shorts she had been rummaging through her suitcase for, puzzling over the look that flashed across Deniz's eyes for just a second. What was wrong with her shorts? He couldn't be that offended that she didn't have a stash of clothes tailor-made to his body type...*Oh*, she thought suddenly. *That wasn't a look of offense, duh. That was...something else. Right. Wow, they were right. I definitely do need to get some sleep and soon if I want my brain to start working again.*

"Right," said Eliza, scrambling to her feet and toward the door, tiny shorts and clean t-shirt in hand. "I'll just...I'll be right back. Make yourself...comfortable, I guess?"

Once Eliza's teeth were brushed, her face was scrubbed clean of every trace of the airplane, and her hair was piled on top of her head in a messy bun, she stared herself down in the mirror. "Okay, goofy," she told her reflection. "It's time to stop making such a big deal out of this. It's not like you've never shared a bed with another person before. Another *man*, even. And this is Deniz...you like him. A lot, remember? Now stop psyching yourself and go cuddle with that man, damn it!"

Entering her room again, the sight of Deniz under her light blanket, lying stock still and staring up at the ceiling like a newly discovered mummy, made her heart knock against her chest. He looked as uncomfortable as she felt, but she had to love the fact that he was still here and hadn't let that discomfort scare him off.

His head turned towards her then. "Um, is this okay? I wasn't sure which side of the bed you slept on, so I just put myself next to the wall to be out of the way. We can switch."

Eliza shook her head. "Believe it or not, I don't have a favorite side." She chuckled to herself. "That's probably because I usually sleep in the middle, come to think of it, but let's try it out like this. If it doesn't work, we can switch."

He nodded. "Okay, then." He turned on his side to face her, lifting the blanket for her. "Come on in, then."

Eliza slid into the bed next to Deniz, the two of them lying face to face with shy smiles flying between them.

"This is weird," she admitted.

He nodded. "It is. But you need rest, and we need to not overthink this right now." He turned onto his back, his arm bent under the pillow so his bicep was near her head. He patted the pillow with his other hand. "Share this with me."

Eliza complied, smiling to herself at the vanity of men and their muscles at the same time she was willing herself not to ogle him. As she nestled into his side, her head sharing his pillow (said bicep was tucked into the open space under her neck) and her arm settled across his chest, she sighed. Home. She was home—again.

Seven

The next morning came soon—too soon. Eliza was vaguely aware of the sun streaming in through the curtains while turning onto her other side, but she forced it down out of her consciousness. If there was ever a day to sleep in without guilt, it was the day after a transatlantic flight.

When her bladder would no longer let her ignore it and the sun had warmed her third-floor bedroom to the point where her small oscillating fan wasn't doing more than blowing hot air around, Eliza groaned and stretched.

As her eyes were still struggling to open, she heard Deniz's smooth, deep voice beside and slightly above her. "Good morning, Eliza," he crooned.

She looked up to see him next to her—right where she had left him—but he was sitting up in the bed, his back rested against the headboard. A book rested in his lap, his index finger marking his page while his attention was focused on Eliza.

"Good morning," she responded, feeling exposed as she fumbled to rub the sleep from her eyes. Deniz was sitting there looking like he had been awake for hours, not a pillow mark or a puffy eye to be seen, but she didn't want to think too carefully about what she looked like right now. She sat up. "Did you sleep alright? How long have you been awake?"

Deniz just smiled. "I did, thanks. I've been up for an hour, but I didn't want to disturb you." He held up the book in his lap, one from Eliza's Kate Austen collection that had nearly lost its cover, she'd read it so many times. "I hope you don't mind that I took this off your shelf."

"Not at all. That's a really great one of hers. It's got some great plot twists...though I probably shouldn't tell you that since you're, you know, reading it for the first time." She put her head in her hands. "I need to drink coffee before I try to make sentences." She peeked up at Deniz. "Did you drink coffee? Or have you just been sitting here, reading and watching me sleep?"

He frowned. "It sounds creepy when you say it like that. I've been here, but I haven't been watching you sleep, so you don't have anything to worry about there. I was just reading and enjoying the quiet morning after all the hustle and bustle in the village and the drama with my sister. I promise I didn't mind."

"Still." Eliza attempted to brush her excessively messy bun back into a tastefully messy bun. "Coffee would have been nice while you were doing that, wouldn't it?"

Deniz shook his head. "The smell would have woken you up. I didn't mind waiting, really. You needed your sleep, and I...well, I think I just needed to be near your grounding presence."

Eliza felt herself melt ever so slightly at his words. "Oh. That's really sweet, actually."

Deniz patted the bed next to him, and she moved there, sitting down next to him as if she were on autopilot. "You don't know what it was like without you here." A faraway look crossed his face, taking him miles away, some place where she couldn't reach him. "It's like I forgot how to be an autonomous, independent man and just slipped right back into the old patterns. A son. A brother. A nephew. A cousin. A grandson. It's amazing I even remember how to be just me again now."

Eliza slid next to Deniz, her arms coming around his waist while his wrapped around her shoulders. One of his hands caressed the crown of her head just before his lips dropped there to press a soft kiss. All thoughts of what she must look like, what she must smell like...for the moment, at least, they were gone. Forgotten. Deniz had needed her, emotionally. She hadn't expected that.

She let herself enjoy that knowledge, the unfamiliar sensation of it, for just a moment until the red warning light flashed in the back of her brain. There were some big important things the two of them hadn't yet talked about. Things he hadn't told her that he probably should. In her uncaffeinated, jet lagged state, she had nearly let herself forget about that, opting to melt into his affection and warmth rather than confront him about it.

But that stopped now. She pulled back from Deniz, forcing herself to her feet at the same time. "Come on," she said, extending a hand to him. "We've got lots to talk about, so we'd better start caffeinating ourselves now."

Deniz's expression sobered, and he nodded, standing alongside her. "We do, you're right. An entire summer's worth of catching up to do, right?" His smile seemed forced, but it was peeking out again underneath his serious brow.

After coffee and breakfast—Crystal had left a bag full of bakery-fresh *poğaça* and *börek* before leaving for the day—Eliza turned in her chair to face Deniz head-on.

"So," she said, forcing the corners of her mouth into an approximation of a smile. "Are we...good? Things seemed a little weird for a while there while I was gone, and...I just wanted to check." It wasn't a full-on confrontation—there had been no demands that he reveal his family's opinions about her or divulge the stress it might be causing him—but it was early, both in the day and in their relationship. She could (attempt to) navigate this delicate situation with some small amount of tact, at least.

"Us?" Deniz's brow furrowed with concern, his hand reaching to grasp hers across the table. "Eliza, we're more than okay. Why wouldn't we be? Is this because I was not communicative enough when I was in the village? I should have warned you about how spotty my connection would be there; I'm sorry I didn't."

She shook her head, wanting to soothe away those lines on his forehead with her words. The last thing Deniz needed was more stress and pressure from her, especially if he was already feeling it from his family. "It's not...I mean, it *is* a little bit about that. I really worried when I didn't hear from you and then...it seemed like I missed something important." She shrugged. "I don't know. I guess I got the feeling that, like, you were trying to keep me a secret from your family or something. And it made me wonder what they would think about me. If they would approve of me." She shook her head with increasing momentum. "I don't know what I'm even talking about. Ignore me...it's definitely way too soon to be thinking about things like this, and I guess I just let it get to my head, and then Crystal said something about Cansu—"

"Cansu?" Deniz interjected. "What about Cansu?"

Eliza waved the question away with her hand. "It's nothing. I don't even know what I'm talking about." She shook her head again. "I shouldn't be telling you about rumors I heard from someone who heard from someone else...I should be asking you if everything is okay between us." She huffed out a humorless laugh. "Which I'm pretty sure I did, right before I started monologuing instead of giving you a chance to answer. So." She gestured between them with her finger. "Are we cool?"

The worry was still evident on Deniz's face, but his warm smile was fighting an epic battle against it. He shifted his grasp so that he could hold both of her hands, his thumbs smoothing back and forth across her knuckles before he lifted one to his lips and kissed it. "We are more than okay, Eliza. I'm so glad to have you back here in my arms that I don't even have the words to express it. My..." He paused, frowning. "Don't worry about my family. You were right that it's too soon to talk or even think about that. A new relationship like ours doesn't need parental expectations on it, right? I mean, you didn't tell your parents about *me*, did you?"

Eliza was shaking her head no, knowing it was the response he wanted...but the truth won out. "I mean, of *course* I did. Are you kidding me? I tell my mom everything, and I suppose that means my dad knows about all of it, too. Did you not want me to say something to them?"

"You...oh. Okay." Deniz's eyes were wide as he found his next words. "That's not a bad thing. I'm just surprised, is all. I guess maybe it's a cultural difference. Wait...that doesn't mean your parents are expecting us to get married, does it?"

Eliza laughed, punching him lightly on the arm. "I'd love to mess with you and tell you they are, but I can't do that to you. I like you too darn much." She rubbed the spot on his arm that she had delivered her swat to. "No, my parents understand the pace and nature of relationships these days. My dad won't be showing up on your doorstep to ask what your intentions are, and my mom won't be texting to ask what she should wear to our wedding. Relax!"

His smile was tentative, his relaxation after hearing her words unsteady but gaining momentum. "That's okay then, I guess." He shook his head as if to clear the screen of his thoughts. "Why wouldn't it be? Anyway..."

But the thought that was occurring to Eliza wasn't comforting her at all. Deniz's reaction to her parents knowing about the two of them seemed to reveal something about his parents and their expectations, and she wasn't sure if she liked it. "If...if your parents knew about us, would they really expect us to get...married? Like, the thought of you dating someone...that's a no go? I mean, totally? There's no flexibility on that?"

Deniz's cheeks were rapidly turning pink. "Well," he began, "I didn't think we were going to get into this topic yet, but we probably should if it's going to be causing you anxiety." He paused, looking down into his nearly empty cup. "It's not as if casual dating...or you know, being an unmarried couple doesn't exist in Turkey. I'm sure you've seen enough *dizis* on TV to know that."

Eliza nodded. She had developed a fondness for Turkish TV series despite her near-complete lack of comprehension of them. Still, it was fun to watch them, enjoy the scenery, admire (or judge) the characters' fashion choices, and fill in the gaps of her understanding by making up her own scenarios in her head. And Deniz was right. They showed plenty of dating and kissing and drama, not at all different from the shows she would have watched back in the US.

"But," Deniz continued, "when it comes to my family, we're talking about life in a village. And that's really different from life in Istanbul or Izmir." He massaged his temples. "Honestly, it might be a culture shock even for a Turkish woman if I took her to the village to meet my parents, no different from how it would feel for you."

"Except that she would speak the same language as them." Eliza quirked an eyebrow at Deniz. "That might seem like a minor difference to you, but it's a pretty major one for me."

"Sure...that's significant." He cocked his head to the side like his sentences were causing him physical pain as they escaped his mouth. "But we *do* speak a dialect. Not just an accent, I mean, some words are just completely different."

Eliza had to smile. Her Deniz was always a stickler for accuracy, even in the middle of a sensitive discussion about why his family didn't know she existed and all the repercussions of that fact. "Right. What about the dating piece? Can we get back to that?"

Deniz exhaled. "Sure. So...well, dating wasn't a thing for my grandparents' generation, that's for sure. It wasn't for my parents or any of their siblings, either. In my generation...well, there are people like me who've moved away and are living in new cities and probably doing all sorts of 'city culture' things. But for the young people who are still living in the village, working on their parents' farms...things are still pretty traditional, Eliza." He finally lifted his eyes to meet hers. "It's still families visiting other families to ask for their daughter's hand in marriage, public engagement ceremonies...it's not the way you do things, and it's not even the way I would prefer to do them...but that's the way it is there."

Eliza was quiet as she took in Deniz's words. His hesitance made sense, but she couldn't shake the feeling that he was embarrassed of her or trying to protect himself from unwanted attention and scrutiny by keeping her a secret from the people that loved him. But today—she offered a silent prayer to caffeine and good sleep—she had the good sense not to say that to him without thinking it through first. "I understand," she said instead, "I think. I guess if things get to that point, they'll find out I exist." She shrugged. "And if things don't get to that point between us, then I guess it's better they never even knew about me."

Deniz's eyes had widened with shock. "That's...no! That's not what this is about." He gathered her into his arms. "I don't even want to think about that, Eliza. About things not...not working out between us. I just want us to enjoy each other, to enjoy being together...without any parents sitting on our shoulders peering over at us to offer their opinions and input. That's all."

She squeezed him tighter, taking comfort from his solid presence and his words. "I'd like that," she admitted. "I think I could really use some enjoyment and fun together, especially after an entire summer of being in a long distance relationship."

"You've got it." She could hear the smile in Deniz's voice. "How about a few days away before the semester starts? Where would you like to go—back to Kaş? Fethiye? You name it, let's go."

Eliza pulled back to look into his eyes. "Really? I mean..." Her pulse was getting away from her, excitement at the possibility of a romantic getaway drowning out her thoughts with a dull roar of static in her ears. "Are you sure? We both just got back here, and I'm sure you need some time to get settled before the new school year..."

She trailed off, but Deniz jumped right in where she had stopped. "As touched as I am that you understand my idiosyncrasies enough to respect my desire to be...shall we say...*over-prepared*..."

As Deniz paused, Eliza chuckled out loud at his understatement, waiting for him to finish his thought.

"Despite that," he continued, "I think we should go. No, it's stronger than that. We *must* go. You've been gone for most of the summer, and so have I. We deserve some sunshine and relaxation before the summer ends and we're consumed by lesson planning and student stresses." He lowered his head, moving his face close enough to hers that their noses were touching. "So I won't take no for an answer. At least, not a no on my behalf. Got it?"

Eliza nodded, biting back a smile. "Understood, sir."

"Right. Good. Then, it's time to answer the most important question." He raised his right eyebrow, fixing his quizzical gaze on her. "Where to?"

Eight

"With all the beaches to choose from, I can't believe you chose *Denizli* for your romantic getaway." Crystal was teasing Eliza, and hadn't stopped since she'd returned home to learn that Eliza and Deniz were leaving for the land-locked province of Denizli in the morning.

Eliza rolled her eyes at her friend. "We're not going to work on a farm or anything like that, Crys." She pulled out her phone, tapping on the screen. "Have you seen the photos of Pamukkale?" She held her phone out, gesturing for Crystal to take it and scroll. "It's unreal."

Crystal stood next to Eliza as she scrolled through image after image of what appeared to be snowy, flat hills covered in people in shorts and t-shirts. "What in the—? How cold is it there?"

"It's not snow," Eliza explained. "But how cool is it that it looks that way? I just love the photos. It's a mineral...travertine, I think? It's a natural wonder, and people come visit and walk down through the pools...can you believe Deniz has never been there, either?"

"I cannot," said Crystal. "It's practically his namesake! I mean, not Pamukkale, even *I* know that means 'cotton castle.' But Denizli...Deniz...that could be confusing."

Eliza scoffed. "Right, I'm definitely going to get confused about who I'm talking to...sorry, boyfriend, I wasn't talking to you. I was talking to this massive province and its entire population."

Crystal shrugged. "It could happen. I'll wait here for you to come back and tell me about all the ways it was confusing and weird. You can owe me dinner if I'm right."

"Like we don't already take turns buying dinner," Eliza muttered.

"What was that? I couldn't quite hear you."

"Nothing," Eliza grumbled, a memory of the previous night's conversation with Crystal resurfacing. "Hey! Don't you owe me a story or an explanation or something about your secret boyfriend? The one you forgot to tell me about the whole time I was in the US?"

Crystal cringed under the weight of Eliza's words. "Yeah, sorry about that. Again. I swear, I wanted to tell you about it before, but just..."

"What?"

"I don't know, I mean..." Crystal shrugged, looking sheepish. "I wanted to talk to you in person. Preferably to have you meet him. I thought if I told you on the phone, you might focus on the parts that sound bad and tell me this is a bad idea." She put her shoulders back, approximating the appearance of confidence with the gesture. "I didn't want that."

Eliza was incredulous. "When have I *ever* done that, Crystal? I just want you to be happy! I'm not going to start criticizing your boyfriend, and certainly not before I've even met him." She shook her head. "Why would you think I would do that?"

"Well, it's not like you've never disapproved of some of my choices before," said Crystal, reminding Eliza with a meaningful eyebrow raise of just how well Eliza had accepted it when Crystal had started working for Nathaniel Collins right after Eliza had turned down the same job.

"This is different," said Eliza.

Crystal raised an eyebrow. "That remains to be seen, I guess." She blew out a breath. "Okay, anyway, so...we're actually sort of talking about getting married so he can move back to the US with me and find a job there."

Eliza shook her head, clearing the screen of her thoughts, trying to shake the obvious mishearing out of her ears. "You...what? Say that again, please?"

"See? I knew this would happen!" Crystal threw her hands in the air, sliding off her chair and away from Eliza. "I knew you were going to look at me like that, like I've made a huge mistake. But it sounds worse than it is, Eliza. There's nothing shady going on here. Chris is a great guy and this just makes so much sense for us. I know it happened quickly, but..."

"Chris? Where's he from? That definitely doesn't sound like a Turkish name."

"He's Canadian," explained Crystal. "From Toronto. He's always wanted to live in the US, and this is one way we can make that happen."

"There are a few things wrong with that sentence, Crys." Eliza barely stopped herself from rubbing her temples to ease the stress accumulating there. "For one thing, you live in Turkey. And this entire plan sounds like it requires you to move back to the States and away from a job and a city that you love so much. And *two*—" She continued speaking, not letting Crystal interject just yet. "—just because someone is from Canada doesn't mean that getting married for a green card isn't sketchy as hell. If anything, it's pretty messed up that most people would be less suspicious about that happening just because he's Canadian and wouldn't extend that same grace if he were, say, Turkish—"

"Spare me the lecture, please," Crystal interrupted, shaking her head. "This is exactly why I didn't want to tell you before. And congrats—I'm already regretting telling you now, so you still got that same result. Well done, you." With that, Crystal stalked from the room, slamming the door of the apartment behind herself as she exited.

Eliza shook her head, talking to herself. "Well, *that* went well."

By the time Deniz texted the next morning, letting Eliza know he was waiting outside to pick her up, Crystal and Eliza still hadn't spoken again.

As she let herself out of the apartment, locking the door behind her, Eliza sighed. She and Crystal had disagreed before—never about something as serious as a potential impending marriage, of course—and they'd gotten over it every time. She wasn't going to let that ruin her precious time with Deniz.

Deniz was standing on the street outside her apartment, leaning against the hood of his car. His neutral—or perhaps even preoccupied—expression morphed into joy as soon as Eliza exited the apartment building, as he pushed off the hood towards her.

"Good morning, you," she said, as he pulled her into his arms, dropping a kiss on her forehead before placing one on her lips.

"Good morning to you, too." Deniz smiled, taking her overnight bag from her and taking her hand in his other hand as they walked to the trunk of the car. "Are you excited for our getaway?"

Eliza nodded, sliding into the passenger seat next to Deniz once he had placed her things in the trunk. "So excited! How long is the drive?" She pulled out her phone, scrolling through the apps on it. "Do we need some road trip tunes? Should we stop for coffee?"

Deniz grinned as he began driving away. "Oh, you're in for a real treat, my dear. We're not actually driving there. I'm just driving us to the bus station. From there, we'll take a bus."

"Oh! Wow. Okay!" It was too early in the day for Eliza to tamp down the surprise she was feeling, so she didn't try too hard. "Um...why, exactly? I just mean, that's not really what I was expecting..."

"I thought it would add to the adventure of it," said Deniz. "Plus, well...sometimes it can be stressful driving in a place you don't know well. And I know it can be stressful being the navigator in those situations, too." He shrugged, his eyes fixed on the road. "This way we can relax and enjoy the journey together, both of us seeing the sights out the window." He flicked a glance her way. "Sorry, I didn't think about this beforehand. Should I have asked you? Told you this was the plan?"

Eliza dismissed his concerns with a wave of her hand. "Please. It's all part of the adventure, Deniz. After all, those of us who don't drive in this country can't be critical of those of us who do. I just hope this bus ride isn't like taking the minibus to Kaş." Her stomach turned with the memory of the small vehicle, its driver's breakneck speed, and the twists and turns of the coastal road.

A laugh escaped Deniz's lips. "I promise you we won't take a *dolmuş* to Denizli. We'll take two buses, one from here to Denizli city center, and then we'll take another one out to Pamukkale. I booked us a hotel room that's within walking distance from the tourist sights there. I hope you'll like it."

"I'm sure I will." Eliza snuggled back into her seat, warmed by the thought of having Deniz—and a hotel room—to herself for the next three nights.

The bus Eliza and Deniz took from Antalya to Denizli was far more comfortable than the airplane journey she had taken just a few days before. The view out the window was certainly more interesting than the endless expanse of clouds she had seen over the Atlantic Ocean, and she was impressed by the driver's assistant's ability to navigate the aisle dispersing hot drinks—and not spilling them on anyone.

There was one stop on their route, and Eliza hadn't realized it was Isparta until the bus pulled into the terminal and she saw the name emblazoned on the building.

"Isparta? Really?" she asked Deniz, looking at the surroundings of the building. "This is your home?"

He nodded. "This is it. Of course, my family doesn't live in the city center here...our village is about a fifteen minute drive from here."

"Cool." Eliza felt a twinge of an unwanted emotion that she couldn't quite put a name on. They were this close to Deniz's home—and therefore to his family—and it felt wrong somehow not to be visiting. But after their previous conversation, she didn't want to push the topic. If he were ready for her to meet his parents, if he thought it was the time for that to happen, he would have acted on that.

Instead, she watched the terminal slip away as the bus pulled back out onto the road, watching the buildings—and then the countryside—around her with a new interest. For all she knew, these were the fields Deniz had run through as a child. Or the streets he had taken to school. Maybe she would know all of those things about him someday...but only if he let her close enough for that to happen.

At the moment, that seemed unlikely. To keep herself from dwelling on that unwanted thought—and the feelings that came along with it—Eliza slipped on her headphones, found an upbeat album on her phone, and closed her eyes. This weekend was supposed to be fun, and that fact required her not to get too maudlin about what might or might not be in store in her future with Deniz.

In her silence, Deniz seemed to have picked up on what she needed. Rather than engaging her in conversation or pointing out landmarks outside the window, he simply took her hand in his, his thumb rubbing across her knuckles. Eliza let herself feel a moment of peace, shutting out the unwanted thoughts that threatened to resurface at every bump in the road.

"We're here." Deniz's stubble tickled her cheek as he whispered in her ear. She tugged on her headphones, rubbing her eyes with the palms of her hands. Jet lag was still kicking her butt, and she had managed to fall asleep in the remaining half hour of the bus's journey to Denizli.

She let Deniz take her hand and lead her off the bus, stopping to collect their bags from the driver before making their way to the local buses. Deniz knew his way around, marching them directly to a small bus—*not another* dolmuş, Eliza thought to herself, her stomach already turning with the impending motion sickness. After speaking with the driver and confirming that the minibus would be departing in ten minutes, they climbed inside to claim their seats.

The journey to Pamukkale was short and nowhere near as full of twists and turns as Eliza's last journey on a minibus had been. The small vehicle stopped in the middle of what looked like a village square, dropping off Eliza, Deniz, and several other passengers there.

From there, it was a short walk to their hotel, with Deniz carrying Eliza's bag over his shoulder, his own bag in his hand, and his other hand reserved to hold hers. If she had felt rejected by his unwillingness to bring her to Isparta, if that had made her feel like he had doubts about their relationship, the fact that he hadn't let go of her hand in hours was doing a small bit of magic to counteract those doubts and fears.

The hotel Deniz had reserved was small—just a few immaculately decorated and cleaned rooms—and family-owned. They were greeted by a woman named Şerife who had a warm face and an ever-present grin that nearly split her face in two. After checking them in, she showed them to a room with a queen-sized bed covered in pillows, a large bathroom complete with a deep bathtub, and a window looking out on a small lavender field, with views of the surrounding mountains in the distance.

Eliza was taking in the view when she felt Deniz approach, seconds before his arms encircled her from behind. She turned to meet him, their lips finding each other as they relaxed into the comfortable intimacy of being alone together. Her stomach fluttered with the reminder that there were no friends, no roommates to steal their attention or make them feel self-conscious. For the next three nights, at least, they were alone.

"Are you hungry?" Deniz asked, pulling his face out of kissing range, to Eliza's dismay.

As if his question had triggered it, she felt her stomach rumble in response. "I guess I am," she said, giving a pointed look in the direction of the sound. "I'd be happy to stay here in this room with you for the night, but..."

Deniz shook his head. "You have to eat. As much as I'm happy to have you all to myself, my plans for the evening will fail if we don't both get some fuel in our systems.

Come on." He stepped away, taking her hand in his once again and tugging her towards the door. "I chose this hotel particularly because I'd heard such good things about their restaurant."

With that promise, Eliza followed him downstairs, where Şerife showed them to a table in the small in-house restaurant. They were the only ones there—a perk of eating early, Eliza supposed, checking the time on her phone and noting that it was barely five o'clock. At Deniz's request, Şerife brought them glasses and a bottle of local red wine while they perused the menu.

"What's good here?" Eliza asked, overwhelmed by the selection and the unfamiliarity of so much of it. Her experience with Turkish food had been limited to a narrow selection of restaurants in Antalya—*kebap*, *pide*, and her favorite, *tantuni*—and to what was served in the university cafeteria at lunchtime. Sitting in this restaurant, she was aware of a need to change that, to taste as many things as she could. She set the menu down, looking at Deniz. "You know what? Why don't you order for both of us?"

His eyes brightened with her words. "Yeah? Okay." His brow furrowed as he studied the menu, making his selections for when Şerife returned.

After a rapidfire conversation in Turkish between Deniz and Şerife, they were alone again. "So, what are we eating?" Eliza asked, twirling the stem of her as-yet-untouched wine between her fingers.

"A little bit of everything," Deniz answered. "We have some *meze* to start with, and then some different things. *İmam bayıldı*—that means the imam fainted, I think you'll like that one—and some other vegetable dishes. One meat dish, too."

"Sounds great. It also sounds like a lot, though. I hope we can eat it all and that your eyes weren't bigger than your stomach."

Deniz chuckled, shaking his head. "That is a truly bizarre expression. But we've got all the time in the world, Eliza. I'm in no hurry to get back to the room. I mean...I am, but. Well. You know. I can be patient, too." He raised his glass in her direction. "To our first getaway, just the two of us. First of many, I hope."

Eliza grinned, raising her glass to meet his. "First of many."

Nine

Eliza had eaten like a queen, the flavors of the array of Deniz's selections far too enticing for her to stop at the point of comfortable fullness. Instead, just one more bite...just one more sip of wine...and a small shared dessert left her pushing back from the table, one hand on her stomach, and a groan escaping her lips. "Sorry," she told Deniz, feeling a blush warm her cheeks. "That was so delicious and I'm pretty sure I'm about to slip into a food coma and sleep for 12 hours straight." She picked up the empty bottle of wine between them, turning it to read the label. "This didn't help, either. I had no idea Denizli wines were so tasty."

Deniz nodded and smiled. "I'm glad you enjoyed it all. Why don't we take a walk? Help digest things a little?" He stood and held his hand out to her, and she accepted it, letting him pull her to her feet.

"Sounds like a dream." She smiled at him, the surrealness of being *here* with *him* once again washing over her. "Lead the way."

They strolled hand in hand up and down the surrounding streets, which were lined with homes and small hotels, gardens, and fields of flowers. The hills—or were they mountains?—that began nearby popped up sharply behind the properties.

"Where is Pamukkale?" she asked Deniz. "I mean, I know this town is called Pamukkale too, right? But, like, the place we're going to visit tomorrow?"

Deniz nodded towards the hills. "It's up there, but we can't see it from here. I wanted to stay someplace where you wouldn't get a sneak peek at it and ruin your surprise for tomorrow." He smiled at her. "You're going to love it."

Eliza smiled right back at him. "Yes, and what about you, sir? Let's not forget that you've never been here before, either." She shook her head. "This isn't just my new experience, remember? We're sharing it."

"That's right," he said, pulling her hand to his chest. "I forgot for a moment there that I get to enjoy this, too. Thanks for the reminder."

"I know I love to make things all about me," Eliza teased. "But just this once, I'll let you share it."

Deniz kissed her knuckles, chuckling softly. "So magnanimous of you, my dear." His eyes found hers then with an exaggerated wink. "Shall we—" He tipped his head back in the direction they had come from. "—make our way back to the room, then? Any other plans or—?"

"Nope, let's go." Eliza spun on her heel, tugging Deniz along behind her. She didn't need to hear that suggestion twice. "It's time for some alone time. Private time. Past time, actually."

When the next morning came, Eliza woke with the sun already pouring in through the windows. She had slept better than she could remember happening for at least the last few months, and judging from Deniz's still body next to her, his deep breathing, he had done—was continuing to do, in fact—the same.

She stretched, an involuntary groan escaping her lips and causing Deniz to stir beside her. "Good morning," she greeted him, when he opened his sleepy eyes.

"Good morning." His face transformed as unconsciousness was eclipsed by pleasure. "I like waking up next to you."

"Hmm." She leaned in and gave him a kiss. "Me, too."

Basking in the absolute peace and bliss of cuddling next to an attractive man—and one who was undeniably infatuated with her, no less—in a bed whose linens had no business being as comfortable and luxurious as they were, Eliza lost all track of time...until her bladder screaming at her made getting out of bed the only thing to do.

"Come on." She gave Deniz a quick peck on the cheek before disappearing into the bathroom. "We've got breakfast to eat and sights to see!"

Pamukkale exceeded Eliza's every expectation. She had seen the photos of the pale blue and white pools, the layers of which looked like they had been engineered by a crafty landscaper, not something that Mother Nature had cooked up all by herself. She was dumbfounded when the full panorama came into view, snapping photo after photo and cursing that her phone's camera wasn't doing the scenery justice, while wondering if any camera could.

"This is unreal," she whispered to Deniz, who was similarly awed into silence. They hadn't yet ventured close enough to the water to dip their toes in, and Eliza was eagerly anticipating that. Despite the late summer heat in the air and the throngs of tourists wearing shorts and t-shirts, her brain couldn't help but expect the snow-like surface to feel like something from the North Pole.

They made their way to the edge of the first pool, slipping off their sandals and stepping into the warm water. Eliza's foot slid on the mineral surface, making an "Ope!" escape from her lips as she grabbed onto Deniz's arm for support. "Sorry about that," she told him. "I'll try not to take you down with me, but some spots are a little slipperier than I expected."

"Not at all," he said, squeezing his arm closer to his torso so that her hand would be sandwiched in the middle more securely. "We'll take our time going down. We're in no hurry."

They shuffled through the pools, making their way through the cascading travertine terraces. When bigger crowds surrounded them, they made their way to the edge of a pool to let the crowds pass, protecting the solitude they craved and letting no one rush them through the experience. Eliza continued to snap photo after photo, until Deniz led the two of them to a travertine wall, took her phone from her and snapped a series of selfies. The two of them with the white wall behind them, the two of them facing the other direction with an endless expanse of sky blue water and white minerals behind them.

At their pace, it took them a couple hours to make it to the bottom of the pools, the exit of the site. Because the day was still young—and because they were having such fun together, basking in each other's attention and in the fact that they didn't have to share it with anyone else—they made their way back up to where they had begun to explore the rest of the site.

The ruins of Hierapolis awaited them there, and Eliza found herself stunned into silence for the second time that day, this time by the ancient history that they were walking through. The steps of the amphitheater, the very same places their feet were walking, had been walked on by others so long ago that Eliza was having a hard time wrapping her mind around it. "This," she said, gesturing around her, "All of it...it's all older than my country. I mean...wow."

Deniz shrugged. "Well, technically, it's older than my country, too." He gave her a cheeky grin. "If we're talking about the Republic of Turkey, it's still just a baby in a lot of ways."

They continued to explore leisurely, walking hand in hand and tugging each other to a stop when something caught their attention. The ancient road, the necropolis full of tombs with Greek letters on them...all of it was humbling, the reminder that humanity had existed for so long before that moment. That people had lived and died and loved each other, that in the time the city of Hierapolis was built, a relationship like theirs would have been an impossibility. People who were born as far apart as Eliza and Deniz had been would never even know the other existed, let alone have the chance to travel, to meet, to fall in love.

"The world is smaller now, isn't it?" Eliza asked Deniz, reverence in her voice. She traced her fingers over the letters she couldn't read on the tomb that had been there for centuries. "People living here, the people who died here...did they know there was life on the other side of the ocean? Did they even know there was an ocean? It's just...it's amazing, really."

Deniz was quiet for a moment. "It is. It's a good reminder, actually. Sometimes I think...ah, never mind."

"What is it? Come on, tell me."

"Well, sometimes I think life in the village is still like that. Staying within a few kilometers of where you were born. Marrying someone you've known since you were a child. I'm not sure it feels like the world is smaller or more interconnected there." His eyes had gotten darker with his words, his forehead creased with lines.

Eliza reached over to run her fingers over those lines before she could stop herself. "It's okay, Deniz. We're here now, together. We're enjoying this. We don't have to worry about the future. Not today. Okay?"

He smiled, though it seemed forced. "Of course," he said. "Sorry for getting maudlin for a second there. I don't know what I was thinking."

Back at the hotel, another delicious and decadent lunch awaited them. Deniz had ordered *beyti sarma* for them to share, a kebab that was unlike any Eliza had yet eaten. The meat was wrapped in lavash and smothered in tomato sauce and yogurt, and she once again ate more than she intended, simply because the flavors mingled with each other in such a way that it was virtually impossible to recognize that she was already full.

Between the digestion that needed to happen and all the walking they had done in the morning, Deniz and Eliza's afternoon plans were replaced by a two-hour nap, back again in their room's cozy linens.

The late afternoon sun was turning the sky a deeper shade of blue, contrasting with the blinding brightness of high noon on a Turkish summer day. Eliza woke to see the shadows of the mountains, the many shades of blue flooding through the open curtains, and turned to look at Deniz's still sleeping face.

His breaths were shallow, his chest rising and falling in a slow, even rhythm. His handsome face was unmarked by the lines that had crossed his forehead with increasing frequency these past few days. Staring at his face, Eliza couldn't help but wonder what was going on inside that mind of his. What was he dreaming, and what was it that was plaguing his waking thoughts? And where was she in all of it? Was he struggling to figure out how she fit into his future...or was he wondering how and when to cut her loose?

She tiptoed to the bathroom before those thoughts could root themselves in too deeply. Deniz didn't seem like he was preparing to brush her off, but the closer she got to him, the more she realized she didn't know him as well as she thought she did. There was untold depth to Deniz Aydem, facets of his being it would take years to uncover. The same was true for herself, she realized, knowing that there were weaknesses she was hiding from him as much as there were good points she was working a little too hard to make sure he could see. She was fun. Easygoing. Not overly emotional. That was what a boyfriend needed to see, the traits that would make him think, *she's not like the other girls. I'd better hold on to this one.*

Eliza shook her head to clear the thought. What was so bad about being like other girls—or *women*, rather...she hadn't been a *girl* in about a decade—that she didn't want to be like them? Maybe the efforts she made to be liked, to be easygoing...maybe those weren't about differentiating herself from other women at all. Maybe they were simply about controlling how far she let anyone in, how deeply she dared to let them look.

From behind the closed door of the bathroom, she heard the vibration of a phone against a wooden table. Wrapping up her pep talk, Eliza splashed cold water on her face, dried it off with a fluffy white towel, then reemerged into the bedroom, where Deniz was just beginning to stir.

He was looking at the phone in his hand, his hair adorably mussed up from their nap and a deep frown marring the smooth forehead she had admired just a few moments ago.

"What is it?" she asked, moving to sit next to him on the bed, her hand finding his knee in a reassuring gesture. "Is everything okay?"

Deniz shook his head, his eyes wide. "I don't know. I missed a bunch of calls from my parents and my sister. Something is going on, I just don't know what." He pulled his hand down his face, giving a brief stroke to his chin before dropping that hand in his lap. "I need to call them. This doesn't look good."

Eliza was nodding before he even finished speaking. "Of course. I'll be quiet—" But something about the look on his face stopped her from finishing her suggestion. He needed privacy, as much as it pained her not to be by his side, to be shut out when he clearly was struggling. "I'll be downstairs. Text me when you're done." She grabbed her phone from the nightstand and bolted out the door without meeting Deniz's eyes.

Ten

When she heard the creak of a footstep behind her, Eliza grabbed her phone from where she had left it in her lap, busying herself opening apps, scrolling through old messages, swiping through the many photos she had taken that morning.

A throat cleared, the familiar sound attracting her attention. "Sorry about that, Eliza," said Deniz, hesitation in his voice as he took a seat next to her.

She pasted on a smile, dropping her phone again to face him. "It's no problem, really." She took one of his hands in her own. "Is...is everything okay?"

Deniz nodded, then shook his head. "Not really. My sister is leaving for London in two days and my parents are stressed about it. My grandma, well...she's in the hospital, not feeling well. One of the young calves escaped from the barn and my dad spent the last hour tracking it down. They're just overwhelmed."

"That's a lot to deal with all at once. Is your grandma okay?"

Deniz smiled. "She will be. She won't let them keep her there any longer than absolutely necessary, so I expect she'll be coming home tomorrow at the latest."

"What about Cansu? Don't you want to see her before she leaves?"

Deniz's eyes finally lifted from the floor, his gaze locking onto Eliza's like he was searching for an answer to a riddle there. He nodded. "I do. I'm sorry...but I think we need to change our plans."

Eliza nodded. "It's okay, I understand. You can...well, you can go there, and I can take the bus back to Antalya. Will you wait until tomorrow, or do you need to go now?"

"Eliza...no." Deniz turned to face her head on, bringing his other hand to meet hers, all four hands now clasped between them. "I wasn't...I wasn't going to ask you to go back without me. I couldn't...I wouldn't do that. What kind of boyfriend would?"

"A pretty shitty one," Eliza admitted, "Or also one who's not ready to tell his family about the aforementioned girlfriend. I'd understand, I swear. I'm not going to hold this against you when you get back to Antalya."

He was shaking his head then, pausing only to kiss each of her hands in turn. "No, you're not going to hold it against me because it's not going to happen. Eliza, I want you to come to Isparta with me."

Eliza jolted, blinking. "Really? Are you sure? I don't want to be in the way, Deniz. It's okay, really. You need to be there for your family, and I can give you that space."

An impish grin spread across his face. "Not only do I not need the space, but...well, if my parents are feeling as stressed and overwhelmed as I think they are right now, it might be nice for them to have a bit of a distraction." Off the look on her face, his next words tumbled out. "Not that I'm setting you up to fail. Not like that. It's a good distraction, Eliza. They'll be thrilled to meet you. My mom always loves to feed people, and they've never had an American in their home before. She'll be absolutely tickled."

"Okay...but what about the part where I'm your girlfriend? Are...are you going to tell them that?" She couldn't quite meet his eyes as she asked, unsure of what she would see there.

Deniz's next words were hesitant. "I...well, I haven't exactly figured that part out yet. I think I'll have to introduce you as my friend, but of course they're going to read more into that. It's just not really a concept I expect my parents to get. They went from being friends to being engaged, and I'm not really sure how this is going to unfold."

"It's fine," said Eliza, tight-lipped. "We'll figure it out when it happens. Now...the most important question of the moment. When are we leaving?"

Deniz ducked his head, biting his lip. "Well, um...the sooner the better. Can you be packed up in the next half hour?"

"No problem." Eliza bolted to her feet, glad for the distraction and for the time to think about their next steps without her facial expressions being scrutinized by her boyfriend.

The journey from Pamukkale back to Isparta via Denizli was shorter than Eliza had remembered. The fields and villages out the window flew by, their destination coming nearer with every passing moment.

She wasn't ready. Not really. What awaited them at the Isparta bus terminal? Deniz had told her his dad was coming to pick them up, but she was so unprepared for that moment and for everything that followed it.

"So...what...I don't even know how to ask this." She stumbled over her thoughts as they struggled to become words, berating herself for the anxiety that she was feeling. "What do I do? I mean, I'm so out of practice at meeting my boyfriend's parents already, and the fact that your parents and I don't even speak the same language..." She fell silent as she once again stared out the window.

Next to her, she felt Deniz wrap his arm around her. "It's going to be okay, Eliza. No one will expect you to speak fluent Turkish. And you've talked to my sister, she'll be there too. It's going to be okay."

"I just wish I knew more Turkish. I wish I had known we were going to do this, go there. I would have brought them a gift or something. Isn't it terribly rude to show up empty-handed? Is your mom going to hate me for that?"

"My mom couldn't hate you if she tried." Deniz's smile was warm, his eyes crinkling at the corner. "And that's both a reflection of how very loveable you are *and* the fact that my mom is incapable of hatred. Really. I know it's hard to believe, Eliza, and I know you don't like feeling unprepared...but this is going to be okay. It might even be fun."

"What about my limited Turkish, though? No one is going to be able to communicate with me, and I will barely be able to understand anything any of them are saying?"

"That will be okay, too." He raised an eyebrow at her. "You're a language teacher, Eliza. You know that making mistakes when speaking a new language is all part of the process, isn't it? Don't tell me you really expected yourself to take a full Turkish course and master the language before you ever had to use it with my family."

Eliza shook her head, chuckling. How had he managed to read her mind? "Guilty as charged, sir. Mistakes are all well and good in my English classroom, but apparently I hold myself to a completely different standard than I do my students."

"You're not the first. I can't tell you how hard it was for me to spend time with you and the other Americans outside of work, before we started dating, I mean. Everyone was talking so quickly and there were so many references I didn't get. Jokes I didn't understand, movies I hadn't seen, pop culture that wasn't part of my childhood." He smoothed her hair back from her face, kissing her on the temple. "I finally had to decide that my attraction to you, my desire to be around you, was more powerful than my fear of saying something stupid in front of you."

"I'm glad you did."

"So am I." He pulled her towards him, hugging her body against his. "And I'm glad you're here with me now, and that you're going to be with me while I'm supporting my family. I just need you to trust me that it's going to be okay, even if you make a mistake or if you don't understand something. I'm going to be right here, right next to you, the whole time."

Soon after, when the bus pulled into the Isparta bus terminal, Deniz's dad was there to meet them, with Cansu perched on the hood of his parked car, waving at them as they arrived. When Ahmet Aydem got out of the car, his expression serious as he walked towards the still-moving bus, Eliza was struck by how much Deniz looked like his father. They had the same strong brow, the same deep, expressive eyes. But where Deniz's face was stubbly, his father was clean-shaven. And where Deniz was frequently with a smile on his face—or at least he had been ever since Eliza got back from Michigan—Ahmet's expression was more stoic, his smiles fewer and seemingly harder to win.

They had barely exited the bus before Cansu barreled into her brother, her small frame rebounding with energy. She hugged Deniz and Eliza in turn, switching between rapidfire Turkish and almost equally rapidfire English with ease. Ahmet approached behind her, greeting Deniz with one of those rare smiles and a quick hug before extending his hand to Eliza.

"*Hoş geldin, kızım,*" he greeted her, welcoming her as a daughter. Eliza knew the term *"kızım"* was used to refer to a younger woman, and it didn't mean he was accepting her into the family as a daughter.

"*Hoş bulduk,*" she responded, shaking his hand.

Cansu squealed and clapped her hands. "Oh my gosh, it's so cute to hear you speak Turkish!" She elbowed her brother in the side. "*Abi,* you didn't tell me Eliza could speak Turkish. Come on!" She turned to Eliza, pulling her overnight bag from her hands. "Let's go back to the house. Mom is going to *die* when she meets your girlfriend!"

Eliza fell into step beside Cansu, leaning in conspiratorially. "Cansu...um. Are your parents going to freak out about Deniz bringing a girlfriend home? I mean, I don't *actually* want your mom to die..."

"Relax! It's just a joke." Cansu's eyes crinkled at the corner when she grinned, just like her brother's did. "Nobody speaks English, and I'm sure Deniz will just tell them all that you're his friend. Everyone's going to talk about it behind your back, but no one will say anything to your face. And if they do, you probably won't even know!" Her expression sobered as she peered at Eliza's face. "Your Turkish isn't *that* good, right? If it is, I'll tell them not to talk about you."

Eliza laughed. "It's okay. They can say whatever they want. If I hear my name, I'll just assume it's something good. That everyone is talking about how funny I am or how great my fashion sense is." She chuckled at the irony of that idea. "It's okay for me. I just don't want to make your mom's life harder, if everyone is going to be gossiping to her about me for years to come."

Cansu had closed their bags in the trunk by then, and she held the back door open for Eliza to slide in before scooting in next to her. Deniz was already in the front with his dad, the two of them engrossed in conversation ever since they had arrived.

"My mom won't mind," Cansu reassured Eliza. "Life in the village...well, you take what entertainment you get, you know? Maybe it's gossip about your son's girlfriend, maybe it's a wedding in the square...and maybe it's a lost calf that *someone* has to chase around, swearing at him to come home."

Eliza nodded. "I get that. It's nice to have something to talk about, I guess." She smiled at Cansu, taking in her bubbly demeanor, the excitement that was virtually radiating out of her pores, then leaned closer. "I heard you're leaving for London soon," she said, wiggling her eyebrows. "Tell me all about it!"

Cansu's eyes lit up even brighter than they already were. "Oh gosh, Eliza, it's so cool. I'm so excited! I'll be working in a hotel in London, learning about the hospitality business there, and there are other people in this program from, seriously, *everywhere*. Other interns like me from Canada, Greece, Poland, Kenya...I don't even know where else. I got so excited and overwhelmed reading the email that I can barely remember anything it said. I can't *wait*. It's going to be such an amazing experience and I don't even know what impact it's going to have. On my career, of course, but on my life, too."

"Totally!" Cansu's excitement was contagious, and Eliza felt herself warming from within with all the possibilities in store for the young woman in front of her. "You must be excited about all of it! There's so much to get used to, living in a new country...and who knows who you'll meet? Maybe your new best friend, even."

"And maybe—as much as my mother hates to even consider the possibility—maybe my next boyfriend! I mean, you never know, right?" She lowered her voice, eyes darting to Deniz in the front seat. "You didn't come here expecting to meet Deniz, right? But you did! And that's so cool. He's so happy with you." She gave her head the barest of shakes.

"I don't know why my parents don't get it. Why my mom is so opposed to the idea of me meeting someone there, why she's going to freak out when she realizes her golden boy is doing exactly what she's afraid of me doing—"

Cansu stopped suddenly, her eyes widening in horror. "That's not what I meant!" She grabbed Eliza's forearm with both hands, her grip strong despite her demure stature. "I don't mean anything about you. My mom is going to love you when she actually meets you. It's the idea of you—not that she even knows about you yet—just like it's the idea of me meeting a nice English guy. She's afraid of losing me to London, and she's going to be afraid of losing Deniz to America, too. But you have to know that's not about you. Not at all." Her eyes were wide, earnest. "If you feel weird at all, like she doesn't want you there...it's not about you, I swear. It's just mothers and sons. Or in my case, mothers and daughters."

"I get it." Eliza nodded. "I'm sure my mom doesn't like the thought of losing me, either. But it's different for her. She's going to travel, come here to visit me and meet Deniz. One of my uncles moved abroad when he was younger, so the idea isn't so new, so scary for my mom." She tilted her head in Cansu's direction. "But you, you're a force to be reckoned with. No one in your family, probably in the entire village, has done something like this." She shook her head in awe, her grin widening with every word. "You're so brave, Cansu, and so damn inspiring. Don't let anyone tell you otherwise. I know it's just that they're worried about you...but I have a feeling you're going to be just fine. Better than fine. You're going to blow us all away."

Cansu's cheeks were prettily pink, her eyes hesitant to meet Eliza's. "Thank you for saying that." She sighed. "It's worn on me a lot in these last few days, hearing how much everyone is worried for me. Like they think I will not survive on my own. I know it's just love talking, but it has definitely made me wonder if I'm making a mistake. Doing the wrong thing."

"I think it would be really unusual if you didn't have some doubts. The important thing is figuring out if you're nervous because your intuition is telling you that you're making a mistake...or if you're feeling that way because you're doing something new and scary and your ego is trying to keep you safe. Keep you playing small."

Cansu blew out a breath. "Yeah. That sounds exactly right." Her voice was small, so quiet Eliza felt herself leaning forward to hear the young woman's words. "How do you know which one it is?"

Eliza chuckled. "Listen to me, telling you this like I've figured it all out." She shrugged. "The truth is, I'm not entirely sure. But I think, on some level, when you're afraid, you *know* what kind of afraid you are. Whether you're 'oh shit, I'm about to make a huge mistake' afraid or whether you're 'holy crap, this is going to be awesome' afraid."

Cansu nodded sagely. "So like the difference between standing up on stage at a singing competition and jumping out of an airplane with someone who *swears* they're pretty sure they know how the parachute works?"

"Exactly. So, which is it for you?"

"Oh, I'm definitely excited-scared. Something amazing is happening, and this is going to be the adventure of a lifetime."

Eliza squeezed Cansu's hand. "You're so right. I can't wait to hear all about it."

Cansu raised an eyebrow in her direction. "Well, that's assuming I actually make it to my departure day. My mom isn't exactly thrilled about this, so...I wouldn't put it past her to hide my passport or lock me in my room until the plane leaves." She took both of Eliza's hands in her own, glancing at the front seat again. "I'm glad you and Deniz are here. I really need your support, and I think it'll help my parents feel a lot more comfortable, having the two of you here."

A mirthless laugh barked out before Eliza could stop it. "Well, it'll help one way or another. Maybe your parents will be so concerned about Deniz dating an American that they'll let you off easy!"

Eleven

For as intimidated as Eliza had been by the mere idea of her, Esra Aydem was a small woman with an unassuming demeanor. She barely came up to Eliza's collarbone, greeted her with a series of enthusiastic kisses on alternating cheeks, and pulled her in for a hug that didn't match her size at all.

Stepping back to regain her breath, Eliza studied the woman who was now greeting Deniz, their routine of hand kisses, hugs and cheek pecks well rehearsed. Esra's head was covered in a practical scarf, and she was wearing the baggy floral pants Eliza had glimpsed on every other woman of her age as they had made their way to the Aydem home in the village.

Esra bustled Deniz, Cansu, Ahmet, and Eliza into the living room, leaving them alone there while she made herself busy in the kitchen. All the conversation had been so free flowing and so rapid that Eliza hadn't had a moment to ask Deniz or Cansu what was going on or what was being said. Now that they were in the living room, perched on couches, both adult children were chatting with Ahmet, with Eliza smiling away in the corner.

It was an awkward thing, not understanding what was going on around you. Eliza was aware of the need to find the balance between smiling politely and misrepresenting just how much Turkish she understood. She schooled her expression to what she thought was the perfect neutral facade, not engaged enough to suggest that she was following what was being said and not bored enough for anyone to feel poorly about her lack of understanding.

Even after a few moments, it was exhausting. And yet, she didn't want to ask Cansu or Deniz for a translation out of fear that switching the conversation to English would come across as a lack of respect for their dad.

Even if she had had months to prepare for this visit, these dynamics would have been challenging. But with only a couple of hours? Well, they'd been there for a matter of moments, and she was already drained.

As if summoned by the thoughts in her head, Ahmet directed his attention Eliza's way with a warm smile and a sentence she didn't understand. Whatever Turkish Eliza had known was out the window with the high stakes situation of wanting to impress her boyfriend's father, and she floundered under the pressure.

Her expression must have been desperate as she chanced a glance in Deniz's direction, and she was grateful when he smiled and spoke. "My dad was asking you how you're liking Turkey so far and how long you've been here."

"Oh." She smiled at Ahmet, nodding her head. "It's wonderful. I've only been here for a year, but there's so much more to see, to experience. It's a beautiful country."

Ahmet nodded along as Deniz translated his words, a small lift of the corner of his mouth giving away his pleasure at her response.

Before he could ask a follow-up question, Esra burst into the room with a small tray covered in tea glasses in one hand, a steaming double decker Turkish teapot in the other. She gave a quick direction to Cansu, who left the room and reentered with yet another tray, this one covered in cookies, pieces of cake, and assorted other baked goods.

Esra seated herself on the floor and began pouring tea into the glasses, first the strong steeped potion from the top pot and then the boiling water from the bottom pot. Eliza was in awe of her bodily confidence as she poured while chatting, barely paying attention to what she was doing and yet the end result always being both the same color—and strength—and not one drop spilled over the edge of the hourglass-shaped cup. This was clearly not her first time pouring this many cups of tea.

The glasses were dispersed on small saucers, one to each of them in the room, and then a dish of sugar was passed around to each to sweeten the beverage to their liking. While Deniz and the rest of his family were sipping away at their tea, Eliza struggled to even pick up the glass, the scalding hot liquid nearly reaching to its rim. When she managed to take her first sip, she was simultaneously tickled with pride for managing it and consumed by regret as the hot drink burned her tongue. This was a skill she was going to need to practice...assuming she passed today's test and was ever welcomed back in the Aydem home—or even in their village—again.

Esra smiled at Eliza, her words slipping out so quickly that Eliza was once again left with a blank stare, unsure of anything that had been said to her. Cansu intervened this time, offering a translation and a reassuring twitch of the corner of her mouth.

"My mom is welcoming you to her house. She's very glad that you're here and hopes that you are comfortable. She also apologizes for not being able to speak English."

"Oh no no no, don't apologize, please." Before she could stop herself, Eliza reached out and placed her hand on top of Esra's. "I'm the one who should be apologizing. We're in Turkey, after all. I should be speaking Turkish a lot better than I can by now."

After Cansu's translation, there were a few small smiles directed Eliza's way, and then the family members continued to talk amongst themselves. Eliza sat back and sipped her tea, willing herself to learn Turkish by osmosis, purely through this experience of being immersed in the language.

Of course, as a language teacher, she knew better than to think that half an hour of sitting in on a family discussion was going to make a serious dent in her understanding of Turkish grammar and vocabulary. But it didn't hurt to dream all the same.

During a lull in the conversation, Eliza leaned over to Deniz, who was sitting next to her on the couch, but not so close that she could whisper in his ear without shifting her position. As she slid towards him, she was aware of every eye in the room tilting in their direction, as well as an unfamiliar tension in the set of Deniz's shoulders.

"What's up?" he asked her, glancing over his shoulder at her—she now realized *too close*—face.

"I was just going to ask how your grandmother was doing." Eliza dropped her gaze, scooting back to her end of the couch without meeting anyone's eyes.

Once she was farther away, safely back in her zone, Deniz's smile was more relaxed. "My grandmother is doing well. She'll be home from the hospital any time now." He asked a quick question to his mom in Turkish, then continued speaking to Eliza. "My aunt and her husband are with her now, and they called just before we arrived to tell my mom they were bringing her home."

Eliza smiled at Esra, trying to convey her relief at hearing the news about Esra's mother, while also feeling self-conscious about being here in the middle of their family as an outsider whose actions weren't necessarily normal—or welcome. The smile Esra returned in her direction mirrored her own, offering the smallest bit of reassurance—not enough to counteract the feeling that was gnawing at Eliza, though. Making her want to crawl out of her own skin, straight to the bus terminal, and back to Antalya. Even if Crystal wasn't speaking to her right now, at least she could understand her when she did.

"Come on, Eliza, let me show you around." Cansu had bolted to her feet and was holding out her hand to Eliza. She tilted her head subtly towards her brother and her parents in turn. "I know Deniz wants to talk to my parents about me and London—" The barest hint of a wicked smirk flashed across her face. "—and I'm sure my parents want to talk to him about you, too. Seems to me like you and I had better get the hell out of here before that happens."

Before Deniz could object—or Eliza could even say a word—Cansu had tugged her out of the room and out of the house. Only when the two of them were out on the street of the village did Cansu drop Eliza's hand and exhale a deep sigh.

"Glad to be out of *that* conversation." She gestured with a tip of her head back towards the room they had come from, their feet already taking them further away from the house with each step. "Better Deniz than me."

Eliza's nose wrinkled as she raised an eyebrow at Cansu. "So...what *exactly* is going on there? I know your parents aren't excited about you going to London, but—"

"Ha! *Not excited* is a massive understatement. It seems like they're taking turns either trying to sweet talk me into staying by reminding me of all I'll miss here or guilting me about my selfishness in abandoning the family." She bit her bottom lip, playing with the fingers of her opposite hand and not quite meeting Eliza's eye. "I'm guessing they're not talking about me, though."

"What?" Eliza spun an about face, looking back at the house as if she could see through its walls to the conversation taking place inside. "Me? Are they talking about me and Deniz? But he told everyone I was a friend! He barely looked at me! And everyone was so nice, so welcoming. This isn't really going to be a big problem, is it?"

Cansu pulled a face. "That's all true...but it's the subtext, Eliza. Him bringing you here, no matter what he told them about you...it sends a message. My parents, and my grandparents, too...they're always thinking about who they want to match him up with in the village. Dropping hints about so-and-so's daughter or granddaughter. Deniz has never pushed back against it. But him showing up here with a beautiful American in tow, well...it's a shock to the system for them, let's just say that."

"I..." Eliza couldn't find the words. "He...They want to match make him with someone? I...this is the first I'm hearing of it, so..." She didn't know what to ask first. Was Deniz *interested* in having a match selected for him? Had he met some of these prospective candidates? Were his parents going to hate her for ruining this plan of theirs? Was she even important enough to warrant ruining their plan, or was this all just a way for Deniz to show them he wasn't on board? Or had she gotten so far ahead of herself that she was making up stories when all that was *really* happening right now was that Deniz had to go to the village and she had happened to be with him at the time?

Cansu grimaced. "Sorry. I think I broke your brain with that." Only then did Eliza realize she'd been silent since her previous sentence trailed off. "It's just...these things are so normal in the village that I didn't really think about how it might be for you to hear something like that." She reached over and put her hand on Eliza's arm. "It was a shock?"

Eliza nodded. "It was a shock. I'm not really sure what to do with it, to be honest. I know it's something I need to talk with Deniz about, probably, but...it's too much. Too soon. Too serious. It's not like he and I are talking about getting married, you know? We've only been together for one summer, and we spent most of that on different continents. I don't want things to be complicated for your parents. I don't want them to think this relationship is more serious than it is. I don't want all that pressure put on Deniz." She looked back at the house. "Should...should we go save him?"

A laugh escaped Cansu's lips. "You could try, but I've given up on that idea after years of experience being unsuccessful rescuing him from anything. No, Deniz can handle himself." She winked at Eliza then. "And maybe things are more serious between the two of you than you think. He *did* bring you here, after all."

"Yes, because you needed help. And your grandmother was sick. Everything was blowing up all at once and so he decided—pretty darn suddenly—that he needed to be here. He just brought me because he didn't have the heart to send me back to Antalya alone."

"Is that really what you think?"

Eliza nodded, and Cansu shook her head in response.

"Eliza, my brother doesn't do *anything* he doesn't want to do. You must remember the days before the two of you fell in love. I'm sure you thought he was terribly stubborn and practically unbearable to be around...right?"

"Maybe a little bit." Eliza chuckled at the recollection. "We did have fun together...eventually."

"Right, but not at the beginning. At the beginning, you only saw the stern, serious side of him. Well, that's all any of us—apart from me, of course, but those are the perks of being a little sister—that's all we get to see. With the older generation of our family, Deniz is so wrapped up in expectations and pressures placed on him I don't know if any of them have seen him *relax*, let alone kick back and have some fun."

"Okay..." Eliza paused for a moment. "That doesn't convince me that he won't give in to pressures placed on him, though. Or that he doesn't want to."

"That's just the thing, though, Eliza. The things he *is* willing to do—like get a good job, come home to help during the summers, be a good son in many of the ways that are expected of him...he's done all of those." Cansu swallowed. "But there's been pressure on him to get married and start a family for years. He's never acted on it. Sure, he's played along to an extent, humoring our mom enough to at least let her talk about it...but he's never actually met with a single prospective candidate."

"I guess there's some comfort in that," said Eliza. "Of course, that's only part of it. Maybe it just hasn't been the right time, or maybe he doesn't want to get married at all." She felt her cheeks flush as she came back to herself, aware of the effect her emotional display was having on Cansu. "I'm sorry. I really shouldn't be unloading all of this on you. We barely know each other and here I am carrying on like you're my therapist. Why don't we talk about something else?" She picked up her pace, Cansu falling into step with her and the Aydem house retreating even further behind them.

Cansu was quiet, contemplative. When she broke the newly tense silence between them, it was tentative. "Are you glad you moved to Turkey? For the job, I mean, but...Deniz, too. Do you ever think things would have been easier if you'd stayed in America?"

A sigh huffed out of Eliza's lips before she could stop it. "Overall, I'm glad to be here. I'm glad I took the chance on the job and that I got to experience everything else that came along with it. Of course, when I was back in Michigan for the summer, it made me realize how much I miss things there, too. My family, mostly, but other familiar things, too. Restaurants with foods from all over the world. Bookstores full of English books, movie theaters full of movies I can understand." She watched her feet trace the cobblestones in front of her. "It's not easy, you know. Moving away from your home country, I mean. It opens you up to a whole new world, which is a devastatingly beautiful thing. But in opening yourself up like that, well…it might be hard to feel satisfied in just one place after that. A part of you is always left behind. I think I understand your parents' concerns for you."

Cansu nodded. "I do, too. I've watched enough movies and read enough books to feel so excited about being in London…the Globe Theatre, the West End, even the silly Gherkin…so many new things to see and experience. But how will I ever be able to move back here and leave it all behind? And how could I stay there and never live here near my family again? Those thoughts have been tormenting me."

"I understand the desire to figure it all out. To know what the rest of your life—or at least the next ten years or so—is going to look like." Eliza stopped, turning to face Cansu. "But uncertainties are unavoidable. And I have to believe that you—and me, too—are equipped to handle whatever decisions come your way. How could you possibly know what's going to happen after this year? This time in London is going to change everything. You'll be a different person at the end of it than you are right now. And that person you are going to become…well, she is going to know what the next right thing for you to do is. I'm sure of it."

Twelve

By the time Eliza and Cansu returned to the family home, they had reached a comfortable understanding. Sharing and finding that there was so much they could relate about with the uncertainties ahead of both of them was reassuring, despite the lack of solutions they could help each other find. As well as Cansu knew her brother, she couldn't tell Eliza what the future held for them. And although Eliza had recently done what Cansu was about to do, she couldn't offer any more insight than what life might look like a year further down the road.

But that was where the comfort could be found. Not in someone else possessing the solution, the magical cure to the source of discomfort. But in the knowledge that someone else was in the same place or had stood where you were currently standing. That the bittersweetness of life was actually beautiful and not tragic. That it was a joy and a blessing to have people to love and miss in two different countries, even if it meant you were destined for homesickness no matter where you were.

"It'll be okay," Eliza reassured Cansu before they slipped back in the door. "Whatever *it* is, I mean. It'll be hard and it'll have downs right along with the ups...but it will be okay."

"I should say the same to you," Cansu whispered back, lowering her voice the closer they came to the door behind which Eliza assumed Deniz and his parents still were. "Though of course I hope things with my brother don't have too many downs in store for you...I like you. I'd like to keep you."

Eliza's cheeks flushed with heat at Cansu's last words, the timing of which coincided with entering the living room and being greeted by four sets of eyeballs staring them down. She willed the blush away as she smiled in turn at Deniz and his parents while Cansu greeted the newcomer. Eliza raised her eyebrows at her boyfriend, hoping she'd be able to interpret what had gone down while she had been gone from his facial expression alone.

Deniz smiled back at her and got to his feet, gesturing towards the person who had joined them while she had been gone with Cansu, a friendly-looking man with a kind, open face who was sitting next to where Deniz had been on the couch. "Eliza, this is my cousin Kaan. Kaan, this is Eliza."

Kaan got to his feet, extending his hand to Eliza. "Nice to meet you, Eliza," he said with a warm smile.

"*Memnun oldum*," she replied, taking no small amount of pride in the smiles and murmurs coming from Deniz's parents at her feeble attempt to speak Turkish. "Nice to meet you, too."

"I hope you don't mind if I crash your party," said Kaan, an apologetic tilt to his eyebrows. "I was just asking my cousin if he would mind me joining him on the trip back to Antalya, but I didn't realize you were traveling together."

Eliza barely restrained a wince. Deniz hadn't even told his cousin that she was here? That much, at least, he should have been able to say in front of his parents. It wasn't like they hadn't seen her with their own eyes. Maybe he had a good reason, she told herself. Maybe she should hear his side before assuming the worst of him.

Yeah, right. This is all perfectly normal. Can't imagine what there is for me to feel strange about.

"That's totally fine!" Eliza smiled at Kaan. "It will be nice to have you join us on the bus." She darted a mischievous grin in Deniz's direction. "I'm sure you have all sorts of stories from Deniz's childhood that I can't wait to hear!"

"Wonderful. I'll pack up some things, so I'll be ready whenever you two want to leave." Kaan turned to Deniz, continuing to speak English either for Eliza's benefit or to keep his relatives from understanding. "How early are you planning to leave in the morning?"

Deniz's cheeks turned bright red. "Oh...uh..." he sputtered. "We're not staying overnight. I mean..." He glanced helplessly, first at Eliza, then at his mother, his eyes landing on Cansu. "Right? We can't stay here. How...?"

"...yeah." Eliza chimed in. "I don't think that would be comfortable for anyone, would it? We should go back. Tonight. Back to Antalya, back to our own apartments..."

"Nonsense!" That was Cansu. "You already cut your vacation short to come here. You shouldn't cut it even shorter." Her grin was wide, evidence that she was enjoying this. She was the *only* one enjoying this. "Stay here. Eliza can stay with me. Don't even try to suggest that the two of you stay together—" She said this last sentence out of the corner of her mouth, for Deniz's ears only. "—unless you are really craving some excitement and drama in your life. No. Eliza can stay with me, and the two of you...er, the *three* of you...can leave after breakfast tomorrow."

Eliza couldn't argue with her logic. It would get dark soon, and someone would need to drive them to the bus station. It wasn't as if she and Deniz could just say goodbye, walk out the door, and be on their way back to Antalya. There were at least a few more steps in the interim. But there was nothing she wanted more in that moment than to be alone with Deniz and on her way back to her apartment, her familiar bed. She needed to talk to Deniz, and she needed to do it without an audience. Even in the short time they had spent with his parents, she could feel a change in the air between them. It wasn't just that he was more reserved, though that was undeniably the case. But so was she. She felt simultaneously like she was invisible and like she was hyper-visible. Like everything she did or said could be seen right through to the heart behind it. But at the same time, no one could see her.

It was probably about not being able to communicate, she realized. Because her words couldn't speak for her, she was hyper aware of everything else—her facial expressions, her gestures, her posture...and under that much scrutiny, they all became unnatural, forced, uncomfortable.

The day had required little physical exertion, but that hadn't stopped Eliza from getting utterly exhausted. She knew that mental activity could tire her out, too—she'd fallen asleep planning lessons and grading papers enough times to believe that particular fact—but she hadn't known until today how tiring just being immersed in a foreign language, desperately wanting to understand it, and being confronted by her failure to do so repeatedly could be.

Her own bed, a dark room, familiar sounds and smells...that all sounded like heaven right now. Like her own personal sensory deprivation chamber, and waiting until tomorrow to get it was making her feel itchy.

Still, Eliza knew making a decent first impression on Deniz's parents—if it was, in fact, possible—hinged on her being flexible and easy-going and culturally appropriate. The last thing she wanted to do was be the diva from a different country who expected things done the way they'd always been done in her experience and worldview.

She put on a smile and turned to Cansu. "That sounds fine to me, but is it okay for everyone else?" She hazarded a glance in Deniz's direction. "Are you okay with that? What about your parents? I don't want to make them uncomfortable staying here, but I also don't want to leave and be rude."

Before Deniz could answer, Cansu stepped forward, looping her arm through Eliza's. "You won't make anyone uncomfortable. Come on, let me show you where we're going to be sleeping." She looked over her shoulder at her brother as she removed Eliza from the room again. "Right, *abi*? You're good?"

All Eliza heard was a grunt from Deniz before the door swung shut behind them. He was left alone again to deal with the repercussions of a decision he hadn't made, and for that, Eliza was tempted to feel guilty. Until she remembered he had brought her here, ill-prepared and possibly unwanted by his parents. The two of them would have a lot to talk about when they had some time alone again, and Eliza hoped with all her might that Kaan would give them the space to have that conversation soon. The tension was growing between them with every passing moment, with every look she didn't quite know how to read, with every inch he pulled away from her under his father's watchful eye.

"So this isn't going to be strange for your parents, right?" Eliza asked Cansu as the younger woman pulled her into a small bedroom. "If Deniz has never brought a girlfriend home before, then clearly he's never brought one home overnight."

"It's fine," said Cansu. "It's not like the two of you are sharing a room. That...well, that could get complicated." She shrugged. "Though honestly, I'm not sure. My parents might be cool with it, but it's not exactly the kind of thing that either of us is going to try. It feels weird, disrespectful, I guess. But don't worry, there's nothing weird about you sleeping in my room. We have relatives and friends of the family sleep over all the time, like when there's a wedding and people come from out of town. It really would only be weird if there were an unmarried couple sleeping in the same room. Which there won't be."

"Right," said Eliza, forcing a sly smile in Cansu's direction. "So you're telling me I shouldn't sneak out of your room and go find Deniz in the middle of the night? I *guess* I can handle that."

Cansu's eyes widened. "I sure hope you can, considering Deniz is going to be sleeping in the same room as my parents."

A bark of a laugh escaped Eliza's lips then, growing bigger and bigger the more she tried to contain it. When she finally got enough air in her lungs—and a straight enough face to get the words out—she spoke. "Duly noted. It would probably be dark in there, anyway, and I might end up snuggling next to your mom. You don't think she would mind, do you?"

"Well, that's one way to warm up to your possibly future mother-in-law!"

And that shut Eliza up. The reminder of what was at stake, of how serious things had the potential to become between her and Deniz, between her and his entire family...the last thing she wanted to do when she thought about that was make a joke.

"I promise I'll behave," she said. "No funny business from me. You have my word."

Cansu smiled. "It'll be fun. Like a sleepover. We can gossip in the dark until one of us passes out."

"I like the sound of that very much."

The family reconvened in the living room an hour later for dinner. Eliza had spent the intermittent time with Cansu, who had been eager to show her all the things she was setting aside for her big move to London. As much as Eliza was enjoying spending time with the younger woman, the fact that she hadn't had a moment alone with Deniz since they had arrived wasn't sitting well with her. If only the two of them could talk...or, barring that, if only she could suddenly be blessed with the ability to read his mind.

But she hadn't wanted to ask Cansu, to trouble her more with her own insecurities than she already had. Tomorrow she would have some one-on-one time with Deniz. Probably. Unless Kaan was with them the whole day, which she had every reason to suspect he would be.

Eliza exhaled her frustrations as she crossed the threshold into the living room, greeting Ahmet and Deniz with a smile. The two men were engrossed in conversation, and Eliza knew she should be appreciative of the briefest glimmer of genuine affection that Deniz sent her way...and yet, she wasn't. It wasn't enough. Not enough to reassure her she belonged in that room or even enough to convince her she was welcome there.

She was tempted to turn around, to slink back to Cansu's room and mope there. She didn't need to be where she wasn't wanted, and she didn't even care if it was childish to make a scene like that. If it was enough to clue Deniz in to the fact that she was uncomfortable, that this was *not* what she had had in mind for their vacation away together...well, it would be worth it. It wasn't as if she had the airspace or opportunity to use actual words to communicate her feelings to him.

But when she looked over her shoulder towards the door, contemplating her next move, a silhouette appeared, blocking her way.

Kaan.

Deniz's cousin smiled warmly, greeting everyone in turn before taking a seat next to Cansu and leaning forward to speak to Eliza. "Hello, again! I've been dying to chat with you some more, Eliza. I hope you don't mind."

"Not at all," said Eliza, surprised to find that she meant what she said. "It will be nice to talk with you, too, and I'm sure Cansu could use the break." She smiled meekly at her boyfriend's sister. "She's been stuck with me all afternoon since there's not exactly anyone else I can communicate with."

"Except Deniz, of course. His English is better than anyone else I know."

Eliza barely stopped herself from rolling her eyes. "It really is excellent, I agree. But he and I have barely been able to say two words to each other since we got here." Seeing the concern flash across Kaan's face, she rushed to clarify. "I don't mean it like that. I'm not frustrated with him, and actually it makes perfect sense. His parents have things they want to talk to him about, and he sort of blindsided them with my existence...I'm fine with all of that. I am just aware that it might be easier and more comfortable for everyone to have the conversations they need to have if I weren't actually...er...*here*."

A deep laugh escaped from Kaan's throat, his eyes filling with mirth. "Eliza, you're thinking like an American, I believe. Which makes sense, considering that you *are* an American."

"Sorry? I don't get it."

"I just mean...well, you know how Americans tend to value things like...well, like privacy. Private conversations. *'It's a family matter. That's not appropriate conversation.'*"

Kaan's impression of a typical American father—no doubt the result of watching the stereotypical role play out in plenty of Hollywood movies—was on point. So good, in fact, that Eliza's hand flew to her mouth to cover the chortle that burst out. Ahmet's eyes darted in her direction at the sound, and she smiled apologetically.

Kaan continued. "In the village, we don't worry about things like that. Look around you. Look at how close the homes are to each other, look at how many people drop in to say hello or to share bread or a bit of gossip. We aren't living in an American suburb where everything happens behind closed doors. Our arguments might happen out in the street, or in a house with the windows open and the neighbors hearing every word." He shrugged. "And I'm not saying that one is better than the other. I think that both ways of life have their benefits and their drawbacks. But I think there's no need for you to feel uncomfortable, even if you yourself are the subject up for discussion between our dear Deniz and his parents."

Eliza cocked an eyebrow at Kaan. "So, you're confirming that, in fact, they *are* talking about me." She jerked her head towards Deniz and his father. "Like...right now?"

"Not at this precise moment, no. But I'm sure they have talked about you at some point today. What's the big deal, though? You don't speak Turkish, right?"

"You don't have to remind me." Eliza held her head in her hands. "I know I should. I promise I'm working on it. But no, my Turkish is definitely not good enough to understand any gossip going on around me."

"Why are you saying that like it's a bad thing?" Eliza could hear the laughter in Kaan's voice even without looking at him. "I'm jealous! I wish *I* didn't understand the gossip. Do you know how free I would feel? Ignorance really is bliss, Eliza."

"Ugh, so true," Cansu chimed in. "It's a lot harder to tune meddling parents out when you understand what they're saying. But if they were speaking, I don't know...Polish? Portuguese? Well, then I wouldn't understand a word. I'd just smile and nod and they'd feel great because they were getting to speak their piece. And I'd feel great because I wouldn't actually have to think about what I'd heard. It sounds pretty great to me."

Eliza just shook her head. "Your points are well received, both of you. And I appreciate the efforts at cheering me up. It's okay. Really."

It was at that precise moment that Esra entered with a tray covered in dishes of food, and the room sprung into action. Deniz placed a large piece of cloth, like a tablecloth or picnic blanket, on the floor, Cansu passed around pieces of bread and *yufka*, a folded, unleavened village bread Deniz had introduced her to, and everyone took their spaces, sitting cross-legged. It was all so natural, every movement unfolding like it was part of a larger machine, that for a moment Eliza was frozen in inaction. Did everyone have an assigned "space" around the tray? Was there somewhere in particular she should sit? Would it be appropriate for her to sit next to Deniz, or would that raise eyebrows in their direction?

And then, as if he was reading her mind, Deniz smiled up at her, patting the floor next to him. "Come on, Eliza, sit here. Let's eat."

Thirteen

Despite all the weirdness of being with Deniz at his family home while not exactly being "with" him, as Eliza lay on the mattress next to Cansu, listening to the young woman's slow breathing, there was a sense of peace, a calm in all of it that was a balm to her soul.

Maybe it was the result of a delicious meal, capped off with a cup of Turkish coffee and a few pieces of *lokum*. Maybe it was the warm smiles from Deniz's mother and his aunts who had stopped by to say hello—and to scope her out, once they, too, had learned of her existence. Or maybe it was just the camaraderie of Cansu, with whom she had slipped into such an easy friendship that, if Eliza were a daydreamer, she could get carried away imagining the two of them as sisters-in-law.

She wasn't a daydreamer, though. Not really. That was more Crystal's territory.

Eliza sighed as she thought of her best friend, who was, as far as Eliza could tell, both swept up in a daydream of her own...and also still not talking to Eliza because of her legitimate concerns about said daydream.

She's been right in the past, sure...about some things. Taking a chance on a relationship, being vulnerable. But that doesn't mean that I need to make her my role model for life or anything like that. In fact, Eliza thought, *she would benefit from listening to me this time around. I just* know *she's jumping in to this relationship with both feet and it's too soon and she's going to end up hurt. Exercising a little caution would serve her well.* She fumbled under the pillow, searching for her phone to text Crystal before she could talk herself out of it.

Hey Crys, it's me. You already knew that. Duh. Anyway. I just...I don't want you to think I don't love you and support you. I just don't want you to get hurt. When I get back, can we talk about it? About taking things a little slower?

To Eliza's immediate surprise, the dots signifying Crystal was typing a response appeared.

Of course we can talk about it. Just know that it's going to be a two-sided conversation. NO WAY I'm sitting through one of your lectures.

And then: Maybe we can also talk about why you're texting me at 11 pm when you're on a romantic getaway with your boyfriend.

If only she knew... Eliza thought. But if she had the upper hand for a moment, the last thing she needed to do was to reveal to Crystal that she was not, in fact, even in the same room as Deniz. That the two of them had barely spoken two sentences to each other and that they'd had an audience for every interaction that had happened since they'd met his dad at the bus station. Still...it wasn't as if she could keep any secrets from Crystal for long.

Oh, I'll tell you all about it, and I'm sure you'll have some choice words for me, too. Only fair.

Crystal responded. Ooh, I'm intrigued...and maybe a little nervous. Any hints? Or should I leave you to enjoy your romantic evening and chat with you when you're home?

Eliza's fingers fired off a response. Oh, there's nothing romantic in the works for tonight. Here's your hint: I'm sleeping next to someone whose last name is Aydem...but her name is not Deniz.

All she got in response to that message was a series of shocked face emojis and three question marks.

Okay, that was unnecessarily cryptic. Spoiler alert: it's Cansu. We're in the village with Deniz's family and...yeah.

The same borderline-hieroglyphic message Crystal had sent a moment earlier came again, this time with a few extra question marks.

That's really all I'm going to give you tonight. Don't want to keep texting and risk waking up Cansu. I'll fill you in on all the details tomorrow.

You guys are coming back tomorrow?! That seems soon...trouble in paradise?

There's nothing to read into here, Crys. I'll tell you everything when I see you. Love you.

Love you too. Night!

But sleep didn't come for Eliza even after she stopped blasting her eyeballs with the blue light from her cellphone. She couldn't help but wonder about Crystal's question. *Was* there trouble in paradise? Had this entire trip—or at least the part that they had spent with his family—been a mistake? Something that had escalated things between them more quickly than they could handle? Would they be okay when they were back in Antalya, or would it be impossible to come back from this, to go back to the way things were before?

Eliza sighed. None of these were questions she could answer herself, without at least talking to Deniz. That was off the table for tonight, though, and there wasn't any progress to be made by thinking the same thoughts over and over again.

If only her brain could get that memo. *How do you stop thinking a thought once you've started? I don't want to keep torturing myself with these questions, but that doesn't exactly drive them out of my mind. That's the trick though, isn't it? Anything you* don't *want to think about, you inevitably* do *end up thinking about. Is that why people count sheep when they can't sleep? Maybe I should try that.*

Eventually, by some minor miracle, Eliza must have fallen asleep, because she regained consciousness the next morning with the sun streaming on her face and roosters crowing outside the window. Before her eyes were even open, a rush of panic gripped her. If the sun was already shining in her eyes, it must be late. Far later than was polite to sleep in the first time you stayed at your boyfriend's parents' house...the first time you even met them, no less.

But as she cracked her left eye open, she glimpsed Cansu's still form next to her and exhaled with relief. There was nothing for her to be missing out on, not when her hostess was right here in the room with her.

Still, it wasn't as if cold panic was the desired state for Eliza's first waking moment, and she spent the next several breathing slowly and deeply, trying to get her pulse back under control and manage the flood of cortisol and adrenaline she imagined were coursing through her veins.

"Nothing like a stress response to get you out of bed in the morning," she muttered to herself, barely audible so as not to wake Cansu.

"Good morning!" At that same moment, Cansu turned onto her side, beaming up at Eliza. "How did you sleep?"

"Er...great, thanks. How about you?"

"Good." Cansu stretched. "I feel great, really well rested." She dropped her hand to her stomach and massaged it. "Hungry, though. And I need some tea." She popped to her feet, swiping her hair back into a messy bun. "Shall we?" she asked, nodding towards the door. At Eliza's blank expression, she smiled. "Breakfast? Aren't you hungry?"

"Oh...sure," said Eliza. "I guess I could eat." In her sudden influx of FOMO-induced stress, Eliza had lost her appetite, or else never become aware of it in the first place. But even if she didn't feel like eating, she was bound and determined that this morning she would make a good impression. She wouldn't emerge from the bedroom fluent in Turkish or anything like that—her expectations for herself were somewhat reasonable, after all—but she could at least eat and drink everything placed in front of her, a surefire way to put a smile on the faces of mothers of boyfriends everywhere.

She found a mirror on Cansu's dresser and frowned at the face that stared back at her as she attempted to rub mascara stains from underneath her eyes. When she had done the best she could do, she slipped her hair from its loose ponytail before retying the same style a little tighter and higher than before. "Okay, then. That's as good as that gets."

Eliza followed Cansu back to the living room, an internal monologue firing off to beat herself up every step of the way. *Why are you following her like a child? Don't you know where the living room is by now? Sure,* she answered herself, *how could I not? But if I stick with Cansu, then I don't risk running into someone and not knowing what to say and the two of us just staring at each other while I wish the ground would open up and swallow me into it. Ah, but what if the person I run into is Deniz? Wouldn't that be great? Well, you'd think it would be, but you never can be too sure about these things.*

Stepping into the living room, Eliza looked up from the floor—why, even her gaze was trained on the floor if she needed further proof that she was feeling small and unworthy and desperately in need of an ego or self-esteem boost—directly into the deep brown eyes of Deniz Aydem.

And for just a moment, a moment in which she zoomed in on his pupils like a special effect in a movie, ignoring everything else that was happening in that room, he was all that existed. He was relaxed, in a way she hadn't seen him since before he had gotten that phone call from his family.

Relaxed, like, "sleeping in with my girlfriend on vacation with no agenda at all for the day ahead" relaxed.

Seeing him like that, Eliza felt a schism in her mind, a splitting right down the middle in two polarly opposed ways. On one side, she felt warm, both all over her body and right down to her soul, at the sight of her boyfriend. She loved him. She knew that without a doubt, in that moment, receiving that smile meant just for her, seeing the peace in his eyes when they landed on hers.

And at the same time, she was livid. With him, for daring to be so carefree and relaxed and comfortable when she'd spent the entire night and most of the day before wondering what the hell was even going on with them, sure. But also with herself, for putting herself in a position where a man—a mere mortal, no less—had the power to make her feel like that. Had the power to sweep her away in love and security and peace...which meant that the opposite was true, too. That without him, she would feel coldness. Absence. Insecurity. Uncertainty.

And there was nothing—*nothing*—that Eliza Britt liked about that. About finding herself in that position, especially at a time like this, when the other people in this room—she glanced around now to confirm that Deniz's parents were, in fact, there, too, looking at her with puzzled expressions on their faces—might not approve of her being in Deniz's life. Might not want her around at all.

And he might just honor their wishes.

No, she didn't like this one bit.

She forced a smile at Deniz, squeezing her eyes the slightest bit to give that crinkle at the corners that gave away an authentic smile. She then turned that same smile to his parents, nodded and said "*Günaydın*, good morning," probably too quietly for them to hear before sitting on the couch at the opposite end from Deniz. She tucked her feet underneath her body and focused her attention on the news program that was playing on the television, refusing to look in Deniz's direction despite feeling his gaze burning into the side of her face.

The two of them, they had a lot to talk about. And now was not the time...but it would be, when they got back to Antalya. There was a lot that he hadn't shared with her in the past 24 hours, maybe even longer than that, and that needed to change.

That wasn't all that needed to change. If he wasn't going to share with her, if his parents weren't going to approve of her...well, then everything needed to change. Before it was too late for her heart.

Who am I kidding? It's already too late, she thought. *I'm attached to him. Hell, I love him, and I'll be crushed when this ends. If it ends, I mean. No...the way things are looking right now, I definitely mean* when *it ends.*

It was hard to pretend that everything was okay, that she was unbothered by her isolation, her lack of comprehension of the conversation, the news anchor, the state of her relationship. Eliza had never been good at pretending, though, and that was why she couldn't look at Deniz right now. She couldn't hide her turmoil, her discomfort, and if she tried, he would know.

And if he looked at her with concern and love in his eyes, if he asked her if she was okay...the facade would come tumbling down. She would fall apart and reveal herself, either with a caustic, sarcastic comment lobbed in defensiveness or with an unwanted tear sliding down her cheek. If his parents already disapproved of her, how much more would that increase when they heard that snarky tone or saw her crying before they'd even eaten their breakfast?

No, that was why her gaze was focused on the television program, like it was the most interesting thing she'd ever seen. Like if she stared hard enough, she might receive some supernatural intervention and be able to understand every word that was flying out of the anchor's mouth rapidfire. Next thing she knew, she'd be speaking fluent Turkish.

Esra handed Eliza a glass of black tea, holding out the sugar bowl for her to take a spoonful. Eliza thanked her and once again commenced the dance of balancing the hot glass on her knee without spilling it or burning her fingers. She couldn't help but miss drinking out of a mug with a handle...

...and come to think of it, she couldn't help but miss having a nice hot cup of coffee with milk in it. Alone. In the silence and calm of her own space, without the stress and pressure she was feeling being around Deniz's family and not being able to communicate with them.

She ached for home—her home in Antalya, that she shared with Crystal, though her home back in Michigan sounded good right about now, too. If she were with her parents, there would be coffee. And quiet. And probably even a cat curling up on her lap. Why did that all sound so good that it nearly made her want to cry?

Eliza wasn't a crier. Not like Crystal, who was in tears watching 15-second videos on her Instagram feed. No, the two friends had often joked that in their friendship, Eliza was the head and Crystal was the heart. They balanced each other out, the detached, cerebral one and the intuitive, emotional one.

But by all accounts, Eliza was messing that up royally now. In the last day and a half—and even longer than that, as she looked back at her relationship with Deniz—she had put herself firmly in the emotional girlfriend category, with her happiness and well-being tied to her boyfriend and the condition of things between them.

Which all reminded Eliza, yet again, that it was time to put things right. To get back in control of her emotions, yes, and to return to more comfortable territory where her relationship was concerned. The last thing she wanted was to be in a codependent relationship where she couldn't be happy unless Deniz was happy. But if they relaxed things between them a bit, took off the pressure and expectation that this thing they were doing was ever going to go anywhere...that could help. They could be casual about things.

Eliza could only assume she possessed the ability to be casual about things somewhere in her being. So far, in the nearly three decades she had spent on planet Earth, she hadn't mastered the art of nonchalance, but if other people could do it, then why couldn't she?

After breakfast was finished, Eliza tried to bolt from the room rather than risk staying behind to feel—yet again—like she didn't belong. Even when the family was tidying up, it was as if everyone knew their place, had a role to play...and she simply didn't know where to fit into that. Or if it would even be received well if she tried. The last thing she wanted to do was come across as an arrogant outsider who was inserting herself into family matters or showing a "better" way to do things.

Before she could make her escape, though, Deniz caught her by the elbow. "Are you okay?" He spoke in a low voice, leaning in for only her to hear. "Is this—" He jerked his head towards the surrounding room. "Is this all okay?"

"Mm hmm." Eliza nodded, responding to him with her lips buttoned shut. Inside, she was screaming, *No, of course it isn't "okay!" How could you think this has all been perfectly normal and has made me feel just wonderful about our relationship?*

Her eyes must have given away at least part of her inner monologue because Deniz frowned, jerking back slightly before he rallied.

"We'll talk later," he murmured into her ear. "It's all going to be fine, I promise."

Eliza nodded and walked away from him. *Of course, it's all going to be fine,* she thought. *It just might not be fine the way* you *think it will be.*

Fourteen

The trip back to Antalya got off to a late start. When they had talked with Kaan the day before about leaving after breakfast, Eliza had envisioned an early breakfast and a quick departure after that, being back in her own apartment by lunchtime.

What she hadn't accounted for—and how could she?—was the way things worked in the village. To start with, she and Cansu had slept later than Eliza had expected...and then no one had been surprised. It wasn't like back in Michigan where she would emerge from a record-breaking long sleep to find her mom had been up for hours and had, in fact, already had breakfast, given the neighbor's dog a bath, and solved three crossword puzzles.

After the family had eaten breakfast, Deniz said he wanted to go say goodbye to his relatives, a task Eliza had agreed to with the assumption that it would be a quick visit, a drop in to say hi and bye, and then they would be on their way. She hadn't accounted for the fact that this was the village Deniz had been born in, as had both of his parents. Which meant that almost every single relative of his lived within walking distance of his parents' house.

The first visit had been to his grandmother, to check in that she was feeling better after her hospital visit the previous day. The elderly woman had been full of smiles and was not at all surprised to meet Eliza, confirming Eliza's suspicion that news traveled fast in the village. Deniz's grandmother had insisted they join her for tea, which Eliza was learning always meant more than one cup of the beverage. While she sipped her drink slowly, one cup for the others' two, she admired Deniz's ability to caffeinate himself without ending up jittery. By her count, he'd had at least five cups since waking up that morning—and those were just the ones she had borne witness to.

After leaving Deniz's grandmother's house, they had made the rounds. His other grandparents, two aunts, and one uncle had all received their Deniz and Eliza visits, too. Walking back to his parents' home, Deniz explained that his other relatives were all busy, already out to work in the fields or at their jobs at this time of day.

"It's lovely," Eliza admitted, huffing under the weight of perishable goods they were carrying back with them, gifts from everyone they'd visited. "Everyone being so close like this, I mean."

Despite her hesitation and discomfort, the morning visits had warmed her from the inside out. Walking in the sun, being the recipient of all those warm smiles, hugs and cheek kisses, and seeing Deniz with these people who had helped raise him...it had worn away at her resolve to feel like an outsider.

Deniz raised an eyebrow at her. "Is this not what your hometown is like?"

Eliza barked out a laugh. "My hometown is *friendly* enough, sure. But it's not full of my family. Not like this."

"Where do the rest of your relatives live, then?"

"They're...well, they're all over, I guess." Eliza shrugged. "My parents met in college, then moved from there when they got jobs. My dad's parents are in Indiana and my mom's parents are in Wisconsin. My aunts and uncles did kind of the same thing my parents did, so they're all scattered, too. Mostly in the Midwest, but...not like this. We're not walking between houses or sharing eggs with each other."

Deniz was quiet, thoughtful. "Did you like growing up like that?"

Eliza shrugged again. "I didn't know anything else, so what could I compare it to? It was always nice to have the larger family together at Thanksgiving and Christmas or for a wedding or a funeral. But it didn't happen more than once or twice a year." She looked around her at the village and all its inhabitants, bustling about on their daily chores. "I think if I'd known something like this was an option, I would have wanted it. But that just wasn't the way it was for us."

"And here I was thinking the total opposite." Deniz looked around him, surveying the familiar sights.

"What do you mean?"

"I always wanted to get out of here. Go away to high school, university, get a job, and never look back. Come to visit or to help when they need me, but...I never wanted to live here as an adult. It can be a lot, you know." He chuckled softly. "I think you definitely *do* know that it can be a lot."

Eliza felt her cheeks burn with embarrassment. "What's that supposed to mean?"

"It means that until a few moments ago, I thought you were going to break up with me the second we got back to Antalya. That my family was so overwhelming that you were going to back right out of it as soon as you got the chance." He squinted at her in the sun. "I haven't quite figured out what changed, but I appreciate it."

With her hands still full of a bag of eggs, jars of preserves, and some homemade cheese, Eliza couldn't bury her head in her hands the way she wished she could. So instead she turned to face Deniz head on. "You're right. I *was* totally overwhelmed, and I was getting frustrated with you."

"With me?"

"Yeah! You didn't exactly prepare me for this, especially not with what you told me about Turkish parents taking relationships seriously and probably not accepting me—"

"That's not what I—"

"Let me finish, please." Eliza sighed. "It felt like everything was stacked against me, and then the whole time we were here, I was just seeing all the ways I didn't fit into your life. All the things I didn't really know about you and all the ways I couldn't connect. I couldn't say more than five words to your mom, for crying out loud!"

"I know." Deniz looked down. "It's not easy for you, and it's not easy for them, either. And I'm sorry I wasn't more supportive."

Eliza shook her head. "You weren't even on the same planet as me once we arrived here. You felt so far away, and I assumed that meant that you were retreating, pulling away. Seeing, like I was, that I didn't make sense in your life. I...I'm not saying I am okay with that. Or that I even understand it. But I'm going to try to. I can at least try to understand you."

"Why the change, though? This is practically the first time you've made eye contact with me since we got here."

Eliza shrugged. "Something was different, walking around here with you. Visiting all those homes. It made me realize you weren't, I don't know...*embarrassed* to be seen with me, or anything like that. I mean, we walked around these streets in broad daylight and you greeted everyone like you were the freaking mayor and they all saw me..."

"And?"

"And you didn't seem bothered by it at all. Sure, you didn't hold my hand or make out with me on the street—"

"Two *very* different conceptions of what PDA looks like...and both not really things you do right here where everybody can see."

"Good to know." Eliza gave him a genuine smile now. "It just made me realize maybe I wasn't looking at the full picture. I was only considering how things felt inside the four walls of your parents' house, and I know I brought a fair amount of my own baggage inside those walls with me. It's worth examining things in different lights...different settings...from all the angles."

He reached out and took her hand, the same one that was carrying a heavy bag full of cheese and preserves, which he slipped out of her fingers and into his own equally laden down hand. The approximation of a public display of affection was there, though, warming Eliza from low in her belly.

"I'm glad to hear you say that," he said. "And I wish I could kiss you right now. If I did that, though, I'd probably get a scolding from my first grade teacher and there would be rumors about our impending marriage by the end of the day today." He winked at her instead. "I'll save it for later, though. You can cash in on that kiss as soon as we're back on our own turf in Antalya."

"I will."

"Promise?"

"I promise."

Deniz's parents and Cansu accompanied Deniz, Eliza, and Kaan to the bus terminal, where they waited outside to wave them off as the bus pulled away. Esra and Cansu had both hugged Eliza goodbye, with the younger woman promising to text her updates about London plans. Eliza had said her farewell to Ahmet, who shook her hand and smiled warmly, wishing her safe travel back to Antalya.

Inside the bus, Eliza sat in a window seat next to Deniz, with Kaan across the aisle from them. She put on her headphones and stared out the window, aware that she was sending the universal signal for "don't talk to me right now" to her boyfriend, but feeling too tired and overwhelmed by all that had happened in the last 24 hours to care.

As far as she could tell, Deniz was having a fine time chatting with Kaan, the two of them laughing together with the easy comfort of brothers or friends who had grown up together. Eliza's cousins all lived out of state and were part of the extended family that she only saw once or twice a year, so she couldn't relate to the relationship between Deniz and Kaan.

Ten minutes into the journey, once the bus was out of the city center and cruising along on the highway, Eliza felt a gentle weight on her knee. Looking down, there was Deniz's hand, palm up and fingers wiggling, beckoning to hers. She smiled and shook her head before depositing her hand in his. His attention was still focused on Kaan, hers once again directed out the window at the passing countryside, but the feeling of his thumb caressing the back of her hand kept her anchored in her seat, rather than floating away with her imagination.

Thanks to a great playlist and the last few chapters of an audiobook, the journey back to Antalya flew by. The narrator was just wrapping up the epilogue of Kate Austen's latest release when the bus pulled into the familiar terminal.

Eliza deposited her headphones back in her backpack and turned to Deniz and Kaan. "That was...fast! I can't believe we're here already."

Kaan rubbed his stomach. "Speak for yourself. I'm starving and have been for at least the last 60 kilometers." He leaned across the aisle to elbow Deniz in the ribs. "Where are you taking me for lunch, eh? Or what are you going to cook for me?"

Deniz chuckled as the three of them picked up their bags, beginning the slow shuffle towards the front of the bus and its exit. "I'll cook for you, Kaan, but not right now. I'm hungry, too. Why don't we take these bags back to my apartment and then go out for lunch? We could get some *tantuni* if that sounds good to you." He looked over his shoulder at Eliza. "Are you going to join us? You are more than welcome." Kaan nodded along, as if he couldn't bear to be alone with Deniz for a moment longer.

Eliza shook her head. "I should go home, check in with Crystal. We left things a bit weirdly the other day, and I need to spend some time with her." She smiled at Kaan. "I'll definitely hang out with you while you're here. How long are you staying?"

Kaan shot a glance at Deniz. "Well...er. We haven't exactly talked about that."

The foot traffic in the bus's aisle had slowed to a stop, and Deniz turned around to face Eliza and Kaan behind her. "You're right, we haven't. So what are you being so sneaky about? Hmm?"

"I'm actually, uh..." Kaan's next words came out quickly, jumbled together. "I'm actually thinking about moving here."

Deniz's face brightened before Eliza's very eyes. "Moving here? Are you serious?"

"Yes, but I wouldn't be staying with you or anything like that. Just until I find a place of my own."

"Kaan, that's great! It'll be so fun to have you around. Won't it, Eliza?"

Eliza nodded. Deniz's joy was contagious, and she was confident that if having Kaan around made Deniz *this* happy, then by extension it thrilled her, too. After all, Deniz's closest friend, Barış, had been pretty unavailable lately, between his job, his research projects, and his relationship with Jack. Even if Deniz was a relationship guy himself, it would be good for him to have another friend to hang out with. Eliza had Crystal, after all, and she wasn't going to give up that relationship anytime soon.

Deniz had left his car at the bus terminal, and despite Eliza's insistence that she didn't mind taking a taxi, he insisted on dropping her off at her apartment before going to his own place with Kaan. From the front seat, she turned around to talk to Kaan.

"I'm sorry if this is rude, but I realized I didn't actually ask you what you do. Are you moving to Antalya for a job, then?"

Kaan glanced up, meeting Deniz's eyes in the rearview mirror and shaking his head. "Er...not exactly."

Deniz spoke up. "Kaan doesn't exactly work, is what he means. He doesn't have to. Must be nice being independently wealthy and retired before you're thirty."

"Really?" Eliza turned back to Kaan. "I mean, I can't relate *at all* and I swear I'm not jealous..."

Kaan rolled his eyes at Deniz. "My cousin is exaggerating, Eliza. I work, I'm an app developer. I just don't work in an office or for anyone else."

"He means his first app was a gigantic success and now he doesn't *have* to work for anyone else anymore," Deniz interjected.

"It wasn't my *first* app," said Kaan. "See, this is why they say people are overnight successes. Because no one pays attention until they succeed, but they probably already tried and failed a bunch of times before that. The app that already took off, that was probably the fiftieth time I've tried. And I still keep working on new ideas, putting them out there to see if another one is going to follow that same trajectory."

"Well, I think that sounds really cool. Really inspiring. What kind of apps are you working on now?" Eliza asked.

"Mostly personal development, like a life coach in an app. I'm coming at it from a few different angles, working on some different concepts. There's nothing concrete that I'm giving my focus to right now, but I thought coming here, having a change of scenery...it could be inspiring." He shrugged. "It usually is."

"Kaan is what some people might call a digital nomad," said Deniz, a note of pride in his voice. "He lives and works all over the place, and Antalya is lucky enough to have him grace us with his presence for a while."

Eliza smiled. "I think just as much as you'll be inspired by being in Antalya, the rest of us might be inspired by having *you* around." She looked back at Deniz. "Right? Especially in our little circle of teachers, there's no one who's done something like that. Definitely no one who is remotely close to being able to retire early." A thought crossed her mind, excitement coursing through her veins. "You have to meet Crystal! Right Deniz, doesn't he have to meet Crystal? Wouldn't the two of them get along so well?"

Deniz nodded, a smile growing on his face. "You know, I think you're right. They could be great friends, I believe."

"Okay, I'll bite. Who's this Crystal?" Kaan had a playful look on his face, like he was humoring a few toddlers by playing along with their charade.

"My best friend. My roommate. Coincidentally, also the closest thing I've ever had to a life coach," Eliza explained. "But I'm not just saying you should meet her because she could help give you app ideas. I think you'd just get along well. Inspire each other with the different ways you think outside of the box."

"So you're not trying to set me up with her?" Kaan's eyes twinkled, and Eliza felt herself pale.

"No! Oh my goodness, no, I wouldn't do that. I swear!"

"If you'll notice, I wasn't exactly complaining. It's just rather uncommon to be told you *have to* meet someone without there being an expectation of the two of you running off together to get married and have lots of children."

"Well, I can assure you, that's not how I meant it at all."

"I'll vouch for that," said Deniz. "Not for the fact that you and Crystal shouldn't get married and have lots of children. I'm still undecided about that." He smiled an impish grin. "I'm just vouching for the fact that Eliza definitely didn't mean it that way."

"Noted," said Kaan, amusement playing at the corners of his mouth.

While they had been talking, Deniz had come to a stop, parking his car in front of Eliza's apartment building. "Should we come upstairs with you and meet the famous Crystal Kim?" He reached to unbuckle his seatbelt, pausing while he waited for Eliza's response.

She shook her head and smiled. "Soon. It wouldn't be fair to spring her big meeting with Kaan on her without even so much as a warning that she's about to have a gentleman caller." She nodded at Kaan in the backseat. "We'll all hang out soon, I promise." She leaned towards Deniz, but he unbuckled his seatbelt and nodded towards the front of the car.

"I can at least walk you to the door of the building," he said. "Kaan, you wait here."

Deniz took Eliza's bag from her in one hand, holding her hand in the other, as he walked her through the gate of her building and up to the door. They stopped in front of the door and he set her bag on the ground, reaching out to take her other hand.

"Thank you for coming with me," he said. "It meant...well, I don't know exactly what it meant yet, but I know it meant a lot."

She smiled, deferring his kind words. "It was my vacation, too, Deniz. I didn't just tag along with you."

"You know I'm not talking about Pamukkale. But I'll say it anyway. Thank you for coming to the village with me. Meeting my parents. Talking Cansu down from all the big emotions she's feeling about London. Drinking my grandma's tea." He stepped closer to her now, dropping her hands to encircle her in his arms. "You didn't have to do that. You could have told me you were uncomfortable, that you'd rather stay behind or...I don't know, come back to Antalya early."

"You're right." Eliza nodded. "It crossed my mind at the beginning. And there I was feeling like I got roped into something I didn't have a say in."

"You always have the power to make a choice, Eliza. I never want to be the person in your life who takes that away from you." He reached up to her cheek, cupping her jawline in his hand. "Don't ever feel like you have to go along with something just because I suggested it or it's my culture or my family…we're in this together, aren't we?"

"We are. It's just…" Eliza looked over her shoulder, back to the car where Kaan was waiting. "It's a lot. What we're figuring out together. And that's before we even add anyone else into the mix. Your family. My family. Future plans and things we haven't even talked about yet." She sighed. "We'll talk about it all. We *need* to talk about it all. Everyone else probably already is, so we might as well, too."

"And we will." He kissed her, first on one cheek and then on the other, before dropping the gentlest kiss on her mouth. "But in the meantime, I just wanted to assure you that it's all okay. We're good. We're going to figure things out, just you and me. We're the ones that matter, the ones that are going to be making decisions about our future. Not my culture or yours, not your family or mine. You and me."

Eliza was breathless, Deniz's words landing in her soul. It was the closest they'd come to talking about the depth of their feelings—the concept of love—and about what the future held for them. It was supremely confusing, especially after the weekend they had had, but only because what she had so recently felt might be the end for them now sounded like something much more serious. Promises. Commitment. A future.

Fifteen

"Is that you?" Crystal's voice called from her bedroom as Eliza entered the apartment. "That better be you. I am *not* in the mood to confront a burglar right now."

Eliza chuckled to herself but didn't answer right away, waiting to see if her silence would draw Crystal out of her room.

Sure enough—

"It *is* you! Hi!" Crystal flew across the room and enveloped Eliza in a hug. "Welcome back! Wow, we've got some shit to talk about, don't we? I'll make some tea. Or wine? Would wine be better?"

"At..." Eliza squinted to make out the time on the microwave clock across the room. "...two o'clock, it would not be better." She dropped her bag on the floor. "Tea sounds great. Then food. Wine later." She flopped onto the couch as Crystal made a beeline for the kettle, a loud sigh escaping her lips.

"That bad, huh?" Crystal raised an eyebrow in her direction.

"Not exactly." Eliza sat up, smoothing her hands over her hair as she worked to straighten her posture, her appearance. "I'll tell you all of it, of course. First, though...are we okay? I'm really sorry for how I left things with you."

Crystal was already waving her hands dismissively, but Eliza soldiered on.

"I should have heard you out when you talked about Chris, rather than jumping on you with my concerns. That's not what you needed from me...you needed your best friend to listen and be excited with you. I just slipped into my protective sister mode instead. I'm sorry." She shook her head. "Really, I am. I don't know what I was thinking."

Crystal was already back to the couch now, setting down two mugs with tea bags still in them on the coffee table before plunking herself practically on top of Eliza. "I'm not mad at you, I swear. I know what you were doing when you were warning me about Chris and about not getting too swept up in things with him." She shrugged. "You were being Eliza. Looking out for me, yes. But also viewing the world through your Eliza eyes, with a certain amount of distrust and healthy skepticism. But that isn't how these Crystal eyes of mine...heh, I like that. Crystal eyes, like 'crystalize...'" She trailed off in thought before shaking her head and continuing. "Anyway, it's okay, and I get it. You don't know him. You're not in here." She pointed to her head, then to her heart. "So, of course it doesn't make sense to you. It will. Eventually."

Eliza took a beat before she responded. As much as she wanted things to just *be good* between her and her best friend, during Crystal's response she had gone from feeling like they were on the same page to being even more concerned about Crystal's relationship than she already had been.

But Crystal was an adult, and she could—and would—make her own decisions. She already had parents, in fact, and therefore she didn't need Eliza to act like a second mother. Only—

"It's not just that I'm jaded, you know," Eliza spat out. "I think when you hear about my whole wild adventure with Deniz over the last few days, you'll see that. I mean...I don't think the difference between you and me is that you're looking at the world objectively and I'm looking at it like a cynic. I think you're just...well, you're more heart-based, more emotional. And I'm more rational."

Crystal's eyes widened as she took a sip of her tea. "Okay then...do you *want* to get into this now, or should we try to keep our truce just a tiny bit longer?"

"You're right." Eliza shook her head, blowing out a sigh. "I don't need to do this right now. *We* don't need to do this right now." She eased back again, rolling her shoulders to release the tension that had built up there in the last few moments. "How have things been with you? Anything fun going on?"

"Oh, you know. Same old, same old." Crystal set down her mug and tucked her feet underneath her, scooting closer to Eliza. "We both know you've got some major tea to spill, so why don't you just get into it already? Huh? Pretty please?"

"If I can even figure out where to begin, then sure…"

"You could start with the fact that you met Deniz's whole family yesterday. That might be a good place to begin."

Eliza groaned. "I sure did. And I wasn't prepared for it at all and probably messed everything up by making a lousy first impression—"

"What kind of lousy are we talking about here?" Crystal interrupted. "Something totally embarrassing? Like you went to kiss someone on the cheek and accidentally got them right on the lips? Spill!"

Eliza shuddered. "Nothing like that, thank goodness. No, I just mean…well, there I was meeting them for the first time and we all know my Turkish isn't exactly good. And even the little that I *do* know, I could barely speak! It was like, as soon as the stakes were high, as soon as there was an opportunity where I really could have benefitted from being able to speak some Turkish…all I could do was say 'thank you' and 'nice to meet you' so quietly that it's a wonder anyone even heard me at all."

Crystal put her hand on Eliza's knee and rubbed it. "I'm sure it wasn't that bad. What else? I bet Deniz's mom loved you. And isn't Cansu great? I only met her for five minutes, but she just seemed like a damn delight."

"Cansu is definitely great." Eliza smiled as she thought of Deniz's sister. "And she is clearly the member of the Aydem family—apart from Deniz—who likes me the most. His parents…I'm sure they like me just fine as a person. But as a partner for their son? Crystal, it was so clear to me. So clear that I'm not what they have in mind for him and…I get it! How could I not? I don't make sense there at all, and why would they want their only son to marry a woman who doesn't speak their language and is still learning the very basics of their culture?"

"Wow. Oof." Crystal looked overwhelmed.

"I know," Eliza agreed. "It's heavy stuff, right?"

"Oh, sure." Crystal waved her arm. "Yeah, boyfriends' parents and their expectations and all that. Combined with the fact that you're trying to interpret their feelings toward you without actually being able to understand what they're saying…and I'm sure you weren't taking things personally *at all*." She stuck her tongue out at Eliza. "No chance in hell that you were assuming the worst and telling yourself all sorts of horror stories. No sir!"

Eliza sighed. "You can tell a lot from people's body language, Crystal."

"Definitely! You're right. We *do* communicate a lot non-verbally…I just think you already knew what you expected them to think about you. So is there *maybe* just a teeny tiny chance that you already believed they wouldn't like or accept you and then just noticed every single little thing that could confirm that?"

Eliza blinked, pausing as Crystal's words washed over her. "Damn it. Maybe?"

Crystal shrugged, holding out her hands. "See? That's all you need. Just a chance."

"It's not that simple, Crystal. Deniz's parents don't love and accept me now just because you made me realize there's a tiny possibility they don't resent my very existence."

"Right." Crystal was looking at Eliza like she had two heads. "I understand how *reality* works. I know we didn't change anything just now, not about anyone else, at least. But we changed something pretty damn important, and that's how you are perceiving this whole situation."

"Yeah, I guess."

"So..." Crystal prodded Eliza's foot with her own. "I don't think that's everything that happened while you were gone. How did you leave things between you and Deniz?"

Eliza groaned. "Really well, actually. Like...the opposite of what I just told you. I'm so damn confused, Crystal. I mean...I love him. That much is becoming clearer with all the time we spend together. But it's not easy, and there are a lot of barriers to us being together." She paused, thinking over her next words before she spoke them. "I almost ended it, Crystal. I was so down on myself after meeting his parents...I had talked myself into the fact that it wouldn't work and was planning to come right back here and cut him loose. Can you believe it?"

Crystal was already nodding. "I know you, hon. Of course I can believe it. It's scary to get close, to get to a point where you're actually scared of what you could lose. It's a lot easier to give up and start over again than it is to go deeper and actually face those fears. And no offense, but you've taken such pride in being strong and rational all on your own that it really wouldn't shock me even one tiny bit if you had reverted back to those factory settings of yours."

"In case you couldn't tell, I'm really not a fan of all this 'feelings and vulnerability' bullshit." Eliza buried her head in her hands, talking to Crystal from between her fingers. "So why did I change my mind? It was after I met the rest of Deniz's relatives, saw him with his grandma and hugged a bunch of aunts and uncles."

"I don't know if you have heard everything you've said to me," said Crystal. "But I seem to recall something about *love*. I didn't jump right on it as soon as you said it and tease you like the time you developed your first crush—"

"Still haven't forgiven you for that, by the way. You could have at least saved the teasing for when we were alone rather than doing it in front of the entire girls' locker room during second period gym class."

Crystal shook her head, but she was smiling. "Truly my biggest regret in life. I do believe I've learned from it though..." She gestured around them to the empty room. "There's no one else here right now, is there?"

"There most certainly is not, and I do appreciate it. Anyway, please continue." Eliza gestured for her friend to carry on.

"Right. As I was saying, before I was so rudely interrupted. You love Deniz. You're thinking about a future with him, and naturally that scares you. But even more than you're afraid of it, you want it. Don't you?"

Eliza sighed, her shoulders dropping. "If I'm being honest with myself...and if I'm not thinking of anything else that's in the way of it..."

"You're not," interjected Crystal. "At least not right now. Finish your thought."

"...then yes. Yes. If I'm allowed to want something, then I want him. I want a future with him and everything that it contains. His family. My family. Language barriers and long airplane rides and goodness even knows what else that I haven't thought about yet."

Crystal smiled. "How does it feel to admit that?"

"Scary as shit." Eliza chuckled. "Lighter though. Good, somehow, even if it's making my palms all sweaty."

"I'm proud of you." Crystal leaned over to hug Eliza, her palm traveling up and down her friend's back. "I know it wasn't easy to say that out loud, but that's the first step, hey?"

"I guess so." Eliza shrugged. "Um...but can we be done talking about me for a while now? What about you? How are things with Chris? I...I'm sorry again for the way I reacted when you told me about him. I should have listened, should have been supportive."

"It's fine, really. I forgive you." A lazy smile spread across Crystal's face. "Things are good with us. Really good, actually. I think maybe you and I are in the same place, for once. We've both found the one. Can you believe it?"

Eliza felt her spine stiffen at Crystal's words, but forced her lips into an approximation of a smile. "That's great, yeah. So when can I meet him? And...I don't know, tell me more about him! Where is he from exactly? What's his deal? How did you figure out that he's the one?"

The one. The words tasted bitter coming out of her mouth. Even as strongly as she felt about Deniz, she wasn't sure she believed in something like soulmates, in there being only *one* right person for you out there. She knew better than to say what she was thinking to Crystal, didn't want to watch her friend shut down before her very eyes.

"Well, let's see. He's Canadian, I think I told you that. He's got a lot of big dreams, big goals...he's actually really inspired me in that realm. We talk a lot about the things we could do and accomplish together. I've never been with someone like that."

"That is...wow, yeah. That's cool." Eliza was humbled. Was she wrong about Chris? Was *she* the one trying to hold Crystal back from something that was only going to lift her up? "What kinds of things are the two of you dreaming about?"

"Oh, all sorts of things. I think if we combine our skills, our brains, all the things we have access to...we could be really successful, actually. Like, starting our own business, I mean."

"What kind of business?"

Crystal gave an exaggerated shrug. "Honestly, we're not that bogged down by details. There are too many possibilities right now, so why limit ourselves to just one idea? As I told you before, we're thinking about going back to the US, actually. Getting set up there to build something together. Obviously, Chris isn't a US citizen, but once we get married, we can work on that. He's just really excited about it, you know? The educational programs, the people he can network with. There's a lot more to choose from in the States than where he's from."

Eliza cocked an eyebrow. "I mean..." She shook her head once. "He's from Canada? Aren't there all sorts of training programs and people to network with there? I think most, if not all, Canadian entrepreneurs and business owners would bristle at the idea that chasing down American citizenship is the key to success in the field."

An exasperated sigh escaped Crystal's lips. "See, I *knew* you wouldn't get it. So did Chris. He said you'd probably think he was just using me for a green card, and I'm honestly afraid to ask the question and confirm that, so I'm not going to. You just need to meet him, okay? You'll like him, I promise. I'm probably just doing a bad job describing him, but he's really great, I swear. A very solid guy, and a very good boyfriend."

"Okay."

"Really? Just like that?" Excitement was eclipsing Crystal's frustration with Eliza.

"Yeah, why not? It's not fair of me to judge someone I haven't even met, and I should have a little more faith in your ability to judge character. Plus, we can all see how out of character my actions have been these last few days..."

Crystal gave her a sympathetic smile, rubbing her arm. "I didn't want to say it, but since you did...yeah."

Eliza laughed. "Why don't we all get together? Maybe this evening? You and me, Chris, Deniz and his cousin Kaan—"

"Deniz brought a cousin back with him? Fun! I'd love to meet him. What are you thinking for this evening?"

"Good question." Eliza shrugged and yawned, forcing herself to her feet. "Why don't I go take a shower and decompress a little bit? I'll text Deniz after that and see what they are up for. Dinner, though? Maybe a few drinks? Would you be up for that? And do you know if Chris is available?"

Crystal was already nodding. "If he's not free, I'll make sure he is. Any plans he has, he can cancel for me. And for you and Deniz too, I mean, of course. I'll call him and let him know to keep himself free or else *make* himself free."

"Right, sounds good." Eliza nodded one more time to Crystal, before scooting back to the entryway to collect her bag and take it to her room. Between her emotions around Deniz and all the concern she was feeling for Crystal, tonight was bound to be interesting.

Sixteen

Eliza and Crystal arranged to meet Deniz, Kaan, and Chris at Castle Bar at seven o'clock, then spent a leisurely afternoon catching up and soaking up the sun on their balcony, both avoiding talking about the men in their lives. Or at least, Eliza was consciously reminding herself not to ask any more questions about Chris, and she got the distinct impression that Crystal was returning the favor.

Fifteen minutes before their meeting time, Eliza and Crystal took off walking, meandering through the streets of Kaleiçi on the way to their meeting point. It was Eliza's first time back in the old city since her extended visit to Michigan, and she couldn't help but notice how familiar it felt. Walking underneath the massive bougainvillea vines, hopping to the side to let cars navigate the roads that were definitely too narrow for pedestrians and drivers to be sharing them.

When the entrance to Castle Bar came into view, three figures were waiting just outside. Eliza zeroed in on the one that felt like it belonged to her, Deniz with his hands in his pockets, attention focused on his cousin, who was talking animatedly, his words keeping Deniz smiling and laughing. The closer she came, it was as if he detected her presence, turning towards her and his entire being opening in her direction. His smile deepened, his hands came out of his pockets as his arms opened in her direction, and his eyes peered deep into hers.

It was as if he was checking on her without words. *Still okay? You didn't overthink things and get scared off in the hours since we last saw each other, did you?*

She gave him an almost imperceptible nod and a much bigger smile, her pace quickening to bring her into his arms faster.

The closer she got to Deniz, she realized Crystal was matching her pace, though her trajectory was just slightly off from where Deniz and Kaan were standing. That was when Eliza clocked the other man standing there, the third figure that had been gracing the entrance to Castle Bar. He was tall and blonde, fresh faced and...young.

She couldn't place where the word "young" had come from to describe the man she now recognized to be Chris, but it had stuck in her mind. It wasn't as if Eliza and Crystal were approaching retirement age, and judging from the five o'clock shadow on his cheek, Chris was at least old enough to be shaving. But there was something about him, a freshness or naivete that had caught Eliza's attention.

"Eliza, Deniz, this is Chris," said Crystal, a grin spreading across her face as she wrapped one arm around his waist. "And you must be Deniz's cousin," she greeted Kaan.

They all exchanged handshakes and warm greetings, Eliza slipping into a comfortable, joking conversation with Kaan as they made their way into the restaurant to find a table. Crystal had fallen back with Chris, the two of them talking quietly and huddling together as they followed the others to their table.

Eliza took the seat next to Deniz, sliding in as he pulled out the chair for her, and Kaan sat at the head of the table, leaving two open spots for Crystal and Chris. When the two of them sat down, then continued to speak in hushed tones to each other, barely interacting with the rest of the group.

Rather than deal with the awkwardness across from her, Eliza reached for Deniz's hand, then turned to Kaan. "So," she said, more loudly than necessary. "What are the two of you planning to do tomorrow? Did you get some rest today so you can get into some adventures?"

Kaan smiled. "More than enough rest. We are ready for whatever opportunities come our way, aren't we, Deniz?"

Deniz nodded. "Certainly. We were thinking of exploring the waterfall or going for a hike. Would you like to join us?"

"That sounds like a lot of fun, actually," agreed Eliza. "Crystal? Sorry to butt in." She forced a smile at the lovebirds. "Would you like to join us tomorrow? Help show Kaan around Antalya?"

"Er…yeah, sure," said Crystal, her attention still focused on Chris. "Would you like to go, babe? I'll go if you do, but I really want to spend the day with you."

Chris looked around the table, a grin on his open face. "Don't worry about it, love. You should spend time with your friends, and if I can swing it, I'll join you all, too. Now what do you say? Should we be a little more social and actually talk to these nice people?" He gave Crystal a teasing wink. "We can talk amongst ourselves anytime we want. It's not every day I get to meet the famous Eliza Britt!"

Eliza scoffed. "Famous? That just makes me wonder what kinds of things Crystal has told you about me. And considering that we had gotten on each other's nerves fairly recently, it may not have all been good. I'm afraid to ask."

Chris let out a loud guffaw. "It was all good, I promise." He put his arm around Crystal. "Honestly, I'm just jealous of anyone who has gotten to spend as much time—as many years—with my Crystal here as you have. And you know I want to hear all about it. Even better if you've got some awkward photos to share from her tween years."

Crystal punched him on the arm, eyes sparkling with enchantment at his charm. "Don't you dare, Eliza. I'm still trying to maintain *some* of my hot girl magic with this one. No need to shatter the illusion with a close-up of my braces and stringy hair."

"I will try to exercise some discretion," she promised Crystal, not missing that over her head Chris was continuing to nod and mouth his eagerness to see those photos.

"Anyway." *Time for a subject change.* "Crystal, Deniz and I were just saying that you and Kaan should meet, and here we are already, making that happen!" She gave Kaan an encouraging smile and nod. "Kaan, why don't you tell Crystal about the app you're working on?"

"Wow, Eliza, I feel like you were making a speech, like I have to deliver the keynote now. No pressure or anything."

There was the faintest blush on Kaan's cheeks as he glanced in Crystal's direction. *Oh gosh, I hope he didn't take our jokes about setting the two of them up too seriously,* thought Eliza. *Especially with Chris in the picture, Crystal is gone. I'd be surprised if she even remembered Kaan's name after the evening ends.*

"Yes Kaan, go ahead. Now I'm curious." Crystal managed to give Deniz's cousin an encouraging smile, though she hadn't extricated herself from Chris's arms, leaning back into his touch. "What are you working on, and why would these two think it would interest me?"

"I believe Eliza mentioned something about you doing some life coaching work, Crystal," said Kaan. "In fact, I think she referred to you as her life coach of sorts." Crystal brightened at Kaan's words, basking in the glow of Eliza's secondhand praise. "And well, that's what I'm working on. Personal development apps, I mean. Sort of a 'life coach in your pocket' concept. There are a lot of people who are trying to make their lives better—who doesn't want that?—but they don't always know where to begin. I'm working on it from a few different angles—habits, motivation, community—to see which is the most effective."

"Or which combination, right?" Crystal asked, leaning forward across the table.

"Certainly," agreed Kaan. "Why do you ask that? Are you catching something I missed?" His excitement was palpable.

"Oh, I'm sure I didn't," Crystal demurred. "I was just thinking, though...those things you mentioned, habits and motivation and community. Aren't they all part of any lasting change? Why zero in on any one of them? As long as you start small enough, granular enough that the app isn't overwhelming users with too many tasks every day…well, I think it would be a powerful combination." She leaned back again, her cheeks flushing as she regained awareness of herself and her uncool level of excitement.

"That's my baby!" Chris crowed with pride as he grinned at Crystal, checking with Kaan that his assessment of the situation was, in fact, correct. "I mean, I didn't follow any of what you just said." He gestured in front of his face, highlighting his blank expression. "I don't know what language you all were speaking, but it put me to sleep with my eyes open, I think. But!" He wagged his finger at Kaan, his smile growing. "Judging by this guy's reaction here, whatever you said, baby. Whatever that great idea of yours was, I think you really knocked his socks off. I always knew you were smart, but I didn't know you were *that* good!"

Eliza looked away from the spectacle that was Chris, secondhand embarrassment over his apparent lack of belief in Crystal's abilities. It was one thing not to have inherent knowledge of Crystal's skills and talents—*that* Eliza could almost forgive. But even if he hadn't arrived to this planet pre-installed with Crystal Kim's emotional, spiritual, and intellectual CV, he could at least have the decency to celebrate them without being so surprised by them.

Her gaze fell on Crystal, and Eliza had to look away. Her friend was eating up every insipid word coming out of Chris's mouth, judging by their matching grins. Eliza had tried—for all of five minutes, to be fair—to be open-minded about Chris, but with every passing moment her concerns about both him and the effect he was having on

Crystal continued to grow. There would be more uncomfortable conversations to come, she reminded herself with a resigned sigh. But it was part of the deal of being best friends. She hoped, after all, if *she* were the one making a fool out of herself over a *clearly* undeserving and immature man, Crystal would be good enough to call her out on it.

I'm not making a fool out of myself with Deniz...right? Sure, the emotions and vulnerabilities of the last few days have been uncomfortable, but I shouldn't jump right to the conclusion that I'm dating someone who's wrong for me. Right? There are doubts there, and as much as pop culture would tell me that those doubts mean our relationship is doomed, I'm pretty sure they say a lot more about me and my openness to a romantic relationship of any kind, rather than some kind of prophetic warning about Deniz.

She shook her head, continuing to take the trajectory of her gaze around the table, where it landed on Kaan. Kaan sat back, listening to Deniz—Eliza had missed what the two of them were talking about, so focused had she been on Crystal and Chris's antics—but his eyes were locked on Crystal.

Interesting, Eliza thought. *Is this just a reaction to the teasing we gave him in the car, or is there more to this?*

It wasn't as if Kaan were just admiring a beautiful woman or wondering how she was sitting next to such a dull young man—as far as she knew, Eliza was the only one guilty of that particular pondering. There was a wistfulness to his expression that Eliza couldn't place. A longing for something lost, something he couldn't have.

Speaking of Deniz, she'd barely given her boyfriend the time of day since they had all exchanged their greetings.

After handing menus around the table so they could all decide on their orders, she leaned over to Deniz and whispered in his ear. "Hi. I missed you."

His face brightened at her closeness. "You did? I missed you, too." He took her hand in his own again, squeezing it. "But we're here together again, with no plans for either of us to head off to parts unknown anytime soon." He gave her a wary glance. "Right? You're not going to scoot off to Istanbul for the weekend or take a quick lunch in Vienna, are you?"

Eliza smiled. "I have no plans to get on an airplane anytime soon, or even a bus. It looks like you're stuck with me, mister. Although..."

Deniz quirked an eyebrow at her. "Although...?"

She shrugged. "I wouldn't say no to taking a trip to Istanbul with you sometime. Apart from the airport, I've never been, and I would definitely enjoy exploring it with you."

"With me? Really? I'm shocked. I would have thought I'd be last on your list after I spoiled our last vacation with a drop-in to drink my mom's tea and kiss my grandmother's cheeks."

A laugh escaped before Eliza could stop it. "Oh, don't mistake my excitement over visiting Sultanahmet for me being totally over the whole village experience. We...might still need to talk about that at some point." She shrugged. "I'm just also pretty sure you don't have a secret second family waiting to spring on me in Istanbul, either."

Deniz nodded. "You've got me there. Just the one mother and father for me. I guess you've probably got one in every state? Is that how you're going to surprise me someday when I travel to America with you?"

Eliza's cheeks hurt from smiling so big. "If you're traveling across an ocean with me, I'll figure out all *sorts* of great surprises for you. Even if it means paying actors to play alternate reality versions of my family members. Why not?"

They leaned away from each other soon after, Deniz and Kaan to talk about which starters they wanted to order for the table to share, Eliza to sit back and bask in the peace of the evening.

It wasn't perfect, not by any stretch of the imagination. There was still the small matter of whatever was brewing between Crystal and Chris across the table, along with the serious relationship talks that needed to happen with Deniz in light of the time they had spent with his family and the expectations that had been raised, at least implicitly, between them.

Still, she couldn't help but smile and feel that the air around her was charged with something. Potential. Possibility. Maybe this time, something good was coming. Hadn't that always been her experience in Antalya, anyway? Even when things had been hard, like the misunderstandings at work last year or all the drama with Cem...when it was all over and the curtain rose, the end result had been good.

Eliza was far from an eternal optimist, but she would never have claimed to be a pessimist. She was a realist. If that meant she was the first in her first grade class to give up on the idea of Santa Claus, then so be it. It was time—*past* time, if you'd asked her six-year-old self—to move on from that particular illusion.

Something had been changing inside her, even if she wasn't sure what to call it or if it was safe to say it out loud to anyone else. The part of her that had opened herself up to Deniz again after she'd been so tempted to storm out of his parents' house in the middle of the night wasn't a part she was familiar with. The part of her that leaned in to him rather than recoiling back to the familiar was there, too. It felt good, even at the same time that it felt scary. And that...that was all she could ask for right now.

Underneath the table, she crossed her fingers and uttered a silent wish that things really were as good as they seemed. That she wasn't about to have the rug pulled out from underneath her.

Seventeen

"I can't believe I didn't ask you last night, but what did you think of Chris?" Crystal asked the question Eliza had been dreading as soon as both of their eyes were open the next morning. Eliza was still taking her first sips of coffee and Crystal had just bounded out of her room, the bun on top of her head just as perky as her morning person personality.

Eliza took another sip to buy herself a little extra time before responding. It wasn't as if she hadn't known the question was coming, and it wasn't as if she hadn't thought about what to say...it was just that she hadn't exactly landed on a final answer.

"Well," she began, "I did wish I got a chance to know him a bit better. I felt like Chris and I barely had time to talk, considering how much time we spent at the same table."

Crystal giggled. "That's my fault, I guess. I'm not very good at sharing him." She sidled over to the French press, pouring the rest of its contents into her mug. "Can you blame me, though?" She groaned. "Ugh, he's just...he's just such a damn delight and I always have so much fun with him. It turns me into a bit of a selfish jerk, though, since I don't let anyone else get any of the Chris goodness." She stuck out her lip in an exaggerated pout. "Sorry about that, Eliza Bean. I'll try to do better next time, okay?"

Eliza steeled herself for what she had to say next. "Is that the extent of it, do you think? I mean...I don't know. I don't want to jump right to conclusions with someone I barely even know." She paused before sharing her next words. "It felt weird, though. You weren't like yourself, and I don't know if he really *gets* you—"

She was interrupted by a harsh laugh from Crystal. "That's rich, from you. Like you *aren't* a different version of yourself with Deniz? Like we didn't spend all afternoon yesterday talking about how his family doesn't get you. And you want to question *me* about my relationship? Please."

"You're right," Eliza admitted. "I know I'm different with Deniz, and I know I'm far from an expert of relationships. I certainly won't be offering marriage counseling services anytime soon. I'm not saying our partners don't or can't bring out different sides of us, different parts of our personalities."

"Then what is it?" Crystal blew her hair out of her face, all of her morning peppiness replaced by the annoyance that was radiating in Eliza's direction.

"Well..." Eliza grasped for an example to illustrate what she was trying to say. "Last night, when you were helping Kaan brainstorm his app concept. That was amazing, of course. We all love to watch your brain work and it's an inspiration how you're able to put ideas together and come up with something new."

"Thanks..." Crystal was tight-lipped, no doubt waiting for the other shoe to fall.

"Did you notice how everyone reacted, though? You had me, Deniz, even Kaan...all of us were quiet, awed, appreciative of what you had shared. But Chris..."

Crystal nodded. "He said he didn't understand anything I'd said but that *apparently* I was pretty smart if Kaan was so impressed by me. Yeah, I heard it, too. And...I mean, whatever. Does it bug me that my boyfriend doesn't try a little harder to pay attention when I talk about my passions? Of course! Who wouldn't be annoyed by that? But does it mean I have to, I don't know, dump him right away and go find someone better? Of course not!"

Eliza tried not to let her surprise show upon finding out things weren't perfect between Crystal and Chris. There were more pressing matters to address. "Don't you think you deserve to be with someone who gets you, though? Who at least listens when you speak and knows that you are intelligent and powerful and wonderful because *he* knows it and not because he sees it reflected back to him on some other guy's face?"

"I knew you weren't going to give him a fair chance." Crystal was shaking her head as she moved out of the kitchen, back to her room. "You said the right things after our argument before. You said you'd give him a chance and get to know him, but that was never really going to happen, was it? As soon as you saw him there, you made a decision about him. And you decided he wasn't good enough for you, for your little circle of fancy friends. I mean, what was Kaan anyway? Some kind of fancy pants inventor? *Please*. At least Chris is a regular guy. That's what I need in my life. A regular guy. As long as he loves me and I love him, we don't need anything else."

"So it's love then?"

Crystal nodded, jaw jutting out in defiance. "Yeah, I guess so. I feel more with him than I do with any of the rest of you cold, emotionless zombies...and that's what I want. I want passion and love and...and the *excitement* of it all. So what if he doesn't share all my interests? Is that the secret to a long-lasting relationship? I hardly think it is. Look at you and Deniz. The two of you have plenty in common, and yet there's still this gigantic gulf between you that's probably going to be the thing that tears you apart."

"Uh, I'm sorry...what?" Eliza sputtered. "How did we get to talking about me right now and also, *what the hell* are you talking about?"

Crystal rolled her eyes. "I'm just saying, Eliza. The more you focus on what you have in common with someone, the more obvious it becomes that not *everything* is the same. You and Deniz are both teachers, you both love your families, you're both stubborn as hell...the list goes on. And yet! There's this big difference between you, right? You're from different cultures, you speak different languages...and you can both try to act like those aren't huge barriers, like they aren't deal-breakers..." Her eyes turned cold as she stared Eliza down, unblinking. "But let's call them what they are. They *will* be what ends your relationship. Maybe not right now. Maybe the two of you will try to work through things and Deniz's parents will try to get on board with the fact that you're, well, *nothing* they ever expected for their son...but how's it going to end? With a 'happily ever after' and a solution that works for you and Deniz, your parents and his?" She scoffed, a mean glint to her eye. "What's that solution supposed to look like? I thought you were too old for fairytales, Eliza."

She couldn't let the tears burning at the back of her eyes emerge, couldn't give Crystal that satisfaction. This was happening because Crystal was hurt by Eliza's words, and like a wounded animal she was lashing out, causing harm to anyone in her immediate radius.

That didn't mean it didn't hurt to hear her words, and that also didn't mean those words weren't affecting Eliza. Was it true? Were she and Deniz already staring down the end of their relationship, prolonging the inevitable?

That was something for her to mull over later, when she was alone with her thoughts. It would only be a few more moments, a few more harsh words, before Crystal stormed out.

"Thanks for the input, Crystal." Eliza schooled her expression into the stoniest one she had available in her repertoire. "I appreciate you being honest with me. I just hope you will be honest with yourself, too." And with that, she left the room, retreating to her bedroom before Crystal could take the satisfaction of a big dramatic departure.

When she heard the door slam a few moments later, Eliza sighed. Alone again, with her thoughts—and some new fears and worries—to keep her company.

•❤ • ❤ • ❤ • ❤ • ❤•

With Crystal out of the apartment and Deniz busy with Kaan, Eliza had time to herself for the first time since she had returned to Antalya. And not a moment too soon, considering she was only a few days away from the beginning of the new school year, which would be preceded by a few days back on campus with just the teachers.

This time around, things were different. She would not be returning to the Mediterranean School of Languages, but had accepted a new position at the Antalya Technical Institute. She would be back in the classroom full-time, no longer taking on any extra administrative responsibilities.

But she would miss the familiar, friendly faces at Med School. Especially...

She retrieved her phone from her nightstand and fired off a text to Jack.

Where are you? How come I haven't seen you yet? When can we hang out? Is now too soon?

Jack had been Eliza's first friend at Med School and the first person she had hung out with outside of work in the days she had been Crystal-less. She felt a twinge at the reminder that she was, once again, Crystal-less...along with discomfort at the fact that she was only reaching out to Jack now. She had blamed her lack of initiative on the fact that he was busy with Barış, but still. It wouldn't have hurt to at least text him.

Not that he seemed to hold it against her.

Eliza's phone started vibrating with an incoming video call almost as soon as the text message had left her fingers.

"It's really you!" Jack crowed, his face covering the full screen of her phone. "I told Barış I had to call and make sure someone hadn't stolen your phone, that this wasn't some elaborate scam to get money out of me or something." He turned away from her, gesturing to someone off camera. "Come say hi! It's really Eliza! I know, I didn't know she knew how to send a text message either!"

A moment later, Jack's face was squished to the bottom half of the screen while Barış hovered over him, grinning at Eliza. "Hello there!" He waved as he leaned closer. "It's nice to see you, and welcome back to Turkey! I heard from Deniz that the two of you were going away for a little vacation. Did you have a nice time?"

Eliza nodded and smiled. "We did, thanks. How are you both? How has your summer been?"

Jack gave an exasperated sigh. "What summer?" He looked up at Barış's chin and shook his head. "This guy doesn't know the meaning of the word 'vacation,' so there's been a lot of work going on here."

"Hey now." Barış was smiling at Jack's good-natured teasing. "We've had plenty of fun. Don't believe him!"

The look Jack was giving her begged to differ from what Barış was saying. It didn't help that he was mouthing "workaholic" to her while raising his eyebrows in Barış's direction. Still, the happiness on his face and the lightness in his eyes were undeniable. He was a man in love, and his teasing only revealed just how far gone he was for Barış.

Eliza was thrilled to see Jack so happy. The ease between the two men was palpable, how comfortable they were in each other's company.

Of course, there was a twinge—just a twinge—of jealousy, too. They had already figured out how things worked between the two of them, clearly. Eliza didn't get the feeling they had some big family drama hanging over their heads, and she couldn't help but wish to be in the same position.

"When can I see you?" she asked Jack, giving as uncomplicated a smile as she could. He could always read her better than she wanted people to read her, and the last thing she wanted was for him to see the jealousy and confusion that were plaguing her.

"I'm free today," Jack responded, glancing up to Barış to check in. "Barış has a lot of work to do, and he won't say it, but I'm sure he'd appreciate having me out of his hair for a bit—"

"Hey now!" Barış interjected, swatting Jack on the arm. "Don't put words in my mouth."

Jack shrugged. "I'm just saying. I know if *I* needed to focus, it would probably be easier to do so if you weren't lounging around the apartment, being handsome and distracting." He put his hands around his face, framing it just so. "And we all know which one of us is clearly the most distracting with his good looks."

"I can't even argue with him." Barış was looking at Eliza now. "He may not be the most humble, but he clearly won the handsome lottery."

"You do just fine, too." Eliza was grinning now. It was impossible not to in the presence of love and carefree, good-natured fun.

"What about the beach?" Jack wiggled his eyebrows. "I could definitely use a beach day. Have you even been in the water since you got back?"

Eliza shook her head. "It's been...a little busy. I'll catch you up on everything when I see you."

"Oh dear. I'm not sure I like the sound of that. Who am I kidding? Your drama is always entertaining, even if most of it is unnecessary."

"We'll see about that. I'll tell you everything and you can decide for yourself."

"Fair enough." Jack nodded once. "So...see you at Konyaaltı Beach in twenty minutes?"

"Perfect. See you then." She waved before ending the call. "Bye Barış! Have a great day!"

By the time Eliza arrived at the beach, she had worked up a sweat. It was shaping up to be a hot day, summer holding on in Antalya for at least another month or two. August might be the dog days of summer in Michigan, but she fully intended to sneak some beach time here well into October if the sun was warm enough for it.

Jack was waiting in their usual spot, sitting cross-legged on a beach towel, flipping through the pages of a novel. When she saw him there, she picked up the pace to a jog, grinning the whole way. If she hadn't realized the extent of how much she had missed Jack before, it was abundantly clear now.

He jolted, dropping his book as she tossed her beach bag down next to him. "Holy shit, you startled me! Warn a guy next time, huh?"

"Sorry." But Eliza wasn't sorry for her joy at the sight of him. How could she be? She flung herself down next to him on his beach towel, encircling him in a bear hug. "Ugh!" she cried. "I've missed you so much it's ridiculous. Never leave me again!"

Jack's chest rumbled with laughter under her cheek before he gently pushed her off. "If you'll recall, *you* were the one that left me, Ms. Britt. I've been here all summer."

"Hmm, is that so? Interesting." She kicked off her sandals and leaned back, propping herself up on her elbows as her gaze focused on the sea, its edge that kissed the sand full of families and children playing. "Tell me about what I missed, then. Don't skip a detail!"

"Oh, I sure will. It's mostly about Barış and it's all terrific." Jack slid his sunglasses down his nose, peering over them to size Eliza up. "First, you should probably get whatever's bugging you off your chest."

She wrinkled her nose at him. "How do you do that? How do you know something is wrong?"

Jack cocked his head to the side. "Well, let's see. There's the fact that you texted me out of the blue after not hearing a peep from you since you got back. You were more communicative when you were in Michigan, friend. So, there's that. There's also the fact that neither Crystal nor Deniz are here with you, so I'd hazard a guess that there's trouble in paradise with at least one of them." He looked up in thought, arching an eyebrow. "Let's see. Is it...Crystal? Barış said you and Deniz were on vacation, so everything is probably good there. Unless..."

Eliza groaned. "First of all, wow. I am a terrible friend. You only hear from me when I'm not busy with my roommate or my boyfriend? That sucks."

"Nah, it's not that bad. If you'll notice, I wasn't exactly breaking down your door to hang out, either." He shrugged. "We both got busy with our boyfriends, and honestly, I'm pretty happy for us. And I knew we would hang out again. I'm sure you knew, too. We've got one of those friendships where you can just pick right up again like no time has passed, and I really love that about us."

"I do, too." Eliza leaned into Jack's side, nudging him in the ribs. "Thanks for understanding and not giving me a hard time."

"Of course. Now, what about the rest of it?"

Eliza shrugged. "You were right about Crystal. Have you met this Chris?"

Jack groaned. "Ugh, yes. The worst. I mean...I get it, he's cute. But that man does not *get* Crystal the way she deserves to be gotten. I don't care, it's the truth."

"Did you try telling her that?" Eliza scoffed.

"Of course not, are you kidding?" Jack shot a glance at Eliza. "Wait. You didn't? Did you? You did! Oh no, how did that go?"

"Well, you see that I'm here alone without her, so...you tell me."

"Yeah, so about how I expected. Eliza, you've known Crystal way longer than I have, right?"

"I mean, yeah. We grew up together."

"Right." Jack was looking at her like she had sprouted a second head. "Have you ever known Crystal to be anything less than fiery and passionate and...how do I say this...not exactly the most receptive to constructive criticism? Does she usually do what *you* tell her? Because that sure hasn't been my experience."

"No, you're right. I just...I just couldn't *not* say something, you know?"

Jack nodded. "I get it. And maybe it was good, what you did. Maybe you planted the seed and she'll think about it and with time, she'll realize that Chris needs to go. But she's going to have to get there on her own. And as much as you don't want to...you're just going to have to be patient."

Eliza groaned. "You're right, I know you are. I don't want you to be right, but it's the truth. And I don't want to be patient, but...I'll try."

"Thatta girl." Jack smiled at her. "What about Deniz? All good there?"

Eliza paused as she looked for the right words. "Do...do you ever feel, with Barış, like there are just...wow, a *lot* of obstacles in the way of the two of you being together? Like...what about his family? Have you met them?"

"Not yet." Jack shook his head. "But that's not a problem, not for either of us. We've both experienced our fair share of rejection, and we've both arrived at a point where no one but us gets to make decisions about what makes us happy. So even if his family isn't fond of me or if mine doesn't like the thought of me falling in love in Turkey, well...that's their problem, not ours. It might sound harsh, but it works for us."

Eliza nodded. "It sounds brilliant, actually. Don't get me wrong, I'm sorry that you've been rejected, both of you. That sucks, and it's not fair. But it sounds like you have healthy boundaries around your relationship. And you know who gets to make decisions about it. That's huge."

Jack leaned in with a raised eyebrow. "Is that...not how things are for you and Deniz?"

"I don't know, but I don't think so. I get the distinct impression his family was pretty shocked to learn about me, and I'm sure they would prefer for him to end up with a nice Turkish girl."

"And what about Deniz?"

"That's the thing." She shrugged. "I know he cares about me, but I can also see how much he cares about his parents. I think he'd like to make them happy, and I don't know what that means for our future together."

"Yikes." Jack's mouth was a straight line, his eyes wide.

Eliza sighed. "Yikes indeed."

Eighteen

Hey, can we talk? Deniz's texts were the stuff of nightmares. Eliza was going to have to work on this with him.

Opting to give him the benefit of the doubt—to consider that perhaps he really *did* just have a light-hearted conversation in mind and wasn't about to tell her she was grounded or that her childhood pet had been hit by a car—she wrote back: Sure! Just checking, though...everything okay? That sentence always has a bit of a foreboding feeling to it. She threw a "tongue out" emoji at the end of the message, playing her anxiety off as a silly question. Deniz would see right through it, but at least in writing she still looked as carefree as she wanted to.

Great! Just the two of us...Kaan is out with an old friend from university. Want to come here? I can pick you up.

Okay, so...did that "great!" refer to how things were be-tween them? Or had he, in fact, dodged that question? Hmm...

I think it would be good for me to get some fresh air. I'll walk over. See you in a bit!

Eliza slid her phone into her pocket and took off out the door. She had the twenty-minute journey to Deniz's apartment to overthink what was waiting for her when she arrived there, and there was no time and no need to delay that.

Though she listened to her most upbeat playlist on the walk over, it didn't stop her mind from going to plenty of not-so-upbeat places. It didn't help that she couldn't remember a time when she'd been told "We need to talk" and a positive outcome had been the result. It was strange, though. It wasn't as if those words had preceded an an-nouncement about her parents getting divorced (they were still happily married) or a loved one dying (her mom had always been good at delivering bad news). Still, that phrase felt like the prelude to a breakup announcement, no mat-ter how Eliza spun it.

She tried to play the "what else could it be?" game, entertaining her mind with only fun possibilities. Maybe Deniz thought they should move in together—but it was too soon for that, as far as she was concerned. Maybe he wanted to redo their vacation—she could get on board with that. Maybe he wanted to know if she preferred gold or silver for her engagement ring—whoa, where had that one come from? *Definitely* too soon for that.

No matter what possibilities she entertained, she still found herself getting anxious again. Either Deniz wanted to pump the brakes between them or he wanted to step on the gas, and both were scary options.

As his building came into view, she stopped, took one last deep breath, and steeled her nerves. Whatever was waiting for her, she would handle it just fine. She always managed to get to the other side of whatever was stressing her out—somehow—and this would be no exception.

"Hey there!" Deniz called down from his balcony as she approached. "I'll come down to meet you and walk you up."

"Awesome." She smiled up at him, warmed from the inside just at the sight of his face, his smile just for her. Even when she wanted to be tough and steely, a badass who was unmoved by his charms, one smile from him melted her right back into gooey cheesiness.

Eliza had reached the locked door at the front of Deniz's apartment, and she only had to wait a moment before it swung outward, Deniz's open face in front of hers and welcoming her inside. He pulled her in for a hug, a kiss on each cheek, then took her hand and led her up the stairs to his third-floor apartment. *An elevator would be nice right about now*, Eliza thought. *Not like my heart isn't already racing enough.*

What was it about walking up flight after flight of stairs that always made Eliza feel like there was some secret shame in panting? Like if she breathed harder than normal, it was a reflection of how out of shape she was. She found herself trying to breathe shallowly and inconspicuously, which meant that by the time they stopped on the landing of the third floor, her chest was rising and falling rapidly, embarrassing her with every inhale.

She couldn't help but notice Deniz was breathing normally—sure, maybe a little deeper than he would if they were sitting at a cafe, but at least he wasn't trying to sneak oxygen like it was a controlled substance.

"Go ahead." He held the door open for her, steering her towards the couch in his living room. "Do you want something to drink?"

"Water would be great, thanks." Eliza sat down, taking the opportunity to get her panting under control while he was out of the room.

When Deniz returned with two water glasses, she accepted hers with a small smile and waited for him to take a seat and share why he had summoned her.

When he didn't speak right away, she nudged him, her knee bumping into his. "So," she began. "I don't know if you're aware of this, but 'we need to talk' is basically the equivalent of telling someone you're about to fire them or break up with them. So...yeah. I'm a little apprehensive to find out which one of them it is." She forced a small smile, playing her words off as a joke when, in reality, she was deadly serious. "I'm pretty sure you don't have the authority to fire me at work, though...and the school year hasn't even started—"

"It's not that." Deniz interrupted her, his hand on hers. "And I'm sorry if my words sounded serious, if they made you nervous..."

Oh good, then, Eliza thought. *Maybe that wasn't actually his intention.*

"But it *is* serious, to me at least. And we do need to talk. I didn't want to make you think we were just going to have a fun date night and then spring this on you."

"Okay..." *There goes that theory, then.* Eliza waited for Deniz to continue, aware of her pulse racing in her chest while also feeling like she was floating above her body, looking down on what was about to happen.

"I've been thinking," Deniz began. "Ever since we got back from the village—"

"A week ago," Eliza interrupted, reminding him that whatever he had been thinking about, he hadn't been doing so for a long time.

"Right." He nodded. "It was...well, it was unexpected, having you there. I'm really glad you were." He rubbed his thumb over the back of her hand. "I was so happy to see you in my hometown, to see you with all my family members."

"I was glad to be there, too. I mean, I was nervous about it and didn't exactly feel like I did a great job making a good first impression on everyone. But I'm still glad I was there."

Deniz lifted the corner of his lips. "Cansu really was so happy to meet you finally, too. She...well, she has made it very clear to me—and wanted me to make it clear to you, too—that she doesn't approve of this conversation we're having."

"Okay..." Eliza tipped her head to the side, a silent encouragement for him to keep speaking.

"I don't know how much you picked up on of the...weirdness, I guess we could call it that. With my parents. I sort of blindsided them with you. They had no idea I had an American girlfriend, and it was not very nice of me not to let them know before I showed up with you. It wasn't kind to you, either. The whole time, they were just trying to put on a good face while they were talking to me out of the corner of their mouths, trying to understand what was happening."

"I never felt unwelcome," Eliza reassured him. "They were very kind. If anything felt weird to me there, it was just about me and my lackluster Turkish skills. Your parents were wonderful. And your mother is such a wonderful cook..." She paused, smiling at the memory. "I think I actually had a dream about her beans the other night. And I can assure you, I have never dreamed about a bean before in my life."

"She'll be happy to hear that." Deniz's smile was more genuine now, but it still didn't quite reach his eyes.

"What is it, Deniz? Come on, dude. You are torturing me here!" The panic was rising in the back of Eliza's throat. "If you're about to drop a bomb on me, then just drop it already. I promise you aren't making it easier by taking longer to get to the point."

Deniz shook his head. "You're right. I'm sorry. It's just hard to say something when it hurts."

"Rip it off like a bandage then, I guess." She leaned over and patted his knee lightly, playfully. "Out with it already!"

"I think we need to take a little break." He looked up from his lap, his eyes finding hers. "Or...to slow things down. I'm not sure how to say it, what to call it. It's just...I owe it to my family. To ease them into this more. To at least consider their perspective. Not to strong-arm them into accepting the way I want to live my life."

Eliza's jaw was sinking towards her chest. Though the words were more or less what she had been expecting to hear, it didn't make it easy. "Did...do your parents want us to break up? Is that what this is?"

Deniz shook his head. "It's not that, no. They didn't say anything. I could see the hurt, the confusion that I didn't tell them about you, about my life with you...and I'm haunted by the fact that we did that. No, that *I* did that to them. I sprung you on them, and that was unfair to everyone. And then my grandma, well, she *did* call me and give me a little piece of her mind about being so secretive. She didn't tell me to break up with you or anything like that, but she did spend a long time talking about her friend's granddaughter and what a nice girl she is."

It was hard to hear anything Deniz said after that. *His grandma wants to set him up with someone? After we drank tea together? After she saw us together?* How could she not take that personally?

"Wow, your grandma must have really hated me." The words came out before she could think about them, feeling herself rising to her feet. "I wouldn't have guessed that. She seemed so sweet, so warm...happy to see me, even. I...I think I should go." Eliza's eyes and the back of her throat were burning with tears that were threatening to spill out at any moment. "We can take a break or whatever. Slow things down. Or just end them here. It seems like that will be the best solution for everyone."

She flew to the door, shoving her feet back into her shoes while vaguely aware of Deniz's presence behind her, his hand on her forearm. She couldn't make out the words he was saying, could only see the sadness on his face, the pleading in his eyes. "I can't," she said. "I can't right now. Can't...hear it. Can't...think straight. I have to go. Go..."

Deniz backed off, no longer standing between her and the door. He said something to her then, perhaps something about talking to her later, but if the words reached Eliza's ears intact, then by the time they traveled to her brain, they were a garbled mess. Shock and embarrassment had filled the screen of her mind, and her only mission in that moment was to get out of Deniz's apartment, out of his line of sight, before the tears came.

And they did come. As she ran down the stairs, she couldn't see a single step in front of her, so full of salt water were her eyes. It was humiliating, finding herself in this position. Believing things would work out between the two of them just because they loved each other, believing the smiles of Deniz's family members as proof that they liked her, that they accepted her, that they thought she was a good match for him. Clearly, that had never been the case.

Leaving the building, some part of Eliza expected to feel Deniz's hand on her arm, tugging her back, telling her he hadn't meant it like that, that she had misunderstood him. But he wasn't there. No one was tugging on her arm. And as she crossed the street to the sidewalk, out of the corner of her eye she could see his balcony, where, sure enough, no one was waiting to deliver a dramatic monologue or beg her to come back.

"Wow, they must have really hated me," she said to herself as she marched, walking as fast as she could back to the safety of her apartment. "I didn't expect them to accept me easily. I know it's a big deal to have your only son dating someone you can't even talk to, but...wow. This takes it to another level. So much worse than I thought. And so fucking embarrassing. I was nodding and smiling along with everyone like we were old friends, like we were having so much fun getting to know each other…and the whole time they were probably talking *about* me and planning how to get rid of me."

If there was one surefire way to make Eliza Britt shut down and shut you out, it was humiliation just like this. Not that she had ever been humiliated just like this. No, it was rare indeed that she put herself in a position so vulnerable that she wasn't master of her own domain and keenly aware of everything going on around her. And it just figured that the one time she let that guard down, dared to get close to someone without the trappings of security that came from sharing a hometown or at least a mother tongue, she got burned. Well, she could put a stop to that.

Deniz may have just been suggesting slowing things down or taking a break, but anyone who knew anything about relationships knew what that was—his attempt at gracefully bowing out, protecting her feelings before he ended things. She would give him what he wanted then, even accelerate it for him. She didn't want a big scene, a dramatic farewell—that wouldn't make things easier or better for either of them.

No, she thought, wiping her eyes and fixing her face in a straight line. *I'll just be* fine. *I'll be so fine that he'll see that it's okay for us to be over. We can be professional colleagues and nothing more. We can transition right back to that relationship and it won't hurt anyone. When he sees how unbothered I am by the whole thing, he'll be able to move on with his life and his parents' wishes. And I'll be able to enjoy my time here without it changing the trajectory of my whole life. When the job ends, I'll leave. Go back home and get back on with my real life.*

And with that, her eyes were dry. Chin high. Gaze fixed forward as she walked quickly and purposefully back to her temporary home, bound and determined to throw herself into her work, do the job she came to Turkey to do, and get out again before it was too late.

Nineteen

I t was a nice change of pace from all the personal drama to have a series of lessons to prepare. It was late Sunday morning, the day before the new semester began at Antalya Tech, and Eliza was perusing her materials—the program had opted to use the latest and greatest materials from an up and coming English publisher—and deciding where to set her focus for the first day.

There would be icebreakers, as much as she wished they could skip them. The students would need to get comfortable with each other and with her, and she would need to establish a baseline understanding of their current English proficiency. While she wasn't exactly in the mood for fun and games—Deniz had been trying to reach out to her for the last two weeks, while Crystal had been avoiding her for the same amount of time—it wouldn't do to put her desires over the students' needs. Especially not on the first day of school.

She poured herself a cup of tea and settled in on the couch, flipping through the new textbook and paging through her folder full of extra lesson materials collected over the years.

The front door rattled, the sound of keys jingling in the door calling her back to the present moment. Eliza lifted her chin, listening, and then fixed her attention pointedly on the materials surrounding her. She had work to do, damn it, and she wasn't going to hide in her room just to make Crystal feel more comfortable.

If Crystal wanted to storm off, she was free to do so. But Eliza lived here—paid rent here—too, and the two of them were going to have to talk to each other again, eventually. Maybe the lesson materials would be an icebreaker of their own...

As soon as the door opened, there was a flurry of activity. Crystal stomped into the room, not even bothering to slip off her shoes, and flopped on the couch next to Eliza, sending a few loose papers flying in the process. "Ugh!" Her groan was dramatic, with flailing arms to match.

"Um." Eliza reached over to move her lesson materials out of harm's way, setting her mug on the table out of reach as well. "What's going on? Are you okay?"

Crystal huffed and puffed, a loud sigh her response to Eliza's questions. "Clearly, I'm not!"

"No, I can see that." Eliza nodded. "What is it? Anything I can do?"

"Well, if you can restrain yourself from saying, 'I told you so,' that would be a great start." Crystal dropped her head on the back of the couch, staring up at the ceiling. "Chris is gone."

"Gone? What do you mean he's *gone*?"

"Just what it sounds like, Eliza. He got an opportunity that was 'too good to pass up'—" Her use of air quotations made it clear exactly how she felt about that opportunity. "—and now he's leaving for New York and we're over."

Eliza shook her head, rattled. "What—? How—?"

"Oh, you're wondering how him getting a job offer in New York requires us to break up?" Crystal turned her head, laying a caustic gaze on Eliza. "Trust me, I wondered the same thing. But it seems like now that he doesn't need me for his visa, he doesn't actually need me at all. He found his own way, and he left me behind." Crystal's eyes were looking glassy now, filling with moisture. "I can't believe he would do this to me!"

It took a great deal of willpower for Eliza to stay quiet, lending support with her presence and her silence, when all she wanted to do was pile on the Bashing Chris train. She didn't find it at all difficult to believe that he would abandon Crystal, that his whole aim in their relationship had been to make it beneficial for his goals. Had he even cared about Crystal?

"I'm sorry, Crys." Eliza leaned back next to her friend, pulling her into an embrace. "I'm sorry you're experiencing this, and I'm sorry for the pain I caused you, too."

"You were right, though. You always are, aren't you? Trust Eliza to be the grounded, rational one, while Crystal is out there being a hot mess of emotions and drama." She squinted up at Eliza. "I should be more like you, shouldn't I?"

A laugh barked out of Eliza's lips. "I wouldn't recommend it, no." Off Crystal's puzzled expression, she sighed and continued. "It doesn't mean I'm happier than you. And it doesn't mean I don't get my heart broken, too."

"Deniz? Oh no...what happened?"

Eliza shook her head. "We don't need to get into that now. It's just...it was too much for his family, I think. And his desire to take a...well, to take a bit of a break...made me realize that this isn't the path we should be going down. This way...well, it's only heartbreak at the end. Better to call it off now before either of us gets too invested. You know?"

"Oh. Oh, no." Crystal leaned back, closing her eyes. "I'm so sad for you, Eliza. I'm so sad for me, too. We just...wow, we're both kind of a mess, aren't we?"

Eliza leaned back next to her. "We've certainly both made a mess of our attempts at love, I can't argue with you there." She nudged Crystal in the ribs. "Maybe we should take a break from it for a while, huh? I don't like to do things I'm not good at."

Crystal's eyes popped open and closed again just as quickly. "What? I know we're both hurting, but no way. Life without love is...frankly...intolerable. No, even when it hurts and I'm miserable, I still want it in my life. I still want the passion and I want the lows, as long as I get the highs, too. If I gave up on love...well, I'm not even sure I'm ready to give up on Chris yet, if I'm being honest."

"Really? Even when he was so clearly using you to further his career goals? When it turns out that's what this was all about?"

Crystal shook her head. "Even that, I could forgive him. I get it...I'm ambitious, too. And things aren't that straightforward, you know? I respect that he has big dreams and wants to live in the city that he thinks would give him the best chance to realize them. But even if it seemed like he was using me to get there, well...I would have been there with him, too. It's not like he would have dumped me at the border and changed his phone number or something. We would have been together. We would have had fun together and loved each other and made it all work." She shrugged. "Maybe we still will, after he realizes how much he misses me."

"You're really serious?" Eliza was incredulous. "You are a far more forgiving woman than I am, Crystal."

"It's not about forgiving, it's about the love. It doesn't just go away because I'm mad at him. That's what makes this feel like such torture." She opened her eyes finally, examining Eliza. "You didn't stop loving Deniz just because he wanted to take a break, did you?" The expression on Eliza's face must have shocked her, because she sat up straight, leaning toward Eliza. "Did you really? How did you do that? How *could* you do that?"

The set of Eliza's jaw was firm as she shook her head, the words coming out in direct contrast to the traitorous feelings in her heart. "How could I not? If someone doesn't want me around, thinks I complicate their life with my mere existence...well, love just flies out the window then. And it's not like I have fiery ragey feelings towards him now...no, that would still suggest a passion buried somewhere. I feel quite neutral towards Deniz. I wish him the best, but I'm very okay with the fact that he doesn't believe that includes me."

Every word was a lie, but she couldn't let Crystal see that. Her cool and rational facade was intended for two purposes—as a "fake it until you make it" effort to convince herself that what she was saying about her feelings was actually true, and as inspiration for her emotional, mercurial friend. Maybe if Crystal believed Eliza was capable of being so calm and unbothered about a heartbreak, she would find it in herself to move on from Chris, too. To not settle for such a lackluster relationship but to wait for one where she was treated—or more appropriately, treasured—the way she deserved to be.

Her words were like affirmations; maybe if she said them out loud enough times and with enough feeling, she'd start to believe them.

What? It could happen. She could get over him. She could feel indifferent about his rejection. She could wish him well and move on, forgetting all they had shared.

People did it all the time. Didn't they?

If she kept thinking like this, Eliza was bound to slip into feeling sorry for herself, and no good could come from that. She leaned forward, slapping her knees before getting to her feet and reaching down for Crystal's hand.

"Come on," she said, pulling Crystal to her feet. "We've got to get out of here. No more wallowing. No more dwelling on what we can't change. We are two single ladies in a city with so many beautiful beaches. I don't even care that I've got lessons to plan; we're going swimming. Get your suit on!"

Crystal looked incredulous. "Really? *You* don't care about the lessons you have to plan?"

Eliza shrugged. "Not right now." She leaned closer, dropping her voice to a whisper. "I'll plan them later, but don't tell my badass self who's all 'screw work, let's play' that I've already decided that."

Crystal chuckled, shaking her head. "You are truly the wildest rebel of them all, Eliza. I bet you gave your parents real hell as a teenager...I shudder to think of the trouble you got into. Staying up late to write papers, sneaking out to the library to check out extra books?"

"Come on, Crys. You were there! You know I never would have snuck out without permission." She smirked at her closest friend. "Besides, I had my own set of encyclopedias—truly wild, life before Wi-Fi—so I barely needed to go to the library at all. Don't tell the library that, though. It's still one of my favorite places in the whole town."

Crystal was already walking away, on a mission to get herself beach-ready and out the door before Eliza changed her mind, no doubt. Little did she know, Eliza was in no danger of doing that. She needed the change of scenery, the distraction, just as much as Crystal did, if not more. She could dress this outing up like she was doing it for Crystal all she wanted, but inside she knew she was doing it for herself, too. There weren't many places in Antalya that didn't remind her of Deniz, unfortunately, but even if she thought of him the whole time they were at the beach, at least she would have sun and salt water taking up her mental energy, too.

Konyaaltı Beach was still crowded with tourists, even though the impending start of the academic year served as a constant reminder that summer was, in fact, nearly over. Crystal and Eliza found a spot a short walk from the shore, positioned their towels there, dumped their bags and tossed their coverups, then made a break for the water.

One of Eliza's favorite things about swimming in Antalya was the fact that she didn't need to worry about her things on the shore. Since the first time she had come to swim here, she had left her bag behind on her towel, and although she religiously checked to make sure everything was unbothered, she had never once had to sprint out of the water to apprehend a would-be thief.

Still, she tended to swim facing the shore, if not to make sure her possessions were left alone, at least to keep anchored as to where they were. She had seen a few tourists at different times, wandering up and down the shore, dripping wet while they tried to remember where they had left their things, and Eliza had no interest in playing out that role herself.

Crystal was floating nearby, lying on her back, working on her tan. She would drift away, then swim back to Eliza to share her latest thought about why men sucked, before floating away again. Eliza split her attention between keeping an eye on Crystal—unclear herself of what she was afraid might happen to her—and on their towels and bags on the shore.

Because Eliza was facing the shore, she was the first to notice the man approaching their towels, setting up his own just a foot or so away. "Really?" she scoffed to herself. "The whole beach, and you've got to set up camp practically on top of us?"

Her curiosity got the best of her, and the next time Crystal resurfaced, Eliza jerked her head in the direction of the man who was now sitting on his towel, reading a book. "I'm going to go see what's up with this guy. It's a little strange that he camped out right by our stuff, isn't it?"

Crystal squinted in his direction, then looked at Eliza with a quizzical expression on her face. "You might need to get your eyes checked, friend. You don't recognize him?"

Eliza shook her head.

"Uh...if I'm not wrong—and okay, there is a *slight* chance I am since I only met him once—I'm pretty sure that's Kaan."

"Kaan? Like Deniz's cousin Kaan?" Eliza groaned. "That might be even worse than some rando deciding to sit right on top of us at the beach." She bugged out her eyes at Crystal. "Do you think he knows about me and Deniz? Do you think he came here to talk to me about it? Oh God, I hope not. Maybe it's just a totally random chance that he happened to sit right next to us. Yeah, that's got to be it, right?"

But Crystal didn't look convinced. "Considering that he's waving at me right now"—Eliza glanced over her shoulder to confirm that the man-shaped blob on the shore was, in fact, waving one of its appendages—"I highly doubt it." She pushed Eliza's arm under the surface of the water so that Kaan—whose vision was apparently much better than Eliza's—wouldn't see. "Go talk to him. It's definitely more awkward communicating via waves and smiles—which you can't even see—than just sitting down with him. Right?"

"Ugh, fine. You're right. I'll go." Eliza looked up at the sky, allowing herself just a moment to wallow in self pity that this was happening to her. "You coming?"

Crystal shook her head. "Not yet. If he's here to talk to one of us, it's definitely you. And I am nowhere near finished with my salt water therapy." She made a shooing gesture with her hand. "Now get out of here, you."

Eliza made her way to the shore, wading around families with small children playing in the shallows, then stepping gingerly onto the larger rocks at the shoreline. Aware that there was a chance she was being watched, she wished she could exude the confidence of someone with much less sensitive feet, but as it was she was tiptoeing, eyes focused on the ground in case a sharp rock was waiting to cause her some major discomfort.

When she had nearly made it to the safety of her towel, she let herself look up. Sure enough, the man sitting next to her bag was none other than Deniz's cousin, and he appeared to be engrossed in the novel he was reading, turning pages while she watched.

Her shadow crossed his towel, and he looked up, closing the book and smiling when they made eye contact. "Eliza! Hi! I was hoping to find you here."

Eliza couldn't help but smile back. Kaan's warmth towards her hadn't changed, and even if she didn't want to think about how much she liked *any* members of Deniz's family, she couldn't help but feel like Kaan was—or at least had the potential to be—a friend.

"I'm impressed that you did!" She looked around her, gesturing to the sea of people surrounding them. "You could have easily parked yourself next to a stranger, and this moment right here could be a lot more awkward than it already is."

Kaan raised an eyebrow. "Awkward? Us? Not at all. But uh...actually." He looked down at the cover of his book, sliding his finger across the raised letters there. "Well, it turns out I'm just good at following directions. Deniz told me where you all usually sit when you go to the beach. And he may have mentioned the rather distinctive towels you and Crystal have." He nodded towards Crystal's "Greetings from America's High Five" towel with a map of Michigan's Lower Peninsula on it, parked alongside Eliza's "I wish I was at Pemberley" design.

Eliza sat down on her towel, covering Mr. Darcy's home with fresh drips of water. "Fair enough. I guess we stick out a bit here. Still, how did you know we'd be here?"

Kaan shook his head, raising his hands. "Oh, I swear I didn't. I wasn't even specifically looking for you. I just wanted to go to the beach and Deniz said this was the best spot. That you happen to be here right now is just a bonus."

"Right." Eliza turned back to the water, looking out at the coast side by side with Kaan. "I didn't actually think you had put a tracker on us or anything like that. And I'm glad you found us." She snuck a quick glance and smile in his direction. "It's nice to see you. How's...um. How's Deniz?"

Taking a sip from his water bottle, Kaan seemed to think over her question before answering. "He's been...quiet. Look, I clearly know that something happened between the two of you. I suggested meeting up with you and Crystal multiple times—multiple times a day, sometimes—and he kept dodging it. Finally, today, he said it's not going to happen. That you aren't really seeing each other right now." Kaan shrugged, twisting the lid back onto his bottle. "Look, I know it's not my business, and I'm not going to ask what's going on, so don't feel like you have to tell me. He's my cousin, and I care about him. And I respect his privacy." He gave a small, mischievous smile then. "But I did still want to hang out with you...and Crystal, if that's okay with you."

Judging by the way Kaan was looking out at the water, that same smile on his face, there was something out there giving him a great deal of joy. Sneaking a glance in the same direction, Eliza's suspicions were confirmed—it was Crystal, carefree and floating, without a clue that she was being admired.

And if for no other reason than the fact that her friend deserved to spend some time around a good guy, especially after everything Chris had put her through, Eliza accepted. "Of course," she told Kaan. "It would be a lot of fun to spend some time together."

Twenty

The plan was for Eliza and Crystal to meet Kaan that night for dinner, and Crystal had been shocked when Eliza had informed her of said plans. Kaan had abandoned his spot on the beach before Crystal had gotten out of the water, and Eliza couldn't help but wonder if it was because of her impending arrival at the beach towels that he had left. Was Kaan...shy? That had been unexpected.

"So we're really going to meet your boyfriend, er, ex-boyfriend or whatever the hell you two are...we're going to meet his cousin for dinner? And Deniz isn't invited? Doesn't that seem totally bizarre?" Crystal had picked up her pace as the two of them were walking home, animated from within by the ridiculous nature of Eliza and Kaan's plans.

"It was Kaan's idea, and he didn't say anything about Deniz. I assume he isn't coming, since I doubt he wants to be around me right now, but I didn't ask. Kaan knew something was up between us, and I guess I'm trusting his discretion that he's not going to put the two of us in an awkward and public situation."

"That's pretty trusting of you," said Crystal. "If it were me orchestrating the dinner, and if I hadn't just sworn off men for both of us, I would definitely play puppet master and try to get the two of you together."

"Good thing Kaan isn't like you, then."

Crystal lifted her shoulders. "Good for you, I guess. My way would be more fun for me, though." She walked in silence for a few moments before turning to Eliza. "What are we going to do with Kaan, anyway? I've barely met the guy and I think you've spent hardly more time with him than I have. Isn't this going to be weird?"

"Not at all. He's really nice, and he's easy to talk to. I promise we have more in common than just Deniz. And you did meet Kaan, you just missed the chance to have an actual conversation with him thanks to the distracting presence of You-Know-Who."

Crystal rolled her eyes. "You can call him by his proper name, you know, Shitty McBoyfriend. No need to tiptoe around it on my behalf."

"Good to know." Eliza chuckled. "The name change suits him."

"I thought so, too. If I ever talk to him again, I might just suggest he change it."

Eliza fell quiet at that statement. As much as she wished Crystal would never speak to Chris again, her words were a reminder that, especially in a moment of weakness, it was possible that she would. It was even possible that the two of them would rekindle their spark one day, and it made it hard for Eliza to be honest about her true feelings about Chris. She wanted to tell Crystal that he was a total jerk, that she deserved better, that she should never speak to him again...and yet, she knew there was a chance she would have to eat those words if the two of them got back together again.

"You got awfully quiet," Crystal observed. "Thinking about what might happen if Chris and I cross paths again?"

Eliza's jaw dropped. "How did you do that? Can you actually read my mind?"

"It's not ESP, it's just BFF." Crystal shrugged. "We've done this dance before, you know. I've dated people, and when things start to fall apart, you step up like a best friend should and talk shit with me." She paused, twisting her lips to one side. "But...sometimes what seems like the end isn't actually the end, and I know you end up feeling so awkward for what you said when it looked like we were cruising for the finish line."

Eliza was flabbergasted. "Yeah...you're right."

"I felt that same way when you were with Alec." Eliza winced at the reminder of her ex-boyfriend. "Every time he did something shitty, and you thought about breaking up with him, I played the 'pile on Alec' game. And then when you would say that he apologized, and you were giving him another chance or something like that..."

"Oof."

"Yeah."

Eliza stopped in her tracks, tugging Crystal's arm to bring her to a stop, too. "Can we both agree that we deserve better than the treatment we've gotten from the vast majority of the people we've dated?"

"Oh, for *sure.* I'd say we deserve better than all of them..."

"But?" Eliza's pulse picked up tempo, anticipating Crystal's next words.

"But I think we both know Deniz was a gem. Still could be, actually."

Even though a part of her wanted to agree, to ask Crystal how they could make things work and come up with a step-by-step plan and bring it into reality, her cynical side won out and she scoffed, the sarcastic laugh barking out. "How, exactly, could he still be a gem? I can admit that when we were together, he was good to me. I have no complaints about Deniz Aydem as a boyfriend. But as a guy who chooses his family over me, I have to say some of the shine has worn off." She spun on her heel, marching once again towards their apartment. "I think we can both agree that in the future I should try to date someone who will not value his family's comfort more than mine."

Crystal was jogging next to Eliza, her shorter stature and shorter legs struggling to keep up with Eliza's pace. "Okay, yeah, that part wasn't great. But—" She grabbed Eliza's arm, yanking backwards with more strength than Eliza had expected. "Can you slow down for one second? You don't have to physically run away from me just because I said something you didn't like. I will not make you date Deniz again. I'm just trying to get you to listen to, like, one complete thought that doesn't agree with the way you've already made up your mind."

Eliza stopped. "You think I can't listen to an idea if it goes against what I've already decided?"

"Ha!" Crystal laughed, then clapped a hand over her mouth. "Sorry, it seems like you weren't joking, judging by that look on your face. But, um...no. No, I don't think you're great at staying open to things—wait, let me finish this. Seriously, Eliza. When something makes you feel emotions you don't want to feel, you shut down like...like a security gate snapping into place when someone tries to rob an art museum. I don't know!" She threw her hands up in exasperation. "*You* come up with a better metaphor!"

"So you're saying that I might benefit from hearing a different perspective? Is that it?"

"Well, yeah. I don't know exactly what Deniz said—ahem, because I don't think *you* exactly heard what Deniz said—but you shut right down on him as soon as he started talking about uncomfortable things. And actually, Eliza, if you'll recall...you almost pushed him away before he could even do that."

Eliza groaned, wishing Crystal didn't know her as well as she did. "Did I really?"

"Uh, *yeah*. In the village...remember? You felt uncomfortable there—again, it's all about the unwanted emotions, isn't it?—and you were ready to push him away, to come right back here and say, 'Thank you very much sir, but that will be all now.' And then something changed when you met his grandma and drank her tea or some shit like that and you decided to be vulnerable—"

"Oh right, Grandma and her tea." Eliza let out a bitter laugh. "A lot of good that did me. She was the one who wanted to set Deniz up with someone else."

Crystal reached over, one hand on each of Eliza's shoulders. "Eliza. Stop it. You are looking at all of this like an American."

Eliza raised her eyebrows toward her hairline. "Of *course* I am. How...how else do you want me to look at things?"

"Well, you could *try* to be a tiny bit more open to the way things work differently in different cultures, for a start. Maybe remember that you're not a character in a movie and everything doesn't have to be so dramatic. Deniz's grandma isn't standing up in the middle of a wedding saying she objects." Crystal shrugged. "She's just telling him she knows a nice girl in the village if he's interested. That's all."

Eliza was incredulous. "Right. But he has a *girlfriend*, Crystal. Or he had one, at least."

"You're not getting it. Eliza, Grandma is just being practical. She and Deniz aren't talking about his *feelings* and his big dramatic love for you. She's just doing what grandmas do in this part of the world. And trust me on this, because I happen to have a grandma of my own in this part of the world, too, and this might not be the big deal that you're making it out to be."

Massaging the bridge of her nose, Eliza shook her head. "Why are you telling me this *now*? Why did you support my 'men can fuck off' meltdown a few hours ago just to tell me I may *actually* have overreacted now?"

"About that." Crystal grinned. "I reserve the right to feel whatever the hell I want to feel. And right now, after being out in the sun and swimming in the sea until I got so hungry I could eat, like, a whole freaking deep-dish pizza...I feel good. Life is good. I have a best friend who cares about me and doesn't want me to be around jerks. And I know Deniz, and in all the time I spent with him, I never thought he was a jerk. Okay, maybe I did a tiny bit at the very beginning, but once he was special to you, he was never anything but the best. I just wanted to do this little favor, for him and for you. Offer my services as a cultural translator, free of charge." She put her hands on her hips. "I'm not telling you to forgive him, and I'm not saying that if the two of you get back together, you won't have things to figure out. But I am telling you to be more culturally curious and less sure of yourself. You don't have all the answers, and some things—most things—aren't universal. You have to ask questions and you have to clarify that you're on the same page. Otherwise, it's never going to work. Ask me how I know that."

At that, Eliza felt a crack form inside her chest. They really were the head and the heart, weren't they? Crystal couldn't help but feel everything, and she, Eliza, ran from anything that felt new or unfamiliar. Right back to the safety of the feelings she'd always felt. Choosing solitude and a middle range of emotions rather than anything too low...or too high. "You're right. And you did nothing wrong with Chris, apart from choosing the wrong person. You're all heart, Crystal, and when I was worried about you, that was about me, too. I was just trying to keep you safe, but you were doing the brave thing and loving fully. He just wasn't the guy."

"Yeah, maybe. Just take what I'm saying to heart, okay? Especially the part about making sure you're on the same page. I thought Chris and I were...thought we were a team united, and it turned out I was just a means to an end for him. And when he found a different means, an easier one that he could take on solo, well, he went right for it. Anyway, enough about him. He's history, and you don't have to worry about me." She reached up and tugged on the nearly dry lock of hair hanging next to Eliza's ear. "If you're going to worry about anyone, worry about you. And Deniz. And take some of that natural curiosity of yours and apply it to your relationship. Don't assume you know what's going on just because you connected the dots. You may have skipped a bunch of dots in between, you know? It's supposed to be a whole freaking picture, and you just made a straight line."

Eliza had to laugh at that. "That sounds like something I would do, as much as I hate to admit it." She looped her arm through Crystal's and they resumed their walk home, much slower now that they both were processing some big thoughts and feelings, rather than running from them. "I'm still going to need some time, I think...but I'll talk to Deniz. I will. He deserves to speak his full piece...and I deserve to know what's going on, too."

Crystal squeezed closer to Eliza, smiling up at her. "Glad to hear you say it, friend."

As the time for dinner with Kaan drew nearer, Eliza could sense Crystal dragging her feet about going out—something she was feeling, too. Whether it was from all the sun they'd gotten that day or the lesson plans that were still hanging over her head, the thought of heading out and waiting on a meal sounded exhausting.

Crystal was the first one to say it out loud, though. "Do we really have to do this? I'm tired, you're tired, and Kaan can probably just hang out with Deniz, can't he?"

Eliza leveled a stern look at Crystal. "We already promised, Crys. How bad would it be for the poor guy if the only people he knows here apart from his cousin just cancel on him at the last minute?" She pursed her lips, looking around the room for inspiration. "Ooh! Would it be super weird if I just invited him over here for takeout?"

Crystal jumped up, looking alive and energized for the first time since their post-beach slump had settled in a couple of hours ago. "I love it! We can get *çiğ köfte* from downstairs, eat on the couch, and stay in our nice comfy clothes. Kick Kaan out once we're done eating and go right to bed. Sounds perfect to me!"

"Some parts of that sound perfect, I'll admit. But if Kaan is up for it, we should still attempt some basic manners and politeness, don't you think?"

Crystal shrugged, looking unbothered. "I mean, I guess. Will you text him now so I know if I need to shower and get ready to go out or come up with a good excuse to be left behind?"

"You're the worst," said Eliza, shaking her head, already pulling out her phone to text Kaan.

Hi Kaan, would you be up for coming to our apartment for dinner? We are both tired after the beach today, and heading to Kaleiçi sounds exhausting. We'll do that sometime, but for tonight, maybe...takeout at ours? Let me know.

Kaan wrote back quickly. Oh, that's perfect! I hadn't realized your classes started tomorrow until I saw Deniz scrambling around to get everything ready. I was going to suggest we reschedule, but you still need to eat. I'll bring dinner! Any dietary restrictions for either of you?

"Huh! Wow. That's really sweet." Eliza was already sending back a thank-you message, but she couldn't stop herself from reacting out loud, so eager was she to catch Crystal up on their plans.

"What's sweet? Are we going out?" Crystal groaned. "Please say no, please say no, please say no."

"We are *not*, so you can relax and stop whining." Eliza shook her head at Crystal, unable to hold back a smile at her dramatic antics. "Kaan is going to bring dinner here. He was thinking of rescheduling since tomorrow is my first day of classes, but he says we need to eat, so he's going to bring something. I'm sure it will be a nice...and also short...visit."

"Okay," said Crystal, visibly impressed. "I love a man who comes bearing food. I guess I am not *totally* against the idea of Kaan coming for dinner then. Still doesn't mean I'm going to change out of my comfy clothes, though."

"And I would absolutely never dream of asking you to do such a thing," Eliza reassured her. "If I ever get married, you should know you are entirely welcome to wear your sweats."

"Good, because you already know I was going to." Crystal winked one eye shut as she grinned at Eliza. "So you're talking about marriage again, huh? Not so 'sworn off of all men and the possibility of romance' anymore, are you? Can we credit that to my *awesome* pep talk today?"

Eliza groaned. "I misspoke, clearly. I should have said, 'If I ever win a Nobel Prize, you can wear sweats.' But...also, yeah, your pep talk was great. Just don't let it go to your head."

Crystal giggled wickedly, sounding like a cartoon villain and steepling her fingers in front of her face. "Excellent. My plan is already unfolding nicely, then."

"Whatever. I'm at least going to shower before Kaan gets here and see if I get some masterful inspiration for my lessons tomorrow while I'm in there. One of us should have good hygiene, or else we'll scare the poor man away before anyone even eats their dinner."

"We can't have that," said Crystal. "I'm hungry. Did he say what he's going to bring? Ooh, or is he taking requests?"

"He asked for dietary restrictions, and I told him we don't have any." Eliza shrugged. "Your guess is as good as mine."

Crystal dismissed her with a wave. "Go take your shower, then. I'll be daydreaming about delicious food. See if I can figure out how to connect with Kaan telepathically and put in a request." She lifted her fingers to her temples and closed her eyes, speaking in a hypnotic voice. "Chicken...and lots of carbs...ooh, *tantuni*...maybe some dessert...and okay, some green stuff, too...maybe a salad...?"

Eliza left her to order her dream dinner and set to getting herself ready. Showering now would save her some time in the morning, and she hoped against hope that tomorrow wouldn't be a typical "Eliza's first day of school" morning. She had been running late on that particular day more times than she cared to remember.

Unbidden, the memory of a different morning crossed her consciousness. A day just the previous spring when she had overslept and missed the shuttle to the Mediterranean School of Languages. She had been waiting for a taxi that never came, and then, just like an actual knight in actual shining armor, there he had been.

Deniz.

He had pulled over his car—shining as brightly as his metaphorical armor—and rescued her, dropping her off at the university and even revealing some important information along the way. It was that information that had revealed what a good man he was, that had been the beginning of things changing between them.

Eliza shook off the memory as she stepped into the shower. She had already decided that a conversation with Deniz was a good idea, if not to rekindle things between them, then at least for closure and clarity. Being reminded of all the ways he had been good to her—better, often, than she had been to him—only stirred to amplify the bittersweetness of it all.

He was good, it was true, and he deserved to speak clearly about what was on his mind, even if it hurt her. But if what he was saying was that his family did not approve of her and he was choosing them over her, it was going to crush her. That was unavoidable. Because she *knew* he cared about her, and she *knew* that if circumstances were in their favor, they would make it work. She couldn't handle hearing that something out of their control was going to turn them into star-crossed lovers.

Eliza massaged the shampoo into her scalp, feeling the salty texture wash away. That was enough thinking about Deniz for one night. Bad enough that she'd be seeing him at work tomorrow.

Twenty-One

When Eliza finished drying her hair and left the bathroom, she was greeted by the sound of voices—voices she hadn't been able to hear over the sound of the blow dryer, and it was a disconcerting feeling entering her own living room like a visitor in the middle of someone else's conversation.

She recognized Crystal's voice, of course, and could only assume that she was speaking with Kaan, not that she was giving him a moment to get a word in.

What she definitely didn't expect, though, was the stoic, unsmiling, but very handsome figure sitting next to Kaan on the couch.

"Deniz? What are you doing here?"

If she had thought it wasn't possible for him to look more uncomfortable than he already was, she had underestimated the effect of her words. She could see it in the redness climbing his cheeks, in the ire he directed towards Kaan.

"I told you this was a terrible idea, Kaan." He turned his gaze back towards Eliza. "I apologize, Eliza. Kaan suggested we go out to dinner, but he neglected to mention until we were outside your apartment that this is where we were coming." He got to his feet. "I should go. I don't want to disturb you."

"No!" cried Crystal, jumping to her feet next to him. "Don't be silly, Deniz. We all need to eat, and we're all adults here. I'm sure Eliza was just *surprised* to see you, not upset about it. Right, Eliza?"

Eliza was already nodding, arranging her face back into an expression that didn't betray what she was feeling. She *was* glad to see Deniz, and surprised, too. What she didn't want to reveal was that seeing him there, so close and yet inaccessible at the same time...well, that was stirring up all sorts of complicated feelings. The kind that made her want to retreat to her room for a good sob into her pillow where no one could hear it.

She smiled and nodded at everyone reassuring them all that this was, in fact, okay. Kaan hadn't done the wrong thing by inviting his hungry cousin—though he may have done a sneaky thing, which she might be questioning him about later. And Crystal hadn't done the wrong thing by letting Deniz inside. And Deniz, well, she and Deniz were going to have to learn to coexist—and even work—together sooner than later. They also had an important conversation on the docket that only she knew about, but if she could get through one evening together, there was a better chance of her initiating said conversation.

"Can I get anyone anything to drink?" Eliza asked the question as she was already moving towards the kitchen.

"I actually brought drinks too, if that's alright," called Kaan, his voice and words drawing her back towards the living room, not letting her retreat from the discomfort she found there. "If everyone's ready to eat, I can get things together." He gave Crystal a meaningful look. "After all, these two have some important work to do before tomorrow, so we'd better get things moving along."

"Absolutely," Crystal agreed. "Let me help you get everything together."

"Is there anything I can do?" Eliza asked.

Kaan shook his head, directing her towards the couch—the same one where Deniz was once again sitting, having given up on the idea of his being allowed to depart. "Just take a seat. Crystal and I can handle it. Maybe the two of you can figure out your first day of class plans together. Wouldn't that be nice?"

Deniz scoffed as Kaan left the room. "The first day is the worst, all that icebreaker bullshit." He looked at Eliza for the first time since she had come into the room then. "I bet you love doing all that *fun* stuff, getting to know the new students."

Eliza laughed out loud, just once. "Not at all! I mean, I love to get to know the new students. But icebreakers and games? It feels like the biggest waste of time, but I know it's essential. If we don't play along, it's just going to take that much longer to get the students comfortable with each other, which is pretty much essential—"

"In a language classroom, yeah." Deniz nodded as he finished her sentence. "A necessary evil, I guess." He hesitated, as if his next words were stuck in his throat. "How have you been? I've wanted to talk to you, but..."

"I haven't made it easy, I know." Eliza gave him her most reassuring smile. "I'm alright, really. And we will talk again...soon. I owe you that. But for now, at least, let's not worry about that. We've got first day things to prepare for and if we can avoid making this dinner awkward for Kaan and Crystal, well...that would be even better."

Deniz raised an eyebrow. "You mean you don't want to join me in torturing Kaan for his badly executed attempt at playing mastermind? Where's the fun in that?"

"Oh, I definitely want to sit him down and ask him what the hell he was thinking..." Eliza shrugged, letting go of just a little of the tension she had been carrying in her shoulders. "I get what he was trying to do, the heart behind it. He cares about you, and I like to think he likes me, too...I think he just doesn't want to see us needlessly hurting ourselves or giving up without at least *trying* to talk things through."

Turning in his seat, Deniz's knees faced Eliza, his arms lifting in her direction before he remembered himself and dropped them back down to his thighs. "Yes. That's what I want, too. I think we both have a lot we need to get out in the open, and I'm ready to talk about it whenever you are."

Eliza nodded. "Good to know. How about we just get through the first week of the school year and we can celebrate being done with icebreakers by going out for a drink and a chat? Or are you going to be planning lessons on Friday, too?"

"No." His tone was forceful, matching the energy he was using to shake his head. "I'll be free. I'll get everything done that I need to do, I just don't want to miss the chance to talk with you. It...it's been hanging over my head like a cloud, following me from room to room. I hate feeling far from you and I can't stop thinking about how I could have expressed myself better, found a way to do so that wouldn't scare you away."

Eliza was quiet, taking in his words. What he had said before, talking about "needing to take a break" or "slowing things down," it had hurt. She had taken it to its natural conclusion and essentially ended things between them. But now it sounded like that hadn't been his intention, and it seemed as if she had only herself to blame for the loneliness and isolation she had been feeling between them.

No, that wasn't true. He'd just said it himself—if he could have expressed himself better, maybe she wouldn't have been scared away.

She wanted to ask what he had intended to say, but now wasn't the time. She could hear Kaan and Crystal shuffling dishes around in the kitchen, and she knew they would rejoin them in the living room any moment now. No, her conversation with Deniz wasn't going to dive any deeper until tomorrow, when they were alone.

"It's okay." She gave him a tight-lipped smile and a re-assuring pat on the knee. "We'll talk about it on Friday. I promise not to do anything drastic in the meantime."

"So you're not booking a one-way flight back to Michi-gan before then?"

Eliza pretended to think about it. "If I do that, it will only be to get out of a day full of icebreakers. So try not to take it personally, okay?"

Deniz threw back his head with unexpected laughter. "Hey, that's not a bad idea. Can I come with?"

She was already nodding. "Absolutely. There's no shame in running away from awkward social interactions, especially not ones where you have to be the adult in charge. The students will be better off without us, and I'm sure they'll get to know each other just fine without being guided through a round of two truths and a lie."

"Oof, yeah. That one is always the worst, though I get a kick out of the way most of them deliver their sentences." He put on a playful, thoughtful expression, stroking his chin. "'Let's see. I'm eighteen years old, I have one sister, and...hmm. Um...I am an astronaut.' Like gee whiz, how are we ever going to figure out which one of those was the lie? Way to keep us guessing!"

Eliza chuckled at the impression. "Yes, exactly! But also, since when do you say 'gee whiz'? What are you, from 1950s America? Don't get me wrong, I love you saying it. I just...uh...didn't expect it." She felt her cheeks getting progressively pinker ever since she'd arranged her words in that unfortunate order: "I love you." She hadn't meant to say that, had she? Was she testing Deniz? Expressing what she wanted to say to him without coming right out and saying it?

She couldn't help but notice he was avoiding her gaze now, too, no doubt having heard exactly what she'd said to him. "I probably got it from a movie, but I can't remember. It just sounded funny and it's kind of fun to say."

"Oh, definitely! We'll have to find all kinds of old slang for you to add to your repertoire. That can be your *thing*, your trademark as an English speaker."

"What are you trademarking?" Kaan was entering the room with a plate in each hand, followed by Crystal and her similarly full hands. "Are you two going into business? Need my help?"

"You and your one-track mind," Deniz chided Kaan, shaking his head. The two cousins took off teasing each other, while Kaan and Crystal arranged the plates around the table. Crystal was shooting some curious eyebrow raises at Eliza, but Eliza didn't want to give her the satisfaction of using her own non-verbal skills to answer the questions Crystal was asking. *What's going on with you two? Was that some flirtatious laughter I heard out here?* Crystal could wait to get her answers, and Eliza would enjoy making her squirm with curiosity. It was only right...and it would also keep the two of them from communicating something nonverbally that might attract the attention of the other two people in the room, something Eliza wanted to avoid.

Instead, she looked down at the plate in front of her, inhaling the aromas wafting her way. "Kaan, this looks delicious!" On the plate in front of her was grilled chicken, a pasta covered in what looked like a pesto sauce, and a beautiful salad loaded with all her favorite veggies. "Where did you get it?"

Before Kaan could answer, Crystal piped up. "He made it all himself! Isn't that impressive? I had no idea we were inviting a chef over for dinner."

"Wow, really?" Eliza raised her eyebrows. "You're just full of hidden talents, Kaan. *Eline sağlık.*" Then, remembering something Deniz had said, she turned a raised eyebrow in his direction. "He told you the two of you were going out to dinner and you didn't clock that he was *bringing* dinner with you?"

"I have learned after a lifetime of cousinhood not to question Kaan." Deniz smiled as he picked up his fork, digging into the plate in front of him. "I'm not completely unobservant, though. I noticed the giant bag he was carrying, but I figured we were just going for a romantic cousins-only picnic on the beach or something." He looked around him, at the cozy room and the company surrounding him. "This was a better choice, though. By far."

"We're glad you're here, too, Deniz." Crystal reached across the table to give him a reassuring pat on the forearm. "It's been weird not having you around, but I'm really glad you're back."

"Thanks, Crystal." He smiled at her but shot a glance at Eliza, as if checking that she shared her roommate's sentiments. Eliza couldn't help but wish things would go back to normal between them, even as she knew she couldn't just skip the awkward but necessary conversations ahead.

Thankfully, with Kaan and Crystal back at the table, there was plenty to distract Eliza—and Deniz, too—from the weirdness that lingered between them.

Kaan's cooking was delicious, and his attentiveness brought out a playfulness in Crystal that Eliza hadn't seen in a long time.

When they had all eaten so much they couldn't fit in another bite, plates were shoved to the middle of the table and stacked there. Eliza insisted no one should carry them to the kitchen to clean up, knowing that the spell of easy conversation would be broken and the reality of Sunday night work apprehension would settle in. It was worth having a sink full of dirty dishes in the morning to soak up more time with friends.

Kaan leaned back against the couch and smiled warmly at Crystal. "I'm glad we got the chance to get to know each other better, Crystal. I had a feeling before I even met you, when these two told me about you—" He gestured to Deniz and Eliza "—that you would be an inspiration to be around, and we all know I'm looking for inspiration lately." He gave a self-deprecating laugh, reminding them all that he still hadn't finalized his new app idea.

"And?" Crystal cringed. "How badly disappointed have you been by the vast difference between the inspiring person you hoped to meet and this reality?" She gestured towards herself, looking down at her limbs like they disgusted her.

"Oh, I've noticed a difference all right. Mostly because while I thought you sounded like a smart and fun and conscientious person, perhaps I underestimated you in all of those areas and even more. You've been a revelation."

Crystal's face turned bright red, her eyes glued on the table as she refused to make eye contact with anyone, even Eliza.

"I don't mean to embarrass you," Kaan continued. "It's just that I believe it's important to recognize and celebrate the goodness we see in others. And sure, a compliment delivered in private is nice, but here, in front of your friends who surely agree with everything I'm saying...well, I think that's even better."

"And I can definitely second everything you're saying, Kaan," Eliza chimed in, lifting her glass towards Crystal.

"Why don't we make a toast? To Crystal and her giant heart, inspiring brain, and the world's best sense of humor. All of our lives would be so much worse without you in them."

After Kaan and Deniz left, Eliza and Crystal exchanged a look.

"I know, trust me. I know." Crystal held her hands up in a gesture of understanding. "We have a bunch of things to talk about after that evening, but..." She grimaced at the words she was about to say. "Don't you need to sleep more than you need to gossip about boys?"

Eliza groaned. "Maybe...ugh, whatever. You know me too well. A good night's rest—especially the night before a big day of work—is pretty much the most important thing in my book." She paused, scratching her chin. "Although...maybe just a cup of chamomile tea to help make us sleepy and a little bit of a debrief with it?" She batted her eyelashes at Crystal. "I'll get up early tomorrow to finish planning my lessons."

"Eliza Britt!" Crystal mimed clutching her pearls in shock. "Are you really putting off *work* just because you want to chit chat about Deniz so much?"

Eliza shook her head. "No way. We're talking about you and Kaan, Miss Kim." She dropped her chin into her palm, elbow planted on her knee as she leaned forward in her seat towards her best friend. "Now, what in the world is going on between the two of you? Was is just my imagination or did I detect some sparks flying? Hmm?

Crystal waved a dismissive hand, but Eliza didn't miss the pink appearing on her cheeks. "Nothing but a new friendship forming there. Though I can tell you, it was definitely a nice change of pace to spend some time with a man who actually listens to what I say and doesn't just zone out."

"Right? And he is such a good cook, too!" Eliza was nodding. "I had no idea we were in for a home-cooked meal tonight, but if there's anything I can do about it, that was not the last time Kaan is going to be cooking for us. If his new app idea doesn't pan out, I'm sure he'd have great success as a chef."

"We'd be regular customers, for sure. And judging by the way he cleaned his plate, I think Deniz would be there at least three nights a week, too. Speaking of..." Crystal wiggled her eyebrows at Eliza. "What were you two talking about out here, anyway? Felt like we might have interrupted something...did we?"

Her tone was so hopeful that Eliza didn't know what to say. Did she have an outcome in mind for how she hoped things would unfold once she and Deniz got the chance to talk? Of course she did. But did that mean she believed that outcome was the most likely one? Not a chance. Eliza was a lot of things, but a hopeless romantic or an unsinkable optimist? She'd never been accused of being either of those.

Time would tell what things could be between her and Deniz, and she wasn't foolish enough to get her hopes up too high this time around.

Twenty-Two

Eliza's first day at the Antalya Technical Institute was off to a good start. She had arrived on time, thanks to the four alarms she had set on her phone, and she was as alert and adrenaline-fueled as she could make herself, thanks to three cups of coffee and the sheer terror of spending the day in front of unknown teenagers.

She had come in early, of course, earlier than many other teachers, judging from the lack of office lights on. Surely when she was more settled into the routine here, she would dare to be a bit later, but on a day like today it served her well to be early. "Early is on time, on time is late," she muttered to herself like a mantra as she let herself into her office.

As she was settling in at her desk, checking and double checking that she had all the materials she needed ready for the day, there was a gentle knock, accompanied by the sound of a throat clearing.

"Eliza?" A familiar voice interrupted her preparations, and she looked up to find a sheepish Deniz peeking in her doorway. "Sorry for the intrusion. I just wanted to wish you good luck on your first day. Not that you need it. I'm sure everything is going to be just great today, and I hope you'll catch me up on all of it soon. How's...today, actually?"

"*Today* today? Like...after work today?"

"We could do that. Or we could eat lunch together. A little mid day check in, just to see how it's all going."

Eliza raised an eyebrow at him. "We have some pretty personal things to talk about, Deniz. Do you really think we should risk getting into all of that here? I'm not sure Dr. Yılmaz would appreciate that."

Invoking Deniz's current boss and former mentor had done the trick, just as she had intended. His face blanched, and he shook his head. "Oh no, I am definitely not suggesting we talk about our...er...*relationship* things at work. We should keep it professional. I just meant, if you wanted to talk about how classes are going or something like that."

She smiled finally. "I figured that, Deniz. Trust me, I'm not going to bring any drama to work." She shuddered at the thought. "I was just wondering if the two of us could be trusted to have a private conversation without getting into personal things, but I think we're both concerned enough about keeping things professional that's not likely to happen."

"Not at all." Deniz shook his head, then smiled at her. "That's settled then. I'll come find you here and we can walk down to the cafeteria together, if that's alright with you."

"Sounds great. See you then. And thanks for the well wishes, Deniz. I appreciate it a lot."

"Oh, uh…"

Was Deniz blushing? He stepped into her office, pulling something from behind his back as he did so.

"It's not just well wishes, it's also first day of school flowers." He deposited the vase on her desk, then darted back towards the safety of the door. "I hope you don't mind."

Eliza bent down to sniff the flowers, thanking Deniz as she did, but when she looked back towards the door, he was already gone.

Something about the way he had disappeared just then tugged on her heart, like she would not see him again. Like she needed to soak up every moment because she didn't know when her supply of them was going to run out.

It was silly, and she knew it. They were both here to teach, both had materials to organize before the first lesson of the day. She shouldn't spend her time hanging onto him, worrying about conversations they needed to have. She should trust that the two of them would see each other at lunch and again after that. That they had many opportunities ahead to talk to each other and spend time together. If not socially, then at least for the duration of the school year.

Only, that wasn't enough for her any more, was it? She wanted to carpool to work together, sit side by side while they prepared materials or graded homework, meet during breaks like a couple of high schoolers in love, leave together at the end of the day and go home to the same place. Take their shoes off side by side and brush their teeth in the same sink before turning out the lights.

Oh, she was in trouble, and she didn't know how it could have gotten this bad. Last year, when Eliza had first met Deniz, she had been consumed by the work she was doing, by the job that had brought her to Turkey. Now, she was practically treating her lessons like an afterthought, something standing in the way of her and time spent with Deniz.

That wouldn't do. She bounced on the balls of her feet a few times, shaking out her limbs to reset her nervous system—something Crystal had shown her once which spontaneously offered itself as a solution to her discontent. Skeptical as she was that it would make a difference, she was still glad to see that no one was peering in her office door when she stopped shaking it off and sat down at her desk to get to work.

By the time the halls were full of the chatter of students on their first day in the English language preparatory program, Eliza was good and ready for her packed day ahead. She had a stash of icebreakers in mind for every class that she was teaching: tailored to the levels she'd been assigned and honed for the skills she was teaching as well. Naturally, there would be more need to get students comfortable chatting in her listening and speaking classes than in the reading and writing ones, but breaking down potential ice between students was essential at any level and in any skill.

In accordance with her level of preparation and confidence, the morning's classes went swimmingly. Eliza found herself charmed by her students, so young, eager, and earnest they all were. She was teaching mostly elementary level courses, and her classes were full of students coming from all over Turkey. At one point, she had a large map of Turkey displayed on the projector in the classroom, while the students practiced introducing themselves by saying where they were from and pointing it out on the map.

It was a geography lesson for Eliza, for sure, and a welcome reminder she wasn't the only one who was far from home.

Because of the configuration of her schedule, she had three lessons to teach before it was time for the lunch break. As the last students filed out, calling, "See you tomorrow, Teacher!" over their shoulders, she felt her stomach rumble with hunger. Time for lunch, which meant...

Time for Deniz.

And she felt so good in that moment, vibrating with the energy from a fun morning getting to know her new students, that she couldn't help but see this impending conversation with Deniz in a new light. A hopeful light. An encouraging light. A light by which, no matter what outcome came between the two of them, she was having a great day and living a beautiful life. Getting to know wonderful students she never would have met had she stayed put in Michigan, and with whom she could look forward to many more days together this semester.

It was going to be okay.

Back in her office, he was already waiting for her. At her entrance, he stood up from the extra chair where he had taken his seat, meeting her on his feet with a smile and a nervous energy.

"How was it?" he asked. "Your first day at Antalya Tech? I'm sure Dr. Yılmaz is eagerly awaiting your report about how much better things are here than Med School."

Eliza chuckled at the reminder of the friendly rivalry between Antalya Tech and the Mediterranean School of Languages, where she had worked the year prior. In fact, she would still be there, if it hadn't been for some unfortunate drama that had turned Dr. Çelik, the director, against her. Even despite that, she couldn't hold it against her old boss. Eliza was still here, still in Turkey teaching the next generation, and still within arm's reach of Deniz Aydem.

"It was great," she answered him. "Best first day I've had in a long time." She rubbed her stomach absentmindedly. "Though I am definitely ready for lunch now. Shall we?" She nodded towards the door, and he took her lead, stepping through it to guide her towards the cafeteria.

Lunch break for teachers and students at Antalya Tech was a gloriously long hour, a full twenty minutes longer than Eliza had gotten accustomed to at Med School. She followed Deniz through the cafeteria line, her plate piled with rice and chickpeas, a large side salad and a bowl of lentil soup that smelled like heaven. The table Deniz led them to had a few smiling faces waiting to greet her, including...

"Barış!" Eliza set her tray down, crossing around to the other side of the table to hug Deniz's old friend and Jack's boyfriend. "I can't believe I haven't seen you all summer. How are you? How's the first day going?"

As she made her way back to her seat across from Barış and next to Deniz, both men sat down as well. "I should be asking you that," Barış answered. "What do you think so far?"

"It's been great." Eliza dug into the soup first, blinking as the spices and flavors played with her taste buds. "The only thing that would make it better is if Jack were here, too." She winked at Barış, who huffed out a sigh in response.

"Trust me, I've tried to convince him, but he always says something about being too distracted if he had to work in the same place as me. Not being able to trust himself to *behave*, whatever that means." Was it just Eliza's imagination, or were Barış's cheeks turning pink? "Maybe you'll have more success changing his mind, though."

Eliza and Barış continued to chat and catch up throughout lunch, with Deniz uncharacteristically quiet, his gaze ping-ponging back and forth between the two of them, smiling or mumbling an agreement when appropriate.

When their plates were cleared, Deniz stood up, tray in hand, and gestured with a nod towards the door. "Eliza? Want to join me for a walk around campus? Help with the digestion?"

"Uh, sure." She darted a glance at Barış. "Barış, are you coming too?"

Barış's gaze was fixed on Deniz, communicating something Eliza couldn't read. "No, I'm good here. You two have fun."

Outside, the sun warmed their backs as they walked the path connecting one end of campus to the other. Around them, students were lounging on the grass, books open in front of some and snacks shared between others. Eliza peered up at Deniz's thoughtful face, finding a frown there that she wasn't sure was from the sun in his eyes. It seemed to reach deeper than that.

"What's going on, Deniz? Whatever's on your mind, it's probably better to just tell me than to torture me with this much pensive silence. I'm only assuming the worst, you know." A humorless laugh came out through her nose as an audible exhale. "How much worse things could get between the two of us, I'm not exactly sure. And yet, here I am waiting for the other shoe to fall. So?" She stopped then, turning to face him head on. "Just tell me. Please."

"I'm sorry, Eliza. It wasn't fair of me to bring things up the way I did, and it's not fair of me now to leave you wondering what's going on, where we stand."

"It's okay," she said. *It wasn't okay, but that's what you were supposed to say*, she thought. "I know you were in a difficult position, stuck between me and your family. Maybe if we had gone there later, taken some more time, things might have been different." She gave him a smile that she knew he could see right through to the sadness underneath.

"It's just..." Deniz paused, looking down at his feet before bringing his eyes back up to meet hers. "You're right, that it's not easy. There are expectations of me, simply because of the way things are done. Have always been done. That doesn't mean those ways can't change, that they aren't already changing. I just...I need some time. Can you give me some time? It's...I don't want to spring too much on my family right now. They're already dealing with enough changes with Cansu leaving, but...we can figure this out. I believe we can."

Eliza's heart leaped with hope just before her rational brain chimed in again. "I'm going to need you to be a little bit clearer there. When you say 'we can figure it out,' who's the 'we' there? Is it you and your family figuring things out? Or you and me?"

Deniz shook his head, reaching for her hands before thinking better of it and dropping his arms back at his sides. "Me and you. That is, if you still want to."

"I...of course I want to. But I'm confused. What was that about your grandma trying to set you up with someone?" She shook her head. "It's all a lot, Deniz. I never envisioned myself ending up with someone whose family didn't like me. I mean, I don't know if I can do that." She ran her hand through her hair, lifting it up off her neck, which was suddenly hot. "I mean, I love you. I do. It's just...it's not as easy as I imagined it would be, you know? I always thought I was good with parents, that of course my boyfriend's whole family would like me. I'd watch football with his dad, steal his mom's cookie recipe, and if he had grandparents, I could hang out and watch old movies with? Well, then I'd be all set. I just didn't imagine that within moments of meeting me, his grandma would suggest someone else to take my place."

Deniz's eyes were sad. "I love you too, Eliza. And this is not how I imagined us telling each other that for the first time."

Eliza laughed. "Is this the first time? I've thought it so many times I felt almost sure I must have already said it by now."

"It's not easy, I know. And I'm not going to tell you that love is enough because I think that might be an idea sold by Hollywood—"

"Hey now." Eliza interrupted him with a pout. "Don't you dare attack my beliefs about love conquering all, especially not in the same conversation that you're breaking up with me."

"Eliza, no. No! Wait, please. That is *not* the point of this conversation, just like it wasn't the message I was trying to convey to you the other day. The last thing I want to do is to break up with you. I just...I just want you to be a little bit patient with me, with my family, while we figure out how to make this work. Please?" His eyes were searching hers, trying to find the answer there before she could speak it.

"I said that wrong, I guess. I know you're not trying to end things, but I can't help but wonder if that's the natural course they're going to take. That they need to take." She gestured between them. "Is this too much? Too much for one family to bear? Especially when they've already lost one child to a different country..."

Deniz scoffed. "Cansu is hardly lost. She talks to my mom every day, so I think their fears of losing her to the big, bad United Kingdom may have been just a bit unfounded."

"Oh." Eliza pursed her lips, rethinking her next argument. "Still. I'm not looking to be anyone's big lesson, big challenge, big difficult thing that they have to learn how to accept. Doesn't it seem like it might be easier for both of us if we just called it? Surely, there are enough challenges in life that even if you ended up with a nice Turkish girl from the village, you'd still have plenty of opportunities for character growth. Same for me with a nice Midwestern boy."

This time, Deniz didn't stop himself from taking her hands in his. "If that's really what you want, I'll back off. I'll let you go. But I won't do it for myself and I won't do it for my family. That's not what *I* want, and I don't believe it's what they ultimately want either. I believe they want me to be happy, and me being happy...well, that's with you. I want to be with you. I just need a little time."

Eliza sighed, her next words coming out against her better judgment. "I can give you a little time. I guess. But if you discover I was right, that this isn't going to work, you need to let me know right away. Don't toy with me, don't waste my time, and don't string me along. You hear me?"

He grinned, relief spreading across his face. "I absolutely do, and I wouldn't dream of doing any of those things." His eyes darted to her mouth, then back up to her eyes. "I *do* dream of kissing you right now to seal the deal, but considering where we are, it'll have to wait."

"Indeed." Eliza nodded. "And don't get any ideas about a 'friends with benefits' kind of situation while you're figuring things out, either. These lips will be waiting for your decision on the other side." And with that, she turned on her heel and headed back towards the English department building, not even waiting for Deniz to catch up with her.

Twenty-Three

"**W**hy does it always end with the two of us here, doing this?" Crystal asked Eliza as she poured her friend another glass of wine. "It's almost too predictable at this point, 'The Tales of Heartache and Woe of Eliza and Crystal.' If it's not me, it's you."

Eliza stopped herself from saying the first thing that came to her mind. *It's usually you, rarely me. One of us is prone to drama and an excess of emotions; one of us is not. It's embarrassing to find myself in this position, to be honest.* Instead, she smiled and nodded. "Maybe they'll make a Netflix series out of it one of these days."

"Tell me again exactly what he said. We're going to Sherlock our way through 'The Case of the Loving Boyfriend Who is Also a Dutiful Son.' Figure out the natural conclusion of this story and beat him to it."

Eliza had already told Crystal what had transpired at lunch with Deniz that day, but she humored her friend anyway. Maybe with each retelling, it would get less surreal; so far, that hadn't been the case. She had retold herself about the rejection on repeat throughout her afternoon lessons, which had been considerably less fun as a result.

"I gave you the gist of it, Crystal. He needs space to figure out things with his family. And we all know what it means when a guy asks for space, right? It's the beginning of the end, or really, it's already the end. It makes no logical sense for me to hold on to the hope of things working out between us when clearly we all know what's about to happen. It wouldn't be the first time that asking for space was really just a nice way of saying, 'I'd like to be on the other side of outer space from you. How about I stay here on Earth and you try out life on one of the gas giants?'"

Crystal shook her head and rolled her eyes at Eliza. "You're ridiculous. And you're missing the point entirely, to exactly no one's surprise." She tapped a finger on the table. "Also, you changed your story about what Deniz said. First, you said he needed *time*, and this time you said he needed *space*. Those are two very different things, so which one was it?"

Eliza sighed. "I don't know. Does it matter? I figured whatever he had to say when he let me down would haunt me forever, so I probably tried *not* to remember it exactly. Alas, I can't forget how it made me feel, which, in case it wasn't obvious, is like total shit, thanks for asking."

"Oh, I didn't ask," said Crystal, brushing her off. "It's not that I'm not *very* sorry to see you experiencing all these unwanted emotions. I just can't help but celebrate ever so slightly that it is, in fact, *emotions* that you're letting yourself feel. Getting swept away in it. I like to think it's good for you to get a little taste of the feeling side of life."

"Gee thanks, I hate it," Eliza sneered. "And I do *feel* things, Crystal. That's not fair. I just...I don't know. I try not to let myself get swept away in them. To remember that I am ultimately in control, right? That I get to choose what I feel. I'm pretty sure you were the one who taught me that."

"Uh...no." Crystal leveled Eliza with a stern gaze. "I think you weren't paying attention in class, if that's what you got from all my talk about emotions and the importance of feeling them. You can't control what you feel, what comes up. But you *can* control what you do with that emotion. You can lose sight of everything else and get caught up in it—"

"Which is *exactly* what I don't want to do," Eliza interrupted.

Crystal rolled her eyes again. "Which is why you should let me finish. You can get swept away in it, or you can treat it as information. A cue that you need to take action to process it. You don't need to be ruled by it, but you do need to acknowledge it, notice what's causing it, and then move through it. Sometimes that means physically moving through it, like, to get it out of your body. Sometimes it means journaling it out or talking it out with a close friend—gee, wouldn't it be great if you had one of those? The only other option is to ignore it and pretend it doesn't exist. Which, frankly, I suspect has been your default setting for unwanted feelings for a good long time now."

"Yikes, Crys." Eliza slugged back a large sip of wine. "At least warn a girl before you go for the jugular like that." She lifted her glass again, swishing a small sip of wine around in her mouth before swallowing it. "You may not be too far off, though. Just, uh, out of curiosity...any tips for a beginner who's just trying to figure out how to do this emotional stuff right for a change?"

Crystal clapped her hands, bouncing up and down in her seat. "I thought you'd never ask! To start with, you're going to have to practice getting honest with yourself about what you're actually feeling. We'll work on how to move through a feeling after that, but until you know what it is you're actually experiencing, how are you going to know how to move it through your body?"

"You've got me." Eliza shrugged, feeling as if Crystal were speaking a different language. All this time—their whole friendship—that she'd felt like she needed to look out for Crystal because she was the "emotional" one...had she been wrong about that? Had Crystal just been more in touch with herself, not fragile in the least? There was a paradigm shift waiting to happen there that Eliza wasn't sure she was ready for yet. Learning that she was flawed was one thing, but learning that she wasn't the strong one in their friendship duo could push her into some real "dark night of the soul" territory.

"Okay, so..." Crystal was still speaking, walking Eliza through her next steps. "Close your eyes. Take some deep breaths. And check in with yourself. See what you find there."

Eliza cocked an eyebrow at her oldest friend. "This is already sounding like some woo woo mumbo jumbo. Can I just tell you that I'm feeling frustrated at my boyfriend, ex-boyfriend, or whatever the hell he is? And maybe skip the self investigation if I already know what I'm going to find there?"

The serene smile on Crystal's face probably came from a place of deep acceptance and inner peace, and Eliza wanted to wipe it off her smug face. Okay, she knew Crystal well enough to know she wasn't smug in the least, wasn't rubbing her emotional abilities in Eliza's face. "Frustration is one part of it, but there's almost always more to it than what's on the surface. Come on, I'll do it with you."

Eliza waited to see that Crystal was, in fact, closing her eyes before she closed her own. Listening to Crystal's deep breathing, she tried to match hers with it, finding it hard to slow herself down, to breathe that deeply.

As if sensing her struggle, Crystal spoke. "Deep breath in from your belly. Breathe through your nose and let your stomach relax and expand as the air comes in. Exhale it out slowly, bit by bit. Then in again, belly expanding. That's it. Just focus on your breathing, and let's slow it down a bit. Listen to my breaths, and stay with me."

Eliza was already feeling more relaxed, her mind threatening to take her away on a tangent as she wondered why something as simple as breathing—something she was known to do every minute of every day—could have this much of an effect on her stress level. And if breathing was such a magic bullet for stress relief, then why didn't she instinctively do it more often? Why were her breaths always so shallow, so quick, so the opposite of what it was she was doing right now?

As if sensing where Eliza had traveled in her mind, Crystal brought her back. "Refocus on your breath with every inhale and every exhale. There's nowhere else you need to be. Just stay right here in your body, right here with the cycle and flow of the air in your lungs. Good."

Eliza heard Crystal shift in her seat and opened her eyes to find that her friend had moved her hands, placing one over her own heart and one over her stomach. Eliza mirrored her actions, no longer caring how she might look as she finally accepted that no one was looking at her, and the only other person in the room with her was the one least likely to judge her.

"Now drop your awareness down into your body," said Crystal, prompting Eliza to think, *How?*

Before she could ask, though, Crystal continued.

"Let your attention travel from your thoughts, your worries, your to-do list all the way down into your torso. It could be the center of your chest, it could be your stomach, wherever feels comfortable to you. And once your awareness is there, get curious. Notice what else is present, what other sensations are around. These could be physical feelings or emotional ones...just notice them. And notice them with curiosity, don't judge them." She was quiet then, pausing for a couple of minutes until her brain, that was *really freaking good at this,* somehow knew it was time to move on. "And then when you're ready, come on back to the room and open your eyes."

As Eliza's eyes opened, she blinked rapidly, surprised by the overflow of sensations arising. "Wow," was all she could say. "That...wow."

"I'm glad it was good." Crystal smiled at her, warm and inviting. "Want to share what you found while you were down there poking around?"

"Definitely." Eliza nodded, her voice coming out subdued. "The frustration was there, yeah, but there was more to it. You were right. I felt this tightness in my stomach, like an anxious feeling. And without even poking at it, really, it was like I just knew."

"Knew what?"

"That it was fear. The frustration was masking fear of being rejected. Being abandoned. Like...I think I want to push Deniz away before he can because it will hurt less to be the one doing the leaving than to be left behind. It already hurt, if I'm being honest, finding out that I'm not good enough for his family."

"Is that true? That you're not good enough for his family?" Crystal's zen vibe was in danger of being replaced with a momma bear violence, it was clear. "Because if he told you that—"

Eliza held up a hand to stop her. "He didn't say that. That's just...well, that's the story I told myself, I guess, based on what he did say. He said it was hard for his family to understand, but that he believes they ultimately will want him to be happy. And that he wants the time, the space, the *whatever* to help them get there." She sighed, exhaling out at least a week's worth of stress. "That's all. He's...he's not trying to end things. He wants to make it work. That's what he said, and I believe he means it. Deep down, I really do." She shook her head at herself, at all the conflicting thoughts and feelings she had observed tangling with each other inside her being. "I'm just scared he's going to change his mind. Decide I'm not worth it."

Crystal moved next to Eliza then, wrapping her in a hug far tighter than would be expected from someone her size. "No matter what happens with Deniz, you are worth it. You're worth working for, fighting for, sacrificing for...whatever the price is to be with you, you're worth paying it." She shook her head then, leaning back to look Eliza in the eyes. "I don't know what's going to happen with Deniz. Neither do you. Deniz might not even know at this point. But the most important thing is for *you* to know what you're worth." She pointed at herself. "I can tell you that, as your best friend, *I* know what you're worth, how special you are. I have a feeling Deniz knows it, too. But that's not the most important thing, or the thing that's going to help you navigate this new scary emotional terrain." She moved her finger from her sternum to Eliza's, poking her there, hard. "*You* need to know it. None of this works if you don't know that about yourself."

"I...oof." Eliza exhaled like she'd been punched in the gut, and the emotional blow felt about the same. "You're right. I know you are. I know that part of what makes the potential for rejection or abandonment so scary is that it might mean something unbearably painful about me, like that I'm fundamentally unlovable or something like that. I know you're right about this. I just..." Eliza sat up stick straight then, as if realizing where she was and who she was with. "How?" she asked Crystal, her eyes searching her friend's face. "How do you know all of this? Here I was so worried about you with Chris, worried that you didn't know how special you were because you were with him...did you know it this whole time?"

Crystal shook her head. "I got lost a little bit there, too. You can't blame me for that, though. He was cute, and it was fun and I bounced back pretty darn quickly, if I do say so myself." She shrugged. "That's part of the deal with me. Just because I'm emotionally intelligent doesn't mean I don't let myself feel things and get swept up in them. Life is a pendulum swinging...sometimes you go too far in one direction and then you correct for it by going too far in the other direction. Hopefully in the end you find yourself nicely in the middle, a good balance of both rather than too much of any one extreme."

"How messed up is it that I thought *I* was the grounded one in our friendship just because I was..." Eliza trailed off, not sure how to finish that sentence.

"More of a robot?" Crystal offered, smile securely in place. "It's normal that you'd think that. Our culture definitely seems more comfortable keeping things buttoned up, thinking over feeling, no big displays of strong emotions. How many times have you seen someone apologize for crying in public? Or try to hide the fact that a movie made them weepy? We're not exactly 'wear our heart on our sleeves' kinds of people, are we? It can be different here, though. In Turkey, I mean."

Eliza pursed her lips, remembering. "Yeah, that came up in the village with Deniz's family, actually. I was uncomfortable, of course, and I wasn't hiding it well." She laughed, looking at the situation with the fresh eyes of her recent emotional revelation. "When I apologized to Kaan, he played it off like it wasn't a big deal and I actually believed him. He made it sound like people weren't so prone to put on a good face for the neighbors, but that being sad or stressed or angry...it was okay to show those things, too." She shrugged it off. "It's not like I could understand anything that was going on around me anyway, though.

He could have just been saying that to be nice and make me feel comfortable. How would I know?"

"Don't." Crystal's expression was serious as she shook her head. "You don't have to downplay yourself or your abilities, you know? So you don't speak Turkish fluently…how long have you been learning? Did you have access to Turkish classes in high school but you slept through them or blew them off? No! It's been a year…less than that, even. Give yourself a break. It's not an easy language to learn, and no one expects you to be fluent."

Eliza's laugh was mirthless. "I'm pretty sure Deniz's family would disagree with you there. If I'm going to be with Deniz, how could they possibly want me to be anything *but* fluent in their language?"

"Do you think their frustration that you can't speak Turkish is because they think you're a failure? Too stupid to learn? Or do you think it's because they wish they could talk to you? Get to know you? Connect with you?" Crystal patted Eliza on the knee. "Communication goes both ways, hon. It's not all on you. And no, I'm not saying they should all learn English or anything like that. I'm just offering a reminder that there are multiple reasons people could be frustrated and they aren't all about who you are as a human. And even if they *are* about that…you don't have to accept it. If someone doesn't want to accept you simply because you're not who they imagined Deniz should be with, well, as long as that person isn't you or Deniz, then who the hell cares what they think?"

For the first time in this conversation, Eliza didn't have a rebuttal. She let Crystal pull her in for another hug, unable to find the words to explain the transformation she had just gone through and with no idea how she was going to assimilate it into her real life.

Twenty-Four

It wasn't easy to give Deniz the time—or was it the space?—that he needed. Eliza saw him every day at school, of course, and it wasn't as if he had said they couldn't be friendly. She often joined him and Barış for lunch, and when there were meetings to attend, an empty seat always materialized by his side.

As much as she wanted to talk through everything with him, to share daily updates on her own journey of self-discovery and to check in on how things were going with his family, she resisted the urge. Crystal reminded her regularly that the work she was doing on herself was like an investment in her future, including in their future relationship. Being centered and grounded in herself would serve her as an individual just as much as it would serve her as one half of a couple.

"You're not looking for your other half, you know? You're whole on your own, and you need to know that now so that you remember it when you *are* half of a couple. Nobody likes being around someone in a codependent, needy relationship." Crystal's sky-high eyebrows had made it abundantly clear just how strongly she felt about that statement. "Ask me how I know that." Then the facade had fallen as she laughed good-naturedly at herself. "Trust me, I know what a lost cause I was with Chris. And I'm working on myself right alongside you, friend."

And the two of them *had* been working on themselves, in tandem somehow. Crystal had insisted that a morning routine was the way to go, and as much as Eliza had been tempted to write it off—didn't she need sleep more than she needed to write in a journal?—it was easier to go along with it than deal with the wrath of a Crystal who couldn't get what she wanted.

That's how it had begun, with an alarm clock set an hour earlier than either of them normally got up and lots of bleary eyes and big yawns, at least at first. They didn't talk much, but they sat next to each other, working through various habits to find what worked for them. Eliza quickly discovered that journaling made more sense to her than meditation, while Crystal was the opposite. Eliza admired her friend's ability to quiet her own mind, to hold a vision, but she had already learned not to be jealous and not to try to make herself be someone she was not. Instead, she sat with the blank page of her journal and poured out whatever thoughts had been swirling around in her mind from the first moment she had woken up.

"You know," Eliza began one morning, when both friends were showered and dressed for the day, sipping coffee like they had all the time in the world. "If our lives were a movie, this would definitely be the makeover montage part, wouldn't it? Can't you just see it? Instead of trying on a bunch of different outfits, getting a salon-quality blowout, taking off our glasses and discovering we'd been beautiful all along, it's...well, it's a little more like the spiritual version of that, I guess."

Crystal chuckled. "You're right...instead of waxing our eyebrows—which you really should, by the way..." She reached over and poked Eliza's left eyebrow. "...we're trying out breathwork and visualization and all the self-help books." She took a sip of her coffee and smiled. "It's definitely the same end result, though. Shiny and beautiful and positively radiating self confidence."

Eliza smiled back. "Definitely. Maybe even a better version of those things. Longer lasting, at least."

"If we keep it up, yeah. That's the pitfall of all this habit stuff, though, so be warned. At some point, you're going to start feeling so great that you think you don't need to do it anymore."

"Yeah? I'm already feeling pretty good, to be honest. How long do I need to keep the whole journaling thing up?"

Crystal shook her head. "That's the thing. When you feel good, you think you don't need the good habits, the morning routine and you forget they are the reason you feel so good. It's like they always say...it's a lifestyle, not a spiritual diet."

"No one says that, Crystal." Eliza rolled her eyes at her friend. "So, you're telling me I've got to keep this up for the rest of my life?"

"I am *not* telling you that. I'm just telling you not to focus on when you can *stop* doing something, like it's a punishment or a chore that you're already ready to be done with. Enjoy the process and keep it up. You can always change what exactly is included in your morning routine, but it's good to have a routine."

"I know...I mean, I *think* I get it." Eliza paused, scratching her head in thought. "It's just...I don't know if you know this, but the word 'routine' isn't exactly as sexy and thrilling and exciting as you seem to think it is."

That got a laugh from Crystal. "Okay, then. Call it something else. Your morning ritual. Self care to start the day. Me time. The point is to give yourself that time, not to argue about the semantics of it. Anyway. You'll figure it out. I'm just trying to spare you from having to make the same mistakes I did before. You know...quitting the thing because you think you're doing just fine without it before you eventually realize that it was the whole reason you were doing as fine as you thought you were."

"Duly noted, and totally appreciated." Eliza smiled at Crystal, getting to her feet to get ready to head out for the day. "Should we go out to dinner tonight? Treat ourselves a little bit, especially since we're really rocking this whole self care glow-up montage?"

"That sounds great." Crystal bit her lip, looking down. "But actually. I had an invitation from someone. I was going to tell you about it."

Eliza should have felt guilty for how quickly her mind raced to the worst possible conclusion. Was Chris back in town? Had Crystal forgiven him that easily? Were they going to go down this same old shitty path again? Instead, she schooled her expression and asked the question. "Oh, yeah? Who?"

"Um...Kaan, actually." Crystal's expression was tentative, checking for Eliza's reaction as much as refusing to reveal her own feelings. When Eliza smiled, she let hers break through, too. "I know! I was surprised, too, but I think it will be nice to get to know him better. He's a good person."

"A good guy, too." Eliza wiggled her eyebrow. "Why don't we reschedule, then? The two of you should go out tonight, have some fun, see what happens."

Crystal's cheeks turned scarlet. "Uh...not entirely sure I'm ready for that. Still learning to trust myself again, you know. Why don't the three of us go out?"

"Are you sure?"

Crystal was already nodding, reaching for her phone and sending her fingers flying across its screen so quickly they were a blur. "I am. Definitely. I'll let Kaan know, so he's not surprised when I bring a chaperone to our date. Ha! That would be the worst, wouldn't it? But no, this way it's just three friends hanging out. Nothing weird about that." She paused, giving Eliza a side-eye glance. "He shouldn't bring Deniz, should he?"

Eliza shook her head. "I don't think so. It's not like it would be weird, but the space is good for us right now. And it's not like we don't see each other around at work. But before we hang out outside of work again, things need to be clearer between us. Where we stand with each other, stuff like that."

"Makes sense." Crystal nodded. "Okay, then. Off to work with you. I'll let you know what I hear from Kaan and maybe we can meet early. Right after work? Catch as much daylight and sunshine as we can after being cooped up in classrooms and offices all day?"

"I love it." Eliza smiled at Crystal. "Have a great day, then, and see you later."

Eliza was earlier than Crystal and Kaan, claiming a table at the cliff-side cafe Kaan had suggested for their pre-dinner coffee and sunset watching. Based on the text message Eliza had received from Crystal, there was a full agenda for their evening, featuring at least three different dining and/or drinking establishments.

And she could use that right about now. As serene as her start to the day had been, it hadn't been easy running into Deniz in the hall today. His face, so unguarded and open when he'd been chatting with a few students in the hall outside his classroom, had closed up when he'd seen her, little more than a tight-lipped grin and a slight wave directed her way. She couldn't help but miss the way things used to be between them and wonder what it would have been to work together when things were that good. The whole time they had been together as a couple and even in all the flirtation prior, they'd either been working at different schools, separated by an ocean, or still on their summer break.

Maybe if things were good between them, they'd be interacting just like this, with small smiles and stolen glances. It would feel different then, though. Like they were sharing a little secret. Keeping their relationship just for themselves, rather than letting their students and coworkers in on it. She had to imagine that would be fun. That it would leave her with butterflies in her stomach rather than a pit of dread and rejection.

Eliza was sipping a latte and admiring the view when Kaan and Crystal arrived—together, to her surprise. "Hey, you two," she greeted them, noticing that they seemed to be finishing a rather intense conversation as they came into earshot. Or at least, they seemed to be sharing some rather focused whispers, only noticing her when they heard her speak, stepping away from each other at the same time.

Crystal took the seat next to Eliza at the four-top table, and Kaan sat across from her, both of them greeting her with warm smiles and pleasantries about the beautiful weather or hoping she had had a good day.

Eliza held up a hand to stop them. "What's going on here?" She gestured between them. "Since when are you two so close? As far as I'm aware, you've only met a few times, so what could you possibly be whispering about so intently?"

Kaan had the decency to look bashful, but Crystal refused to bite back her grin. "Oh, we're old friends now. Kaan and I have been working on a project together. I thought I told you?"

"No, you definitely didn't." Eliza shook her head, skeptical. "What kind of project?"

It was Kaan's turn to speak. "Crystal has been kindly helping me with a new app idea, actually. I got her phone number from Deniz and we've been texting, occasionally meeting up during her lunch hour since she works so close by. Though, actually, I spend lots of time working on my laptop in cafes, so we usually meet there. Sorry, I'm rambling..." His bashfulness had been replaced by full-on blushing, and Eliza narrowed her eyes in suspicion.

"Why does it seem like there's something you're not telling me here?" Her eyes darted between the two of them, though that didn't bring her any closer to an understanding of what she was missing.

Crystal shrugged as she got to her feet. "I'm going to go find the bathroom. Anyone want me to order anything while I'm up?"

"I'd love a cup of tea, please. And whatever you want, too." He handed a few bills to Crystal with a warm smile and—was that a wink? Turning to Eliza, he continued. "It was my idea for us to go to all these places tonight, so it's on me. Thanks for humoring my whims."

She tried to protest, but her attempts were dismissed.

Once Crystal was gone, Kaan leaned closer, dropping his voice. "You're right to notice something going on with me and Crystal. I'm sorry I didn't talk to you about it before, make sure it wasn't weird for you, but...it just sort of happened."

"What exactly?"

Kaan's teeth found his lower lip, digging in. "The specifics...well, I'm not sure. We haven't 'defined the relationship—'" He used air quotes around the phrase "—or whatever the kids are calling it these days, but...well, something more than just friendly app-building collaboration."

"Oh!" Eliza's eyebrows lifted in surprise. "Are the two of you...?"

"Just some flirtation. But where I'm concerned, I'd definitely like it to be more. Ever since you and Deniz told me about Crystal, I just found her fascinating, and after meeting her, that only intensified. She's a special person, and I'm really enjoying getting to know her so far."

Concern flashed across Eliza's consciousness. "And you haven't talked to her about this at all? It's just…Crystal's so friendly, such a ball of light. I hope you aren't misreading her friendliness as flirtation. I don't want you to get hurt, you know."

Kaan held up a hand, allaying her concerns. "Don't worry, I haven't picked out her wedding dress or anything like that. I do, however, like to think I'm a pretty good study of human character and that I can recognize the difference between flirtation and friendliness."

"Of course," Eliza agreed. "I didn't mean to imply that you *were* reading it wrong, just that…well, speaking from recent experience, I'm extra cautious, I guess. Wouldn't want anyone else to get hurt."

Kaan's expression softened, whatever affront he had felt at Eliza's questions vanishing. "Ah, yes. That's exactly what I was afraid of, why I didn't want to rub any of this happiness in your face. How *are* you?"

Eliza shook her head. "It's okay. I want you to be happy, and Crystal, too. And Deniz and I, well…we might still work this out. We'll see what happens after our break is over." She forced what she thought was a hopeful smile onto her face. "And even if we don't, it won't be weird. We'll figure out how to be friends eventually, I'm sure of it."

"That won't happen." Kaan shook his head, his expression stern. "I'm sorry. I don't mean that the two of you won't be friends. Or rather, I mean you won't *just* be friends. I know my cousin, and he's miserable without you. I know—and he knows—that this is important, taking this time to figure out how you can have a future together, but it doesn't mean that he's enjoying it. He wants to be around you, to hear about your day, to share things with you. Trust me, he's having to fill that void with me." Kaan laughed humbly. "And it's definitely not the same. That much is clear."

"I hope you're right..." Eliza began, "But I'm also trying not to put too much stock in hope. I'll be okay with whatever happens, and as much as I'd like a guarantee that things are going to work out between us, no one—not even a psychic—could give me that." She chuckled at her bad joke.

"You sure about that? I can order you a cup of Turkish coffee and read your fortune if you'd like?" Kaan moved his hands to the arms of his chair, as if he were about to leap into action.

That got a genuine laugh out of Eliza, who nodded adamantly. "I'm sure, but thanks for the offer. As much as I'd enjoy seeing your fortune telling skills in action, I think I'll have to take a rain check."

"Fair enough." He leaned over conspiratorially. "Even without the coffee, I can give you one assurance. Something will happen after this weekend."

Eliza jolted back. "What's that supposed to mean?"

Kaan shrugged like he didn't have access to the very knowledge Eliza coveted. "Just that Deniz is taking a little trip to Isparta this weekend. So I can say with some confidence that no matter what happens there, we'll know more just as soon as he's back."

Eliza bit her lip. "I guess we will." She couldn't help but wonder if it was going to be good news or bad waiting for her on Monday morning.

Twenty-Five

Something was brewing between Crystal and Kaan, that much was undeniable by the end of their evening out together. Eliza had tried to tap into her nearly telepathic ability to communicate nonverbally with her best friend, raising an inquisitive eyebrow in her direction when Kaan was reading the menu at the restaurant...but the look she got back from Crystal was blank. Either her friend wasn't aware of what was percolating between her and Kaan, or she wasn't ready to divulge.

No matter; Eliza could be patient. Throughout the course of the evening, she frequently found herself sitting back and observing, a secret smile spreading across her face as she watched her best friend enjoy the attention and appreciation of a good, caring man.

They would talk about it later, Eliza and Crystal. There was no need to rush ahead to that part, to make Crystal aware of what was happening on the off chance that she thought Kaan was just a good friend. Eliza knew too well how disconcerting it could be to discover that what you thought was just a friendly encounter was actually a flirtation, and the last thing she wanted to do was give Crystal cause to be skittish around Kaan.

After the cafe, they had dinner at a small restaurant only Kaan had been to before. Eliza hadn't even known it existed, tucked away on the top floor of a hotel, and she would have assumed it was for hotel guests only, even if she had known about it.

"Are you sure this is open for just anyone?" Eliza had asked in a hiss as they followed Kaan up the stairs.

"It's fine," he had assured her. "I come here a lot; they know me."

The food they had eaten there had been next-level delicious. The chef had trained in an Italian kitchen for years, Kaan had told them, and the result had been a menu that infused the best of both Turkish and Italian cuisine. The view from the rooftop terrace had been equally delicious, and Eliza had once again—it was a frequent occurrence in Antalya—found herself flooded with gratitude and humbled by the fact that she got to experience such beauty firsthand.

The last stop had been a hookah bar in Kaleiçi. Eliza raised an eyebrow when Kaan brought them to a stop in front of the establishment. "Uh...I'm not a big hookah fan," she said. "I mean, I don't mind if you guys want to smoke, but actually I should probably just head home then. It's not that much fun to sit and watch people smoke, and it would probably just cramp your style having me there, wouldn't it?"

Crystal was already shaking her head. "We're not going to smoke here." She looked to Kaan for confirmation, and he nodded. "This is the place Kaan has been telling me about. They have a great drink menu, if what *he* says is to be believed..." The look she gave him then was downright flirtatious, and Eliza filed it away for future questioning.

"Alright then, lead the way." She followed Kaan inside, where he led them to a small table in the corner.

"I'll be right back," he said, walking towards the bar.

"This place is so cool, isn't it?" Crystal leaned across the table towards Eliza, her voice hushed as her eyes darted around. The inside of the bar was small, the walls covered in photos, art, and knick knacks. It was like everything a chain restaurant back in the States wanted to be, except it was clear the adornments on the walls were authentic, collected over the lifetime of the restaurant rather than distributed by corporate headquarters upon the opening of a new franchise.

"It's definitely charming," Eliza agreed. The lack of menus was interesting, though. How was someone supposed to come here for the first time if they didn't know how things worked? "What kind of things do they even serve here, though?" She craned her neck to see if there was a chalkboard covered in specials or anything displayed that would provide a clue.

"Kaan said it was unusual like that. Almost like a speakeasy, where you kind of have to know someone in order to get in or know what to do once you do." Her cheeks colored. "He offered to bring me here a while ago, when we first started texting, and I've been excited about it. I'm glad you're here too, though."

Eliza arched an eyebrow. "About that...texting? The two of you? Something going on there you want to share with the rest of the class?" She made sure to smile, dialing her tone down from her sincere feelings of frustration. Crystal should have told her, it was true. But saying that to her face was a surefire way to shut her down, right when Eliza wanted her to be opening up.

"Not right now," Crystal hissed, darting her eyes above Eliza's head just as Eliza became aware of the sound of approaching footsteps. Crystal leaned back, grinning at Kaan as he placed three glasses on the table.

"Mojitos!" He announced the word with such fierce pride that Eliza had to smile. He was a hunter-gatherer, bringing his bounty back to the women in the tent, even if that bounty had changed ever so slightly in the intermittent years.

"Thank you," she said as she reached for her glass, raising it to clink with the others at the table.

As she took a sip, she understood Kaan's pride. The first swallow of cool liquid washed across her tongue and dusty synapses in her brain started exploding. "Fresh lime!" she exclaimed, her face breaking into an unconscious grin. "I didn't even know I missed it, but *wow*. Now that I have it again, I can't imagine letting it go!"

"I know," Crystal chimed in, eyes bright with excitement. "I thought I was buying limes at the bazaar, but they turned out to be tangerines with green skin." She wrinkled her nose. "Definitely not the same. Not interchangeable, in case you thought they were. Ruined a perfectly good batch of guacamole."

"Ahh, but that guacamole was already in trouble, wasn't it?" Kaan asked, as he raised his glass to his lips. "It's not that easy to find good avocados in Antalya, or at least you have to be pretty patient with them. And you, darling, don't strike me as a patient person." His smile was affectionate, and Crystal's face burned bright red.

"It's easier to blame it on the citrus than to admit that the avocado was *a little* on the crunchy side." She turned the force of her gaze back to Eliza, almost as if she were pointedly ignoring Kaan. "Anyway. This place is pretty cool, right? I'm glad we finally came here." She jerked her head in Kaan's direction, still not looking at him. "He's been crowing about it for long enough, and I'm glad it finally happened."

Perhaps it was the rum in her glass that had given her the courage to blow past social niceties, but Eliza couldn't help but seize the opportunity when it was presented to her. "I have to ask," she said, "How long have the two of you actually been chatting? I had no idea." She directed her gaze at each of them, enjoying the thrill of seeing the discomfort that passed across Crystal's eyes first and then Kaan's. "Seems a bit strange that neither of you would mention it before today."

That got Crystal to look Kaan in the eyes again, something unspoken passing between them.

"Not long," she responded. "So I guess I misspoke when I said he's been talking about it for a long time. I mean, knowing Kaan, he *has* been talking about it for a long time...but to me, specifically, it's probably only been a week or so. Still, he repeats himself a lot, so it feels like it's been ages."

Kaan clutched his chest. "You wound me, Crystal." But his eyes were warm and kind as they found hers, a vulnerability so startling there that Eliza had to look away. "I just really wanted to share it with you, and now that you're here, I think I made the right call."

"You definitely did," Eliza interjected. "And I won't push—for now, at least—about whatever is going on between the two of you. I just want you to know that I see it...and that I'm totally on board, for what it's worth."

"Good to know," said Kaan, lifting his glass to take a sip and hide a smile, which Eliza heard in his voice.

"Ugh, whatever," Crystal sighed, sounding exasperated but giving herself away with the pink hue in her cheeks.

Happy—and surprised—as she was for them, it all made Eliza feel just a bit alone. Only time would tell if Kaan's prediction about an impending change with Deniz would prove accurate, and she was more than ready to leave the uncertainty—and all the discomfort that came along with it—behind.

Kaan had left them at their apartment, despite Eliza and Crystal's insistence that they were perfectly capable of walking home alone.

"Trust me, I know that," he had said, "It's just that *I* definitely need a walk to digest all of our indulgences this evening, and my options are to walk the two of you home and then take myself home...or walk directly home and do laps around the building until I feel ready to go inside. This is the less conspicuous of the two."

"Less strange, for sure," Crystal agreed. "And we don't mind the company at all, do we, Eliza?"

Eliza shook her head, walking determinedly—and just a bit faster than her companions, letting them fall into step and conversation with each other while she led them home to the apartment.

At the front gate, she thanked Kaan for a fun evening and told Crystal she'd meet her upstairs.

She had already changed into her pajamas and was just washing her face when she heard the door open and Crystal's dramatic sigh announcing her entrance.

When Eliza reentered the living room, she found Crystal sprawled across the couch, hand flung over her forehead and eyes closed.

"Crystal? You okay?" Eliza was still rubbing moisturizer onto her face and neck, no hand free to shake Crystal awake or rest a reassuring palm on her shoulder.

Crystal sat up, shaking her head. "I am *not*, Eliza. I actually find myself with all these damn *feelings* again. And for Kaan, of all people! He's nice, and he's a good person…it's just very inconvenient, especially in the middle of all this self improvement. I don't want to go down this path, not right now. I need at least a few more months to sort myself out, and then I'll be ready. But right now? Right now's not exactly good timing, is it?"

Eliza sat down next to Crystal, forcing herself to stay silent when all she wanted to do was deliver a pep talk that was bound to turn into more of a lecture.

Silence won out, though, and Crystal kept going.

"I know I'm missing the point." She let out an exasperated sigh. "Like, I get that people in relationships—even if I narrow it down even farther than that and just say people in healthy relationships—didn't all finish working on themselves before they got into those relationships. I get that it needs to be messy, that I'm always and forever a work in progress and at no stage of this life am I going to feel like I've *arrived*...I get all of that, but I still hate it."

"Hmm." Eliza nodded in agreement, still resisting the urge to chime in, still attempting to use her mere presence to encourage Crystal to keep going.

"I just want to be done with this particular stage of growth, I guess. I want to feel like the main character, not the funny sidekick best friend. I want to be the one who's the star, who went through her cute little transformation montage and now even when she's just making coffee or taking her dog for a walk it's, like, so clear that the camera loves her and she's adorable and her meet cute with Prince Charming is just around the corner. Like...her dog's leash is going to get tangled up with his dog's leash and they're going to bump into each other and laugh about it and be inseparable from that day forward."

Eliza couldn't keep her silence any longer. "Does that mean that *101 Dalmatians* is the pinnacle of love stories as far as you're concerned?"

"Duh! You can't tell me you haven't wanted that exact same thing to happen to you ever since you were a little girl watching that movie for the first time."

"I think it mostly made me wish I had a *ton* of puppies..." Eliza trailed off, thinking back. "But yeah, I remember that couple being cute. And animated, so...you know...something less than relatable. I think in real life, if some guy's dog wrapped its leash around my legs, I would fall down and be pretty pissed off at him by the time I got back on my feet. I don't even care how cute he is. There's nothing attractive about poor leash handling skills."

"These are all valid points." Crystal shifted in her seat, sitting up and looking less flustered with every moment that she spent debating the merits of living out the love story from a movie for children. "Okay, but even if we put that aside." She gestured around her to their surroundings. "Does anything about this look like the life of a main character? I moved to Turkey because of *you*, for crying out loud! What kind of non-sidekick does that?"

"Stop that." Eliza's tone was firm, stern. "You are *not* my sidekick...or if you are, then I'm just as much yours. We are both main characters in our own stories, and we both deserve everything that goes along with that—both the good stuff *and* the character growth stuff. The transformation stuff that we've been working on the last few weeks. Crystal, you've got main character energy all over you! You've definitely got your shit way more together than I do, too." At that, something occurred to her, and she shifted forward, turning to face her best friend head on and taking her hands in her own.

"Crys. Humor me for a minute here," said Eliza. "For just a moment, forget that you're probably the wisest person I know, okay? Just be one of us regular folks for a minute."

"Okay..." Crystal looked skeptical, but she humored Eliza, shifting in her seat to get more comfortable.

"Okay then. So...what if I told you that Deniz got in touch and he's ready to give things a try? See where it could go."

That got Crystal's attention. "Did he?" She leaned forward, her eyes searching Eliza's. "Why didn't you tell me this sooner? That's amazing! Friend, I'm so happy for you!"

As much as Eliza wanted to interrupt her little thought experiment and clarify what was actually going on, she pressed forward. "What if it doesn't feel like great news to me, though?"

"What do you mean? This is what you've wanted, isn't it? Why not be excited about it?"

"It's just...I feel like I just started working on myself and...well, I'm not exactly done yet, am I? Don't I need to make some more progress on my whole self-discovery journey before I'm ready to be in a relationship with him?"

"Are you serious? That's not how this works at all! You're not going to feel ready, and you're not going to be perfectly equipped to be in a relationship—neither is he, by the way—but you're still going to do it, and the two of you are going to figure out a whole bunch of shit together. Just when you think you've figured out all the things you need to figure out, something new is going to pop up and you'll figure it out together, too. I have total faith in you that you'll do that. Now *you* just need to have a little faith in you. Not even a lot, just a little. A little would be a great start." She reached over and rubbed her hand up and down Eliza's forearm. "You've got this, really."

"I hope you're right." Eliza nodded, looking down for a beat before lifting her eyes to meet Crystal's. "That hasn't actually happened yet, by the way. Hopefully soon, though." She shrugged, playing it off like she didn't care one way or the other what happened between her and

Deniz Aydem. "I hope you heard everything you said to me, though. Seems like most, if not all, of it could also apply to..."

"Me." Crystal breathed the word, shaking her head. "That was not even that sneaky and yet I fell for it like the silly sailor that I am. Seriously? All it took was one mention of Deniz's name and you got me totally distracted from my own life!"

"I know, and I'm sorry about that. If it's any consolation, I did listen to your wise words and am filing them away for if and when the day comes that things are good between us again." She bit her lip. "You're not mad, right? I just figured if I stated it as a hypothetical, you wouldn't quite receive it the same way."

Crystal was already shaking her head. "Not mad at all, or at least not mad at you. Perhaps a little frustrated with myself. It's like...I *know* all this stuff, you know?"

Eliza nodded emphatically. "Where do you think *I* learned it from?"

"So I know it's important to talk to myself just as kindly as I'd talk to a friend, to be patient with myself...to take a dose of my own medicine, as it were. It's just harder when it's *actually* happening and not just hypothetically happening."

"Out of curiosity, *is* it actually happening? With Kaan, I mean. Have you two gotten past the flirting stage and into the 'things are actually brewing between us' stage?"

Crystal threw her hands in the air. "Who even knows? At this point, it's entirely possible this is all just happening in my mind and he doesn't even see me like that."

"No chance. I saw how he looked at you. From the first time you met, actually."

Crystal looked skeptical, and Eliza knew there was nothing she could do to convince her. She could only hope that both of them would have some clarity about their relationships soon.

Twenty-Six

As Kaan had promised, Eliza didn't have to wait long for word from Deniz. Unfortunately, the particular words she received weren't as decisive or reassuring as she would have hoped. Instead, it had been a simple text message.

Eliza, could we meet after work today? I hope you're having a nice day.

The text had arrived between her first and second lessons in the morning, and Eliza had felt a simultaneous thrill and dread at the same time upon reading it. As much as she was eager to know where things stood between her and Deniz and if the two of them had any hope of a future, there was a certain amount of fear that came along with it. Yes, she would know one way or the other...but it was possible that the way in which she would know would be one that would crush her...leave her reeling and heartbroken.

Naturally, she fired back an affirmative message, making plans to meet Deniz at the front door of the university and to walk together to a seaside cafe.

There wasn't much time to spare before she needed to be back in her classroom, so Eliza closed the office door and gave herself ten seconds to center and become just a little more present and relaxed. Three slow, deep breaths. A grounding exercise she'd been practicing in times of anxiety—observing the room around her and noticing what she could see, hear, smell, and feel. Thankfully, there wasn't much of anything to smell, but even noticing the light shining in through the window, the sound of students laughing in the hallway, the feel of the smooth desk under her fingers...all of it brought her back to the moment.

It was no use to dwell on future moments that hadn't even happened yet. There was no way of knowing what Deniz would say today, just as there was no way of speeding the day along and bringing their meeting time any closer than it already was. The clock would tick away at the same speed it had been all day, and Eliza would be where she was needed, focused on what was happening around her.

She had students who needed her guidance, colleagues to exchange friendly banter with, and plenty of goodness that was already taking place. Better to focus on that—on what she could be grateful for—than on what may or may not come to pass.

Of course, all of that was easier said than done. Still, she was making her best effort, bound and determined to put all the work she had been doing on herself to good use. What was the point of mindfulness and self-care practices if they only worked when everything was going well? Stress relief tactics were intended to be used in times of stress more than in the times with no stressors present.

On the way back to her classroom, Eliza fired off a quick text to Crystal, an update on what was to come.

Meeting with Deniz after work. Send me some chill vibes, please. Doing my best, but definitely freaking out just a teeny tiny bit.

Crystal sent back a thumbs-up emoji, which almost made Eliza laugh. She didn't have any more to say than that?

She noticed the three dots in Crystal's text message popping up and disappearing, signifying that her friend was drafting a longer response. But Eliza had arrived in her classroom and it was time for her to take attendance; therefore, also time for her phone to be switched to silent mode and placed in the drawer of her desk.

"Good morning, class!" she greeted the students with a smile, pleased to see a number of eager faces looking back at her. This particular group of students were nearly halfway through their current class with Eliza, which meant midterm exams were hovering on the horizon. A review lesson was scheduled for today, and the classroom was fuller than normal as a result. Students who had been skipping class more often than not had turned up for the review session, no doubt to make sure there weren't too many surprises waiting for them at exam time.

Eliza passed out a review sheet she had prepared—she had, in fact, spent a good chunk of her weekend preparing—and heard the groans as it made the rounds. There were essay topics to practice writing, discussion questions to prepare for the speaking portion of the exam, and a long recap of the grammar points they had studied. She had crammed a lot of information into a small space, and wasn't surprised by the less-than-warm reception it had received in the classroom.

"Alright, then. I know you're all very excited for the exam. To make the best use of our classroom time, we're going to focus on grammar and speaking today. That doesn't mean that writing and listening aren't important—it simply means I am going to expect you to practice those topics *at home*." She looked around the classroom and found about five students listening and nodding, the rest either looking at the review sheet like it had personally hurt their feelings, or sneakily looking at their phones under the table.

"Quick!" Eliza interjected. "Who can tell me what your homework is?" She looked around, ignoring the two hands waving in the air and calling on one sleepy-looking boy in the back of the room. "Enes? Can you tell us what your homework is?"

"We don't have any," he answered, deadpan. "The exam is soon, so that means we're supposed to study."

"Right..." Eliza responded, leading him to continue with her tone. "Which skills are you supposed to practice at home?"

Enes shrugged. "Probably whatever we're not that good at. Isn't that how studying works?"

Eliza couldn't help but smile. "That's a little sassy, but I guess you're right. Though I did advise your classmates to focus on listening and writing at home. Are you going to practice writing an essay tonight, Enes?"

Enes shook his head. "If I use up all my essay writing skills tonight, I might have a very hard time at the exam,

Teacher. And no offense, but I would like to do very well on the exam. Homework is not so important for me."

"That's fair. Though I don't think it works that way. I'm pretty sure practicing the skill outside of class will help you get better at using it *in* class." She shrugged. "But I can't control what you do at home. And if I have learned anything in life, it's that there's no point in worrying about something that you can't control."

She wiggled the mouse to wake up the computer on her desk, slipping in her flash drive to open a file. "Without further ado, then, let's play a game!" Looking out at the students' non-reaction to the idea of playing a game, she felt the briefest flash of missing teaching younger students. While it may have been exhausting work, back in the day when she had done her student teaching in an elementary classroom, at least the word "game" had always worked to garner some excitement.

Still, there was a lot that she preferred about teaching university-level students. The topics they were able to discuss were a world away from what came up in a third-grade classroom. And even if games weren't a sure-fire trick for getting students on their best behavior and fully engaged...there was often an intrinsic motivation that inspired her. These young people were trying to find their place in the world, to set themselves up for success in careers and relationships that hadn't even begun to blossom yet. As set in her ways as Eliza could feel at times, it was exciting to be surrounded by so much potential and possibility.

Even if it didn't translate into eagerness to play grammar and speaking review games.

At the end of the day, Eliza stopped by her office only briefly to collect her things before making her way to the front door to meet Deniz.

Sure enough, he was waiting there, leaning against a pillar near the door, looking outside with his profile facing in her direction. It was a distinguished profile, too, even if his posture conveyed exhaustion more than confident handsomeness. He was leaning against the pillar like it was the only thing keeping him upright, and Eliza wondered for the first time today what his weekend, his time with his family, had been like. She hated to think of him suffering for her, even if some part of her welcomed the idea of suffering together, a Shakespearean tragedy of their very own.

She shook her head to clear that thought as she approached him. Romeo and Juliet might have been star-crossed lovers, but more than that, they were impulsive teenagers who would have benefitted from some clearer communication and listening to a voice of reason or two. Those were both things she was determined to do better with Deniz—both to express and to listen.

"Hey you." Deniz had turned at the sound of her approaching footsteps, a smile spreading across his face, replacing the tiredness she saw in the circles under his eyes.

"Hi." Her voice was small as she smiled back at him, an unfamiliar shyness rearing its head. "How was your weekend? You look..."

Deniz chuckled. "You can say it. I look exhausted, I know. It was a busy weekend, and I definitely didn't get enough sleep." He smiled at her. "It's okay, though. My own fault for driving back this morning rather than leaving last night."

Eliza's eyes widened. "You drove back this morning? That must have been so early! Oh my gosh, Deniz, have you been awake since four o'clock or something like that? What were you thinking? Why did you stay that long?"

"The night got later and later and I didn't want to drive then." He stopped, correcting himself. "That's not entirely true. I would have driven then, but my mom was too worried about me. She insisted I sleep for the night there and leave early in the morning. Of course she woke up with me and made me drink ridiculous amounts of tea—and that's me saying that, as a Turkish person—until she was sure I'd be fine and stay awake." He nodded towards the door. "Anyway, shall we walk? We can catch up on the way."

"Sure," said Eliza, falling into step beside him. "Was there a problem last night? Is everything okay with your grandmother?" A thought occurred to her, making her turn to him in a near-panic, stopping just short of grabbing his arm. "Is Cansu okay?"

Deniz was already shaking his head. "My grandmother is as healthy as a horse, which is the proper expression, I believe. Seriously, she's probably in better shape than I am. And Cansu is great. We had a video chat with her last night and she showed us around her apartment." He laughed again. "It's tiny—I mean, it's London, and she lives with three roommates, and it's pretty much what it sounds like. Me, I'd rather live way out in the suburbs and have a full-size bedroom and a functioning bathroom...but she's happy." His smile was proud, wistful. "That's the most important thing. She's doing what she wants to do, and she's happy about it. My parents and I could all see that, and we had a long talk about it."

"Oh? Is that what kept you there that late?" Eliza couldn't help but wonder if the appreciation for Cansu's happiness had translated into a conversation about Deniz's happiness and if that was something that had included her. Had he been up all night arguing with his parents about keeping his American girlfriend around?

Deniz shook his head, then shot her a mischievous glance. "One of the calves got out of the barn, actually. The same one as before. We were chasing it around for a long time. You wouldn't think it would be hard to find an animal that big, but..." He shrugged. "Especially once it got dark, it was a real challenge. She was scared, too, so it took some time to corner her and convince her to come back."

"Ah." Eliza nodded like she could relate, like she had ever trailed a large farm animal around the streets of a village in the dark. "I'm glad you were successful. That must have been a relief for all of you."

"It was." Deniz crossed the street, reaching for Eliza's elbow with a soft touch to guide her to cross with him, both of them picking up their pace to a slow jog to make it to the other side before the light changed and traffic started flowing again.

They walked together comfortably, catching up on the minutiae of their day-to-day lives, all the little happenings they hadn't shared with each other over the past few weeks. If Eliza hadn't already been painfully aware of how much she missed Deniz's larger presence in her life, in getting to share more than just passing smiles and pleasantries in the hallway, she would have been abundantly, painfully tuned into it now. Having him there by her side felt like a exquisite torture—if she knew she'd be able to have it longer than today, it would have been nothing but delicious. But the fact that it might be the end? Well, that was what made it torture.

But either way, she would know soon. And there would be freedom and release in the knowing.

Deniz took them to a cafe she hadn't been to before, which had several outdoor tables, all with great cliff-side views. "Why don't we get some drinks and walk a bit?" Deniz offered. "There are some benches down the way, could be nice to sit there without too many other people around."

"Sounds great," Eliza agreed, hoping his desire for seclusion didn't mean he anticipated a scene. Lots of tears and heartbreak and embarrassment.

Once they had their drinks in hand—an iced latte for her, a hot Americano for him—they made their way to the bench Deniz had his eye on and sat next to each other.

"I can't wait any longer," Eliza blurted. "I have to know. What's the verdict? Is...is this the end? Is it good news? How did things go with your parents?"

Deniz smiled and closed his eyes as he took a deep breath. "I'm really sorry it's taken me so long to come out and say it. I know it's probably been hell for you, waiting for the answer." He opened his eyes then, and reading something on her face, his expression sobered. "It's good news. Sorry. I started to monologue a little there, and I was going to take way too long to say it." His smile was sheepish. "So...there's a spoiler for you, I guess. It's good news. The best news. Assuming, that is, that *you* still want to be with me."

Eliza was overcome with relief, with the emotion of the past weeks washing over her and out again. She had gotten what she had been waiting for and it was every bit as sweet as she had imagined it would be. "Really?" Her eyes darted back and forth between Deniz's, reading the expression there, her view blurring as her eyes filled with water. "What happened? How did you get your parents to accept the idea of me?"

"It was never about that." Deniz shook his head, reaching for her hands to take them in his own. "Anyone who wouldn't accept you isn't worth your time. You know that, right? And my decision to be with you...it was never about whether my parents would be on board with it or not. I love you, Eliza. And one way or another, we were going to be together. It would either have been with the approval and support of my parents, or it would have been without it." He paused, pulling his lips into his mouth for just a second. "I just wanted to give them the respect that I owed them. To face them on my own and give them a little time to warm up to the idea of me having an American girlfriend, rather than...well, rather than the way I did it initially. Showing up there with you, without warning either you or them of what to expect, well, it wasn't really fair."

Eliza nodded in agreement. "It wasn't great for any of us, was it? So what did they say? What did you all talk about?"

"Well, that's the thing. I showed up there, having psyched myself up to face all this opposition from my family. Grandparents and aunts trying to set me up with random girls in the village, my parents crying or shouting at me...no one but Cansu on my side, and a lot of good that does with her all the way in London..." There was a twinkle in his eye giving her a hint that his expectations couldn't have been further from the truth.

"What was it? It didn't happen like that?"

Deniz shook his head, a grin splitting his face in half like the sun peeking over the horizon. "Everyone was thrilled about you. The only shouting came from my mom, asking me why I hadn't brought you and if I had done something wrong to make you mad. They were all just happy to see me happy, I guess."

"I don't understand. How can someone like me if they don't even know me? Especially with the first impression that I made there?"

"Ah, well." Deniz rubbed the back of his neck. "I'm sure we can credit Cansu for doing some campaigning on our behalf, and maybe Kaan, too. The people we were comfortable around could see how we were together. It was as clear as day to them that there was nothing but love and respect flowing back and forth between the two of us, and that I was more myself with you than I'd ever been before."

"So they're not all disappointed that I don't speak Turkish? That I'm not from the village?"

Deniz laughed at that. "They're only disappointed that you don't speak Turkish in the same way they're disappointed that *they* don't speak English. One way or another, they want to communicate with you. Admittedly, there's a better chance of you taking a Turkish class than of getting the entire village enrolled in English lessons, but—"

"I'll do it," Eliza interjected. "I've been working on Duolingo and a couple other apps every day, but…" She felt her cheeks heat at the admission that she'd been making an effort, though she could play it off as an effort to get by in the country where she lived rather than an effort to win over Deniz's family. "I'd really like to take a proper class. See how it goes."

Deniz nodded right along. "Absolutely. I'll help you find one, and if you ever need help with your homework…"

"I know just who to ask." Eliza leaned into him, his arm wrapping around her shoulder as she settled back. "Is…is this really happening, then?"

She felt more than saw Deniz nod next to her. "It absolutely is." He leaned away, craning his neck down to meet her eyes as she turned her gaze to his. "Are you in?"

"I absolutely am."

His smile matched hers, like they had both weathered the same heavy, challenging storm and come out on the other side with a new appreciation for life, for love. He leaned his forehead against hers, eyes closed. "Me, too. Farther in than I even realized."

And with that, their lips found each other, soft and tender and full of all the longing and emotion they had borne on their own these last weeks, yet conscious of the fact that they were in a public area and one that was likely to be frequented by their students.

"Come on." Deniz got to his feet, offering a hand to help Eliza to hers. "Let's get out of here."

She took his hand then, knowing she would gladly hold it in her own for as long as she possibly could.

Epilogue

Nine Months Later

The plans for summer break are a little different this time around, Eliza thought, as she waited at the Antalya airport for her parents to clear customs and exit the main door. She hadn't gone back to Michigan during her time off, but had enjoyed the first weeks in Antalya, spending as much time at the beach as possible and relaxing and de-stressing after a school year that had been full of work, exams, and no small amount of stress.

It had been full of love, too. Ever since she and Deniz had gotten clear on where they stood with each other, the flow between them had been natural, almost easy. Sure, there was work involved in any close relationship—especially in one with two different languages and cultures at play, but they were both happy to do that work after they had almost missed out on their opportunity to do so.

"Still waiting, love?" Almost as if her thoughts had summoned him, Deniz's voice had materialized a few feet behind Eliza.

She turned to greet her boyfriend, shaking her head. "They landed about ten minutes ago, so we probably still have some time. Did you find a good parking space?"

Deniz nodded. "Yes, it's not too far. Assuming your parents didn't bring too many big, heavy suitcases, we should be able to get them there with no problems."

Eliza smiled up at him as she wrapped her arm around his waist, his longer arm coming around her shoulders. They stood like that, facing the gate, her scanning all the faces passing by while Deniz did the same. Considering that he had only met Susan and Dave on video chats, it was unlikely that he would be the first one to spot or recognize them. He'd never even seen them in three dimensions, after all.

"Is that...?" Deniz stood on his toes, pointing over the crowd, before his face broke into a smile and he started waving enthusiastically. As Eliza looked where he was pointing, she saw her mother sporting a matching grin and waving at least as energetically as Deniz was. Dave was trailing ever-so-slightly behind her, struggling with the suitcase Susan seemed to have dropped—her hands were empty, after all—in her excitement to be reunited with her daughter and meet Deniz in real life.

Eliza and Deniz made their way through the crowd, Deniz making a beeline for Dave to offer a bit of relief at the same time Susan wrapped Eliza in a bear hug—the exact bear hug she had missed for the last nine months and could have really used in some of those challenging and emotional days of the previous summer and fall.

"Hi!" Eliza wiped the tears that were spilling from her eyes at the mere presence of her mom. "How was your flight?"

"Good. Long. We're so glad to be here." Susan released Eliza, reaching for Deniz to give him a hug, too. "So glad to meet you, Deniz, and to be here with our girl."

Eliza hugged her dad, not missing the emotion in his eyes, too. A lot had changed since the three of them were together last. Not the least of which...

"So," Dave sized up Deniz, a humorous expression on his face. "My daughter tells me you're going to get engaged, and I have to tell you, I don't really understand how that works. Where I come from, someone gets engaged when they ask the question, and I'm confused about that. Does that mean you're about to ask her the question? And if so...if she knows the question is coming, doesn't that mean she's already answered it? Or is this just a formality? Waiting on a ring?"

"Dave," Susan chided. "Isn't it too early—and aren't we too tired and jetlagged—for the third degree? I'm sure everything will make sense to us soon. Probably after we eat some good food and get some good sleep. Right, Eliza? Deniz?"

Deniz was nodding already. "We will absolutely get you some food. Why don't we take you back to Eliza's apartment and get you settled in there?" Crystal was staying with Kaan in his apartment—he had moved out of Deniz's place months ago, and she stayed there with him often. She said she was doing it this time to free up the room for

Eliza's parents, but Eliza expected any day now to learn that her best friend was, in fact, moving out to live with her boyfriend full-time.

The four of them started walking back to the car, Eliza and Deniz wheeling suitcases and only allowing Susan and Dave to hold their carry-on bags. As they walked, Deniz spoke up. "Mr. Britt," he began. "I'll try to explain how the Turkish engagement ceremony works. For what it's worth, in American terms, we *are* already engaged. I mean, I have asked Eliza to marry me and she has said yes."

Dave puffed up with emotion. "Call me Dave, first of all. And I knew the two of you were talking seriously about marriage, so that's not exactly news. Why else would Susan and I fly all the way to Turkey?"

"For a great vacation!" Susan crowed. "To see our daughter! To meet her boyfriend...er, I mean fiance! We don't need a reason to come to Turkey, and I'm sure this won't be our last visit. Right, Eliza?"

Eliza shook her head. She harbored secret hopes of convincing her parents that regular visits to Turkey were a must, but she could wait a bit before springing that on them.

"How do your folks feel about this marriage?" Dave asked, raising an eyebrow. Eliza had to stifle a smile. Even as an adult, there was no avoiding her dad's protective tendencies, his need to question everything and decide for himself. Even if there was a part of her that bristled at the implication that she couldn't handle herself, she knew there was no need to go down that path. Dave Britt loved her, his only daughter, and he had his own unique way of showing it. She could respect it and receive his love in whatever way he sent it.

Thankfully, Deniz seemed to understand this, too, and didn't take any offense at Dave's line of questioning. "They're thrilled." He nodded. "I know at the beginning they were a bit surprised I had an American girlfriend, but they've really gotten to know and love Eliza in these past months." It helped that Eliza had been taking a Turkish course two days a week, too. She had gained the confidence in her speaking skills to at least have some basic conversations, even if there was still plenty of the village dialect that sailed right over her head.

"It's always fun for them to have a celebration in the village, too," Deniz continued. "And just think of how the wedding will be, if they're this excited about an engagement celebration." They had made it to the car by now, and Deniz opened the trunk to place the suitcases inside.

Eliza opted to sit in the back seat next to her mom, leaving the front for Dave so that he could appreciate the view and continue grilling Deniz. Susan was clearly thrilled just to be near her daughter, and Eliza scooted to the middle seat so that the two of them could be as close as possible, talking in quiet voices as they made their way to Eliza's apartment.

Susan and Dave had plans to stay in Turkey for a full month, and their agenda was jam-packed. In addition to exploring Antalya and spending a week in the village leading up to Eliza and Deniz's engagement celebration, they were going to travel around the country as well. Eliza and Deniz planned to take them to Istanbul, Cappadocia, and a number of famous ruins on the Aegean coast, as well.

They had enough time scheduled for this trip that they could do it all without emerging at the other end exhausted and in need of a vacation from their vacation. Eliza was looking forward to it at least as much as her parents were.

"What's an engagement ceremony called again?" Susan leaned forward in her seat to ask Deniz in the driver's seat. They were in Isparta, and it was the day of the celebration.

"It's called *nişan töreni*," Deniz responded. "And Eliza is my *nişanlı*, my fiancee. Or, I guess, she will be after the ceremony is over." He winked at her in the rearview mirror, letting her know exactly how he felt about what she already was to him in that very moment.

"And walk me through what happens," said Susan, wanting every detail of the impending event to prepare herself in advance. "You give Eliza her ring, right?"

"Ah, that's where it's different," Eliza spoke up. "This is my favorite part, so let me explain it. Okay, Deniz?"

"Of course, my love."

"We both have rings," she explained. "We got matching ones, actually. Plain bands. I'll wear the sparkly one, too, but I just *love* that we both have engagement rings. It feels so...I don't know, so evolved, I guess. Like some serious gender equality on display there. Because dudes can be engaged, too, duh! So why shouldn't they get to wear rings, too?"

"I love that," Susan agreed. "I could barely get your dad to wear a ring even as a married man, so I have great respect for the young Turkish men who are wearing engagement rings."

"It's not just the wearing of the rings," Deniz explained. "Though of course I am looking forward to wearing it, so everyone knows I'm spoken for." He winked at Eliza. "We'll tie the rings together with a ribbon, and one of the elders will say a few words before cutting the ribbon and we all celebrate it together. Eliza and I will make the rounds to thank everyone for their support, for being there. You'll be standing up next to us, but during this part is really the only time you'll have to *do* something."

"What will we have to do?" Eliza glanced at Susan, reading the tone of her voice that suggested she was feeling anxious about *doing* something and potentially doing it wrong...and finding that same sentiment was written all over her face.

"It's very easy," Deniz reassured her. "Just hold out a hand. Eliza and I will take turns kissing the back of your hand and then lifting it to touch to our foreheads."

"Your *foreheads*? But why?" Susan was aghast, and Eliza bit back a laugh.

"It's a way of showing respect. Trust me, your part is easy." Deniz found Susan's eyes in the rearview mirror, and Eliza knew the reassurance in them would ease Susan's nerves. "Just let us take your hand and then lift it at the end. Don't freak out and pull it back or slap me or anything like that. Deal?"

"Deal." She exhaled, relaxing back in her seat.

Deniz brought the car to a stop in front of the village square and they all filed out. There were still hours until the celebration would start, but the chairs were already being arranged, a space cleared for the DJ to set up for all the dancing after the event. Eliza felt a thrill of excitement—and a bit of nerves, too—in her stomach. This wasn't going to be like anything she'd ever experienced before, and she was so glad to have Deniz by her side for it.

And not only Deniz.

"Eliza! I've been looking for you!" Crystal's voice sailed across the square as she jogged towards Eliza, Kaan following along behind her at a much slower pace. "Are we going to go get beautiful or what?"

Eliza opened her arms to welcome her best friend into them at a pace a little faster than she'd expected, the two of them nearly falling over together. "We already *are* beautiful," she reminded her friend, "but yes, we're going to head to the salon soon. Are you ready?"

Crystal nodded. "Ready and willing. Think I can get them to shape my eyebrows too? And maybe yours?" She reached for Eliza's forehead, Eliza batting her hand away.

"I'm sure you can. Okay, let me go find Cansu and say hello to Deniz's parents."

"I'll come with you."

Eliza made her way to Deniz's parents' home, surrounded by her parents, her fiance, and her best friend in the world. Kaan had already gone ahead of them and was no doubt already drinking Esra's tea. He and Deniz would be on translation duty while the young women went to the salon together to prepare for the evening's celebration. Susan and Dave had been to Esra and Ahmet's house every day this week, and the couples had gotten along swimmingly, the language barrier between them barely even an obstacle. Mutual love for their children and mutual joy and relief at seeing them happy could go very far to bringing people from different worlds together.

Esra came out the door before they could get there, her arms open as she welcomed her son's future in-laws. Kisses on the cheek and warm embraces all around had Eliza feeling a sudden rush of emotion, blinking moisture away from her eyes.

Deniz, of course, noticed. "You okay?" he asked, leaning down to say the words for her ears only.

"Never better," she answered honestly. "I'm just so happy that we're really doing this. And that they're all a part of it. We're really lucky, aren't we?"

"The luckiest. But let's not forget that we worked for that luck, too. And I have a feeling that if we keep working at it, we'll keep being lucky together."

Eliza liked the sound of that a lot. Deniz kissed her on the temple, squeezing her hand once before making his way into the house to find Cansu. They were going to be late for the salon if she didn't come out soon.

Esra pulled Eliza in for one more hug, patting her hair and smiling warmly while Eliza caught about a third of what she was saying. More motivation to keep up with those Turkish lessons, but her comprehension skills were already getting better all the time.

The meaning of it wasn't lost on Susan, though, who linked her arm with Esra's, the two of them heading in to the kitchen to begin working on the universal language of love so many moms had mastered: food. She knew that the fusion of their talents would lead to delicious results.

Dave had followed Ahmet to the barn and was looking at the cows inside with more interest than Eliza had expected. When he started to roll up his sleeves to offer help, she knew she had seen everything.

Finally, Eliza, Crystal, and Cansu were on their way to the salon to get ready for the events of the day, with Cansu driving.

"Look at us," she said as she turned onto the main road taking them to the next biggest town, where the salon was located. "Who would have guessed we'd be here?" She pointed to each of them in turn. "About to get engaged, somehow in love with my weird cousin, and living it up in Londontown."

Crystal *hmm*ed along in agreement. "It's only getting better from here, isn't it? We're all getting just what we deserve."

Eliza nodded, taking in the scenery out the window as they passed by. "It's so good, Crystal. So much to be grateful for. So much growth, and so much joy I feel like I could explode."

"Pssht," Crystal scoffed. "You're not going to explode. Expand your capacity for more and more joy, girlfriend. Appreciate what you've got and be ready for more."

"Oh yeah? More goodness is coming? How can we top this?"

"Just you wait and see, my dear friend. It's always coming, just pay attention."

And Eliza was resigned to do just that. To appreciate and celebrate today—she already knew she wouldn't be able to sleep tonight because she'd be positively vibrating with all the love and goodness—and to wait in anticipation of

what tomorrow could bring. That was her new philoso-
phy, and she knew it couldn't let her down. Even when
things were hard, there was always so much to appreciate.
But especially on a day like today, when everything was
beauty and joy and love, the list of blessings was endless.

Author's Note

Thank you so much for sticking around for the conclusion of Eliza and Deniz's story. This was the hardest project I've written thus far, but it was worth it to see these two get their happy ending.

I'm so grateful to everyone who read and enjoyed *Pride, Prejudice, & Turkish Delight*. It has been a surreal and wonderful experience to watch that book slowly make its way around the globe.

If you enjoyed this book, please consider leaving a review, as that is one of the best ways to support indie authors like me. Reviews left on major retail sites (wherever you bought this book is a great start!), The StoryGraph, GoodReads, and BookBub will help other readers discover this book, too.

To stay updated on other works in progress, please visit my website at kcmccormickciftci.com and subscribe to my newsletter. I send out monthly updates on upcoming releases, books I'm loving, and other recommendations.

KC McCormick Çiftçi is an English teacher turned romance writer. She spent the majority of her twenties living and working abroad, collecting the experiences that inform the stories she tells. She enjoys telling multicultural and international love stories through romantic comedy and women's fiction. She lives in Turkey with her husband and a herd of cats.

Prior to diving into the world of romance, KC published two self-help books for intercultural couples, *Loving Across Borders* and *The K-1 Visa Wedding Plan*. Both are available wherever books are sold.

For updates on upcoming releases, behind the scenes news, and all my favorite book recommendations, visit kcmccormickciftci.com (or just point your phone camera at the QR code below).

Also By KC McCormick Çiftçi

Austen in Turkey
Pride, Prejudice, & Turkish Delight

Home (Abroad) for the Holidays
Christmas on Inishmore

Intercultural Relationship Self Help
Loving Across Borders
The K-1 Visa Wedding Plan